MARAZAN

Nevil Shute was born in 1899 and educated at Shrewsbury School and Balliol College, Oxford. Having decided early on an aeronautical career, he went to work for the de Havilland Aircraft Company as an engineer, where he played a large part in the construction of the airship R100. *Marazan*, his first novel, was written at this time. After the disaster to the R101, he turned his attention to aeroplane construction and founded his own firm, Airspeed Ltd, in 1931. In the war Nevil Shute served in the Navy, doing secret work for the Admiralty. He still found time to write, however, and during this time produced several novels including *Pied Piper*, *Pastoral* and *Most Secret*. These were followed in 1947 by *The Chequer Board* and, in 1948, *No Highway* which became a great bestseller and an extremely popular film. In 1948 he went to Australia for two months, a trip that inspired his most popular novel, *A Town like Alice*. He returned there for good with his family, and remained until his death in 1960. His later novels include *In the Wet*, *Requiem for a Wren*, *On the Beach*, and *Trustee from the Toolroom*.

D1150286

Nevil Shute
Marazan

Pan Books London, Sydney and Auckland

First published 1926 by Cassell & Co Ltd
This edition published 1964 by
Pan Books Ltd, Cavaye Place, London SW10 9PG
11 13 15 17 19 20 18 16 14 12
Copyright by the Trustees of the Estate
of Nevil Shute Norway
All rights reserved
ISBN 0 330 10343 1
Printed in England by
Clays Ltd, St Ives plc

AUTHOR'S NOTE

THIS was the first of my books to be published, and in re-issuing it after twenty-five years of obscurity I feel that it may interest young writers if I put down a few reflections about it. It was published when I was twenty-seven years old, and it was preceded by two novels which were quite unpublishable, because everybody has to learn his trade. It was written in the evenings while I was working at Crayford in Kent on the preliminary design of the airship R100, as chief calculator, or mathematician. The whole book was written through from start to finish three times, so that it took me about eighteen months.

So much is published in this modern age about murder, detection, and prison that a young writer who has yet to learn the nature of drama tends to turn to these threadbare subjects for his story and I was no exception. I don't think I knew a great deal about any of them. The aircraft scenes were built up from my experience with the de Havilland Company in its very earliest days. The character of Philip Stenning derived from half a dozen pilots of that Company's Air Taxi service: in those pioneering days of civil aviation pilots had to be tough.

In spite of its immaturity the book got good reviews. I think it sold about 1,200 copies. In revising it for publication I have struck out a few outmoded expressions, such as 'topping' and 'ripping', which I suppose were current at that time, but I have made no other alterations.

NEVIL SHUTE

THE SONS OF MARTHA

It is their care in all the ages to take the
buffet and cushion the shock,
It is their care that the gear engages, it is
their care that the switches lock.

RUDYARD KIPLING.

Chapter One

IT BEGAN in June. I was one of the pilots of the Rawdon Air Taxi Service then; as everyone knows, a civilian pilot, like a dramatic critic, is merely a young man who is too lazy to work for a living. I claim no exception. I had nobody to think for but myself; in those circumstances I didn't see that it mattered much how I earned my living so long as there was plenty of it, and the work not too hard. Moreover, I was a pretty good pilot in those days. I was thirty-two years old that June, and making an income of just under a thousand a year for an average two-hour day. I used to play Rugger for the Harlequins and was making some progress with my golf, though I was never so near to the Amateur Championship as I thought I was. For the rest, I had a small bachelor flat off Maida Vale, and led about as dissolute a life as was consistent with keeping reasonably fit.

I came down from Manchester that afternoon at the conclusion of a photographic tour. It was a Wednesday, I remember, and a very hot day. I flew all the way in my shirt-sleeves with my arms bare to the elbow, and without a helmet. Even so I was hot. The air was very bumpy so that we had a rough trip; from time to time I would look back at the photographer in the rear cockpit, white to the gills and retching and heaving every time we hit a bad one. I wasn't sorry to see him like that again; for a fortnight I had been cooped up with the wretched little man in indifferent hotels. If the devil had flown away with him I could have borne up under the blow, I think. Rather he than I.

We got to London at about three in the afternoon. There was thunder about down there; great masses of cumulus were rolling up from every point of the compass, heavy-looking and pink at the edges. It grew more bumpy than ever. I wasn't at

7

all sorry to be home; it had grown suddenly cold, for one thing, and I wanted my coat. I had a thirst on me that I wouldn't have sold for a fiver. I looked forward along the long bow of the machine to the familiar hangars and the aerodrome as I put her on the glide down to land; Collard had got his car out on the grass of the aerodrome in front of the Pilots' Office and was tinkering with the engine. To announce my arrival I opened out my engine again and dived on the car; he looked up and waved an oilcan at me. I passed within a few yards of him, zoomed up again and finished with an Immelmann turn at the top for the sake of that wretched photographer. Then I throttled again, came round in a wide sweep, side-slipped her in over the hedge, and put down gently on the grass by the hangars.

I got out of the machine, cross and tired. I was as deaf as a post through flying without a helmet, and I felt as though my eyes were full of oil. I was shivering. The ground felt as heavy as lead. I'd had a pretty thick night the night before. Annesley had turned up in Manchester and had produced a couple of Flossies; before the night was out we'd done Manchester pretty thoroughly – dealt faithfully with the town. If there was a low dive in the place that we hadn't been in, Annesley didn't know it.

I handed the machine over to the mechanics, swore at the photographer, collected the log-books, got all my stuff out of the rear cockpit, carried the lot across to the Pilots' Office and dumped it all on the floor.

'Had a good trip?' asked Collard.

I told him in a low monotone, while I sorted out my stuff upon the floor and put on a cardigan, what I really thought about my trip, Manchester, the machine, and the photographer. He heard me to the end, and then —

'Been missing his Kruschens again,' he observed. 'What you want is a holiday.'

I stood up and let fly. 'If you think I'm going to take a ruddy holiday,' I said, 'just because Mr ruddy Collard thinks I

8

want my Kruschens, you're barking up a rocking-horse like the puppy.' Then I saw he'd got a Bass there, and I remembered I was thirsty. 'Give that here,' I said. 'I'll show you what to do with that.' There was a short struggle before I put him on the ground and got it away from him; there was no corkscrew and I cut my lip against the broken neck of the bottle.

While I was trying to stop the bleeding and thinking what a rotten world it was, the office girl came down to the hut.

'Mr Morris wants to see you in his office, Captain Stenning,' she said.

I mopped at my lip and turned to Collard. 'If he wants me to do another job of work today,' I said, 'he can go and —' but the child was there. Then I followed her out of the hut and up through the works to the main office.

I never really got to know Morris, though I quarrelled with him every week. He was Chief Pilot and Technical Editor and Lord High Everything Else in the Rawdon firm. He was one of those lean, saturnine fellows that go about with an air of 'I keep myself to myself, damn you.' He was a pretty good sort in his own way. A married man; he lived in a house overlooking the aerodrome. I believe he married money.

I went into his office and found him at his desk. 'Afternoon, Stenning,' he said. 'How d'you get on up north? I've got another job for you – want you to take a machine down to Devonshire this evening.'

'Damn it,' I said. 'I've only just come back.'

He raised his head and looked at me like a corpse, so that I knew that there was trouble coming.

'Well,' he said quietly. 'You're going away again.'

It was poisonously hot. I could hear thunder rumbling in the distance, but the rain still held off. The air was close and heavy in the office, so that I was sweating and sorry I had put on my cardigan.

'I'm ruddy well not going away again today,' I said. 'I'll go first thing tomorrow morning, if you like. At dawn.'

'That won't do,' he said. 'You've got to start from there

9

tomorrow morning at dawn, to take the passenger first to Liverpool and then back here. I'm sorry, but the machine's got to go down tonight.'

I laughed shortly. 'You're going to be unlucky,' I said. 'I've done three and a half hours' flying today, and I'm tired. You work us too hard, Morris. I'm fed up with it. Besides, you haven't got a machine to send.'

'You can take the one you've had up north,' he said.

'You can leave me out of it,' I replied hotly; 'as for the machine, she's due for overhaul in three hours' more flying time, and from what you say this will be an eight hours' job. And the engine's running rough – damn rough.'

'Are you putting in a formal complaint about the engine?' he said.

There was a sudden flurry of wind about the building and the first drops of rain splashed heavily on the window-sill. I could see that he was getting me into a corner, but couldn't for the life of me see how to get out of it.

'No,' I said. 'It's no worse than some of the engines I've had to fly since I've been here.'

He disregarded that. 'You can refuse this job on medical grounds if you feel you aren't fit,' he said. 'In that case I shall take the machine myself. You know that won't count against you.'

'Damn it,' I said sullenly, 'you know I'm not as bad as that. But you work us too hard, Morris – by God you do. It's going to be a perfectly filthy evening for getting down west.'

'If you call three and half hours' flying a day's work,' he replied, 'I don't. But there it is. You can take it or leave it.'

At that I lost my temper. 'I'll take it,' I said. 'But you don't give us a square deal, Morris. You don't play fair. I'll do the job – but I'll tell you this much. I'll take the machine down empty, but if you wanted me to carry passengers this evening I'd turn it down. Now that's straight. Where have I got to go?'

He looked at me doubtfully for a moment. 'Are you sure you're fit?' he said.

'If I wasn't I should send in one of your ruddy pink forms,' I said irritably. 'Come on. What have I got to do?'

He turned to the map on the wall. 'You'll go to Westward Ho!' he said, 'and put down on the golf links for the night. And, for Heaven's sake, keep off the greens.'

I turned on him. 'Damn it – you know it wasn't I who went over that green.'

'Didn't say it was,' he replied. 'What I said was – don't. The passenger is Sir Arthur Bardsley, who is staying at Carew Hall, near Northam. You'll report to him, or there may be a message at the club house for you. In any case, I understand he wants to make a start soon after dawn.'

Well, that was that. I took my instructions, got my ticket, and stalked out of the office in as vile a temper as any I've ever been in. I wasn't particularly annoyed with Morris; one couldn't help liking the man, and he certainly did work like a nigger to put the show on a dividend-paying basis. No, oddly enough the man I really was annoyed with was Collard for suggesting that I could do with a holiday. The worst of it was that I knew that it was true. For a long time I had been burning the candle at both ends to a greater extent than was altogether healthy, and lately there had been warnings that I should have been a fool to disregard.

'Things can't go on like this,' I muttered sullenly, as I walked down to the Pilots' Office. At the same time, I didn't see any real reason why they shouldn't.

I saw the foreman of the mechanics and told him to get the machine filled up again, and then I telephoned for my tea. Then I went to look at the oil, my latest venture. There is not much left now in France of the stuff that was taken over there for the war, but Collard, having occasion to land near some little French village that had been behind the line, had discovered fifty barrels of (alleged) motor lubricating oil mouldering in a pasture. I went into it with him, and we were engaged in tentative negotiations for buying the lot at a price that worked out at a little over a halfpenny a gallon. It certainly

11

had the viscosity of oil, but it was far too light in colour to attract a purchaser; in these circumstances Collard was trying the effect of various pigments in an endeavour to turn it into such a colourable imitation of good oil as to catch some poor simp up from the country and sting him for at least a shilling a gallon. After all, in most motor-car engines the function of the oil is to wash the heat away from the bearings, and for that this oil would probably do as well as any other liquid.

There was a little pan of it there. I dipped my finger in the oil and drew a little picture on the wall in the style that Collard finds amusing. I laughed at it myself, then went out on to the aerodrome and found the rugger ball and started punting it about in the rain. Then my tea came. By the time I'd finished that, a mechanic was in the hut to tell me that the machine was ready; I told him to get her started up and began to look for my leather coat.

By the time I was all togged up it was half past four; I had none too long if I was to get my job done before dark. The flight down there would take me over three hours against the stiff westerly wind; after that I should have to find a car and drive it to Bideford to collect fifty gallons or so of petrol, return to the links and fill up the machine. Besides that I should have to report myself at Carew Hall and find myself something to eat and – if the gods were kind – a bed. It was still raining in buckets; the clouds had thickened up and come lower and the barograph showed the glass dropping a little bit – not much. It looked perfectly beastly outside; in any other circumstances I would have put off starting for half an hour. There was none too much time, however, and I felt that, having indulged in the luxury of speaking my mind to Morris, it was up to me to carry the job through without quibbling. So I started.

I felt better when I was in the machine. The rain and the wind had cooled the air and freshened up things a bit. I ran the engine up, waved the chocks away, and moved over to the lee hedge to take off. I have been flying for over ten years and one would expect by now to be getting a little stale, a little tired of it. Yet as I swung her round into the wind that day in the rain and saw the aerodrome stretching away in front of me, misty and very wide, I felt as strongly as ever the queer indescribable charm of this piloting, the feeling that I should never entirely give it up.

At the same time, I knew that I was very tired.

Then I opened her up and went rolling over the grass and into the air. I never waste much time in getting on my course; ten feet up I swung her round through forty degrees with one wing tip steadily balanced eighteen inches above the grass. Before I was out of the aerodrome I was on my course and climbing steadily as I headed just about due west.

I didn't climb far before I hit the clouds. They were down to six hundred feet or so; I went trundling out over Buckinghamshire at about that height and wished I was in the Long Bar of the Troc, as I might have been but for Morris. Cross-country flying at any time is boring; cross-country flying in the rain can be perfectly devilish. Sometimes I while away the time by writing letters in pencil on a block strapped to my knee, and in a machine with a good windscreen one can always smoke. But in the rain when the clouds force one down to within five hundred feet of the ground one must keep so much on the alert for a possible forced landing that letter-writing becomes impossible. And a cigarette gets wet and comes to pieces in the wind.

All went well as far as High Wycombe, though the clouds were gradually forcing me lower, so that by the time I was over the town I was down to three hundred feet. I could see the Chilterns ahead of me; it proves how low I was that I could distinctly mark the rise of the ground by Dashwood Hill. The clouds seemed to be sitting right down on top of the hills; for a moment I hesitated, and thought of turning away south and following the line of the hills till I hit the Thames and the railway at the Pangbourne Gap. But it was out of my direct course and time was short enough as it was; I could tell by my time to High Wycombe that there must be a stiff south-westerly wind against me. Looking back upon that decision now, I can hardly realize the effect that it had upon my life. As it was, I looked at my watch, swore, and went on.

I came to the hills about three miles south of the Oxford road. The rain had eased off to a drizzle, but the clouds hung so low upon the hills that I was forced down to within a hundred feet of the treetops. Even at that I was flying through wisps of cloud so thick that I could only see the ground immediately below me. The air was terribly bumpy.

Then there came to me what I suppose comes to every pilot sooner or later, whether he be good or bad. The sweet, rhythmic drone of the engine faltered. There was a moment's screaming, and in an instant the whole bag of tricks had gone to glory and was shaking the machine as a terrier shakes a rat. At the first hint of trouble I had jerked back the throttle, a stream of boiling water came spurting down the fuselage and over the windscreen, and I sat dithering at every leap of the engine and wondering if it was going to stay in the fuselage or tear away the bearers and fall out. I had seen that happen once. The machine came down like a falling leaf, turning over and over so fast that the pilot must have been unconscious long before he hit the ground.

In a second or two the vibration began to die away; I swung the machine round in an S turn back on my tracks. Immediately below me there was a small field in the middle of the woods, or rather two fields divided by an iron railing that ran across the middle. It was an impossible place for a landing; a field that nobody in his senses would dream of trying to put down in under normal circumstances. As the matter stood, however, and at the height I was, it was either the field or the treetops. I chose the field.

I made a mistake there, though in equal circumstances I think I should probably do the same again. When I was an instructor, I used to put that very case to my pupils; I had a little speech that I used to make to them. In case of doubt, I

14

used to say, choose the trees, because they're soft. If you put down on the treetops, I would say, you won't hurt yourself and the machine may be repairable. If you stall in trying to get into the little field beyond the trees the machine will be a write-off and you'll probably be dead.

That's what I used to tell my pupils. In the event, though, one can never overcome a natural reluctance to crashing the machine. If there is a possible chance of getting down undamaged one will always take it, no matter what the risk. Before I fully realized what I was doing I had swung round and was judging my distance for the final turn that would bring me close over the railings into the larger of the two little fields.

I still think that if I had been myself I might have pulled it off. But I was tired; I had flown round the Midlands on photographic work that morning, and then down from Manchester. And Manchester itself – well, I suppose Manchester had something to do with it too. Certainly I made a mess of that forced landing. It was a bad show. I missed the railing by four feet instead of four inches, at a speed of fifty miles an hour instead of forty-two. After that I hadn't a chance. We were nearly into the far hedge and the wood before I could put her on the ground. I swung her round violently in an attempt to miss the wood. She rose from the ground again, cart-wheeled over on one wing tip, and fell heavily on her back.

I can't say that I have a very clear recollection of what happened during the next ten minutes. I was conscious for most of the time, I think, but my memory of the incidents has become blurred with pain. I wasn't strapped in, and as she went over I grabbed at my seat to prevent myself from being thrown out. As it was, I was chucked half out of the cockpit and crashed my head down on to the padded edge of the instrument board. Then the machine turned right over on her back, and the ground came up and pushed me back into the cockpit again upside-down. I remember a keen, agonizing pain in my neck, and then I think I went off for a little. Very likely I was stunned.

I came to myself pretty soon, however. Petrol was running over the seat of my trousers and soaking through my clothes up to my waist; I think it was the cold of it that revived me. I was crammed into the cockpit upside-down, with my shoulders in the grass; I was pretty far gone, I suppose. I remember wondering how soon it would be before anyone found the machine, or if anyone had seen us come down. I knew that I wasn't going to last long in that position.

It was evident that if I was to get out I must act quickly, before I became unconscious again. I could feel the weight of the machine pressing me down into the grass. I got one arm free above my head, summoned all my energy, and with a violent heave managed to lift the machine a little. The movement dislodged my weight; my legs fell down in the cockpit and my body shifted sideways; the machine lurched a little and collapsed on to me again, pinning me in the cockpit.

Then I got my feet drawn up against the floor of the cockpit and tried to raise the machine that way. Again I raised her a little, and again she seemed to hesitate, swung, and collapsed on me again.

That was my last effort. In the new position I could not use either hand to free myself; if I had had the full use of my hands, though, I doubt if I could have got out. The thundering in my head grew terrific.

That, so far as I was concerned, was the end.

I think it was the pain in my neck that roused me again, that and the change of position as I rolled out of the cockpit on to the grass like a hermit crab when you touch the end of his shell with a cigarette. Somebody had lifted the tail of the machine and, there being nothing to hold me in the cockpit, I had tumbled out on to the grass. I lay where I had rolled; I couldn't move, and at first I couldn't see. Then I began to pick up my surroundings, the woods and the hurrying clouds racing past above. At last somebody came and rolled me over and unfastened my helmet and my collar, and began feeling me all over for broken bones.

Finally, I sat up and discovered that apart from the necessity of holding my head on with both hands I had come out of it with very little damage. I tried to get up without letting go of my head, and started falling about like a puppy.

'I'd take it easily for a bit if I were you,' said somebody.

I turned painfully towards the voice. 'I must have done it a bit of no good,' I said vaguely. 'Is the machine a write-off?' And then I managed to look at him.

'Good God!' I said weakly.

He wasn't a bad-looking fellow but for his clothes; a slight, dark-haired man of about my own age. As for the clothes, I've never happened to wear them myself because – for some obscure social reason – when I did my month it was in the second division.

I never really regretted that month. For one thing, the importance of a term of imprisonment depends entirely on the circle in which one moves, and my circle was never exalted. Moreover, I think it was worth it. It came as the result of a very pleasant little evening after a show at one of those places in Jermyn Street; there were about half a dozen of us there, all pilots. It was one of the best little suppers I've ever been at. Everyone was comfortably full but nobody made a pig of himself; it was funny without being vulgar, and this much I can truthfully say, that none of the girls went home next morning any worse than when they came.

At about two in the morning Maddison and I got restive; it seemed to us that an obstacle race in cars would provide a little excitement for the ladies. His car was some old racing chassis into which he had fitted a three-hundred-horse-power German Maybach that he had snaffled off some aeronautical scrap-heap, and he was very proud of it. Mine was nothing like that, but I was pretty sure that I could give him fits when it came to dodging round the lamp-posts. So we started from Jermyn Street.

17

I'll admit that we were pretty far gone, because I can't remember that we even fixed up a course to race. I had one of the Flossies with me in my two-seater. I forget her name, but she had a bag of oranges in her lap, and whenever she saw a pretty lady she threw an orange at her – whether from fellow-feeling or superiority I was unable to determine. For myself, I was very happy. I had one fixed idea running in my head: that I must on no account run over anyone, because then, as I explained to the Flossie as we shot down Haymarket, I should not only be drunk in charge of a motor-car, but drunk in charge of a manslaughter. I remember impressing on her that this was an epigram.

I am a little hazy as to exactly where we went. I remember a furious game of touch-last at the bottom of Whitehall which had to be abandoned for fear of running over the policemen who were trying to get on our running-boards, and I remember telling the Flossie as much as I could recollect of the Secret History of the Court of Berlin as we went round and round the Queen Victoria Memorial in front of Buckingham Palace. I think we got into Piccadilly by St James's Street, because it was in Air Street that we met our doom. I spun in here to get to Regent Street, meaning to go up and have a look at Madame Tussaud's. But there was a taxi in Air Street that impeded my cornering; I did the best I could, braked heavily, ran up on to the pavement, and impinged upon a lamp-post. Maddison, following close behind me, ran into my stern and – there the police found us.

I am not very clear about the proceedings at Vine Street. I imagine they were purely formal; I know they let the Flossies go after a bit, but Maddison and me they popped into the cells for the night. I decided then that it was time I pulled myself together; a little cold water and a cup of black coffee that they got me made a new man of me, and by the end of half an hour I had decided that my best line was to plead guilty. Maddison was worse than I. I could hear him in the next cell entertaining with song a small, discreet audience of constables in the passage. He was telling them all about the Yogo Pogo, I think, and I remember that he was particularly insistent on the fact that

> *The Lord Mayor of London,*
> *The Lord Mayor of London,*
> *The Lord Mayor of London wants to put him in*
>   *the Lord Mayor's Show.*

Since then I have often wondered about the Yogo Pogo, but I never learned any more. For myself, I went to bed and slept soundly till they came to call me.

Now the sequel to this had certain elements of humour. I hadn't a chance to speak to Maddison till they stood us up together in court. The magistrate asked me first what I pleaded, and I said that I pleaded guilty and would accept the findings of the court.

Maddison kicked me on the shins, pleaded not guilty, asked for a remand, and was taken away.

A policeman got up and said that my car mounted the pavement. Apparently that set the fashion, because in a minute everyone was saying that my car had mounted the pavement. It was evidently a far graver offence to mount the pavement than to run into the taxi. In fact, that was about all the evidence there was. In extenuation I said that I might have been a little excited, but I was very far from being incapable of driving a motor-car. I pointed out that I hadn't endangered anyone but myself. The magistrate said I had endangered the policemen who were trying to get on my running-board. I said that wasn't my fault, and got sternly rebuked. Then they asked me how much I had had to drink. I asked: Since when? and that didn't do me any good. They said, since six o'clock the evening before. I could see that it was hopeless by that time, so I gave them the account in chronological order so far as I could remember – two cocktails, half a bottle of sherry, about a third of a magnum, a glass of port, six whiskies (during the intervals of the theatre), another half-bottle of champagne (at

19

supper), and after supper a few more whiskies. That finished it. The magistrate told me that he greatly regretted that his powers were limited to a sentence of one month in the second division, and they took me away to Brixton.

Maddison, on the other hand, retained Eminent Counsel for his defence at a perfectly incredible fee, and got off. Maddison was never very bright at the best of times. With a touching faith in the integrity of the Law he paid Eminent Counsel to get him off and gave him a free hand. The result was perfectly appalling. Eminent Counsel started away back in 1915 and took the court through every little crash Maddison had had in ten years' flying. He must have been a pretty dud pupil; we heard that he wrote off two machines in 1915, three in 1916, and two more later in the war. Eminent Counsel was a little hard up for post-war crashes to account for Maddison's mental state, but he made such play with the material at his disposal that by the time he'd finished Maddison was a clear case for detention during His Majesty's pleasure and the Bench were inquiring how it was that the prisoner was apparently licensed to carry passengers in aeroplanes for hire or reward. At that point Eminent Counsel began to hedge a little. Maddison got off, but the evening papers made such play with him that the Air Ministry had to cancel his licence. That was a pity, because he was quite a good pilot.

The Air Ministry had a smack at me when I came out, but nothing like such a hard smack as that. The firm looked a bit old-fashioned at me, too; I didn't really blame them. They were all good sorts, though, and I think each of them felt secretly that it was up to somebody who had never happened to be drunk in charge of a motor-car to cast the first stone. In a month it had all blown over.

But all this is a digression. I sat on the ground in the rain for a bit and looked at the convict, and the convict looked at me.

'What the devil are you doing here?' I said.

I noticed that he was keeping his eyes open for anyone that

might be coming to have a look at the machine. He didn't seem to have heard me; I spoke to him again.

'What are you doing here?' I said.

He looked down at me as I sat on the ground, and smiled at me vaguely.

'What a damn silly question!' he said gently. 'I'm looking for the Philosopher's Stone; or – the Tree of Knowledge. One should have learned the difference between Good and Evil by this time, though, don't you think?' His voice drifted away into silence. 'But I doubt if it grows in this wood....' He roused himself. 'I don't think you're much hurt.'

I blinked at him. 'You'd better get back into that wood and go on looking for it, pretty damn quick,' I said. 'There'll be people here in a minute.' It was a wonder the crowd had not arrived already.

He nodded. 'Perhaps that would be wisest,' he said reflectively. I noticed that he spoke like an educated man. 'Are you sure you'll be all right now? That's good.' He moved towards the trees.

'Half a minute,' I said weakly. 'What about you?' I tried painfully hard to collect my wits. 'Do you want any help – is there anything I can do?'

He asked me if I meant it.

There was a sort of wheel and ratchet going round inside my head and I was feeling very sick. I wasn't at all sure that I did mean it; at the moment I hadn't enough go left in me to pull a sprat off a gridiron. I climbed slowly to my feet and stood there swaying gently in the breeze; he ran up and caught hold of my arm to steady me.

My head began to clear a little. 'Of course I mean it,' I muttered. 'One thing I ... one thing. What did they get you for?'

He looked at me in a way that made me feel pretty rotten for having asked.

'Embezzlement,' he said shortly.

I planted my feet farther apart on the grass and found it an assistance. 'Well, that's a good clean sort of crime,' I said vaguely. 'So long as it wasn't anything to do with dope or children. . . .' I pulled myself up; I was beginning to ramble.

But he looked at me curiously. 'You don't like dope?' he said.

I made an effort and pulled myself together a little. 'Get back into the hedge and don't stand talking in the middle of this field like a ruddy fool,' I said. He scuttled back to the edge of the wood. 'Now see here,' I said, 'I'll do whatever I can to help you get away. I owe you that. What is it you want – food and clothes? Do you want to get out of England?'

He looked at me suspiciously. 'You're not going to give me up?'

I told him to talk sense. 'For one thing,' I said, 'I could give you away now without bothering to get you into a trap, simply by going away and telling people that I'd seen you here. But here I am. I'll do what I can for you if you'll let me, or if you don't want any help I'll go away and forget I've seen you. Now that's square.'

He motioned to me to come close; he seemed suddenly afraid. 'It's most frightfully good of you,' he said, 'and I do want a bit of help. It's a thing that you can do quite easily, without any risk to yourself. There's a house about four miles from here on the other side of Stokenchurch. The house is called Six Firs. It's not my home – I daren't go near home. They'll be on the look-out for me there. But there's a cousin of mine lives with her people in this house – a girl, oh, a damn good sort. She'll fix me up if she knows I'm here. Go to the house and get hold of her, and tell her. Don't let her people know – they're too old. Tell her I'll be outside the house from eleven o'clock onwards. Tell her to leave the morning-room window open and to switch on the light in her bedroom when it's safe for me to come in.'

'She won't believe me if I go and tell her that,' I said. 'No girl would. She'd think I was trying it on.'

He gripped me by the arm. 'You've got to make her believe,' he said. 'You've got to – you simply must. I must see her – she may have heard – she may know something. Man, I tell you, I've got to be free for the next ten days. After that. . . . But she may know what's happening.'

He was becoming rapidly incoherent. I freed myself gently from his grip on my arm.

'I'll do the best I can,' I said. 'Six Firs, at eleven o'clock, with a light in her bedroom window. By the way, what's her name?'

'Stevenson,' he said, 'Joan Stevenson. My name is Compton.'

'Right you are,' I said. 'I'll go there and do the best I can. And see here – if I can't convince her I'll be near the gate myself at eleven o'clock tonight. Now you'd better cut off into cover.'

He turned and ran into the wood through the trees till he was out of sight. I noticed that he ran with a limp.

Well, there I was – and the devil of a fine position to be in, too. I turned and walked unsteadily towards the machine. She was in a shocking mess. I looked first at the engine. One of the connecting-rods had poked its way through the side of the crankcase and made a hole big enough to put my head into; through the hole one could see the mincemeat inside. I judged the machine to be a complete write-off; the port wings crumpled up and the fuselage badly injured close behind the engine. It was the worst crash I had had since the war.

I stood looking at it all for a minute, and it struck me that I was very lucky to have got out of it alive. It was now a quarter of an hour or more since it had happened, and nobody had arrived in the field. And then I thought that if Compton had not turned up I should still have been in the machine, pinned upside down, unconscious and dying – if not already dead. The thought of it fairly made me sweat with fright.

I was feeling much better by now. My neck had had a beastly wrench, but I could walk without holding on to it, and apart from that I was hardly hurt. I left the machine and began to walk along the edge of the wood in the direction of Stokenchurch. In all the half-mile that I walked through the fields to the road I never saw a soul. It was evident that nobody had seen me come down; that wasn't difficult to understand, because it was a brute of an evening and I had been flying very low above the trees, half hidden in the clouds. As I went on through the fields and met nobody I realized that I owed my life to this fellow Compton. I don't imagine that my life is worth much or that I've ever done much good with it; at the same time – it's all one has. And then as I walked on I knew that it was up to me to see this business through to the end and to back Compton in every way I could – even if it were to mean another spell in quod for me. Looking back now over the years I'm glad to be able to remember that I stuck to that decision, and backed him till he had no further need of me.

I went on, and presently I came to a road. A little way along it I met a Ford van delivering groceries to some outlying village. I stopped it and asked the boy for a lift in to Stokenchurch. He stammered and looked at me as if I was a ghost, said something in refusal, and tried to drive on. I jumped on to the running-board, leaned in over the wheel, and soon put a stop to that. And then I realized that appearances were against me. The hand that I switched off his engine with was covered in blood and oil; I had no hat and I could feel that something had happened to my hair. I discovered later that there was a deep cut over my right eyebrow that had bled all down the side of my face; it was drying now and my hair was all stuck up with blood on my forehead. I had been feeling so generally ill that I hadn't noticed it.

I told the boy what had happened. When I got him to believe me, his one idea was to go off and have a look at the machine. I told him I was going into Stokenchurch in his Ford whether he drove me or not. He perked up a bit at that, but I pretty soon unperked him, and at last we got going on the road to Stokenchurch

We got to Stokenchurch at about half past five. I went straight to the inn, postponed giving an account of myself and got on the telephone to Morris, while the crowd fluttered about outside and peeped in at me through the door of the room.

I told him what had happened. 'I hadn't an earthly,' I said. 'The clouds were right down on to the hills – I was only a hundred feet up when the engine conked. I told you it was running rough. What? Oh, yes, the machine's a write-off – absolutely, I'm afraid. What's that? Well, I can't say that it worries *me* much – only too glad to be well out of it. I don't give a damn about the machine. Yes, I dare say you do, but that's your worry. Oh, nothing to write home about, thanks. I got shaken up a bit and cut my eyebrow – nothing serious. I'm sorry it's happened, but I'm not taking any responsibility for it at all. I told you I wasn't fit to go. As a matter of fact, fit or not, it wouldn't have made any difference to what happened.' Which was a lie.

Rather to my surprise he said he was sending down the breakdown gang at once, and told me to fix up a meal for them. I rang off, and immediately found myself the sensation of the evening. I should think half the village crowded into the passages of the pub, all eager to see me and condole before I had my face washed. I managed to get away from the crowd, and the landlord's wife took me upstairs and bathed my eyebrow for me; I would have preferred the barmaid, but didn't like to say so. It was a clean cut and she made quite a good job of it for me, fixing it up with a bit of lint and sticking-plaster. Then I went down and saw the landlord and arranged about a meal for the mechanics over a stiff whisky.

Presently I began to throw out feelers about the Stevensons, and the house called Six Firs.

I said that I thought I knew some people called Stevenson who lived near Stokenchurch; at least, I knew of them but had never met them. He said that they would be the people at Six Firs. I was told that the house was about a mile from the village; with a little encouragement he told me the whole family history – so far as there was anything to tell. Arthur Stevenson, Esq., CB, was a man of about seventy, several years retired from the Treasury. His wife was only a little younger, and both were passionately fond of gardening. They always took first prize for sweet-peas at the local flower show. Before moving to Stokenchurch on their retirement they had lived for thirty years in Earl's Court. Their pew in church was close under the pulpit because the old lady was getting very deaf. There was a son in India, a major in the Indian Army. There was a daughter about twenty-five years old who lived at home and painted pictures – water-colours, I gathered – which had been exhibited at High Wycombe. They had a Morris Cowley which the daughter drove. The barmaid had a cousin who was their cook. That was all.

I said that my father had been at school with old Mr Stevenson, and I thought that I would walk up and call on them. He offered to send a boy with me to show me the house, but I got out of that and got directions instead. I borrowed one of his hats, and set off up the street.

As I went I realized the utter futility of the whole thing. It was impossible that such a household should shelter an escaped convict. It struck me at once that it wasn't fair on the old people; at all costs they must be kept out of it. It was evident that if there was any help at all coming from that house it must come from the girl; I can't say that I was too sanguine about her. From the landlord's description she sounded a blue-stocking of the most virulent description; it seemed to me that water-colours and escaped convicts were unlikely to go well together. Evidently I must try the house, but I thought it was more probable that Compton would have to stay in the woods for a day or two till I could get some clothes for him and smuggle him away.

As I drew nearer to the house I began to wonder how I should get hold of the girl without her parents. A succession of ideas passed through my head and were rejected one by one. I might say that I was soliciting custom for a projected milk round – but that wouldn't work in the country. Nor would the gas-meter do, where there was probably no gas. Finally, I fixed on the car as being the one thing in the house that would be solely the domain of the daughter, and decided to make that my line of attack.

The house was a pleasant-looking place on the wooded side of a hill, standing well back from the road in three or four acres of land. It was not a large house, but it was beautifully cared for; the gardens were small, but very neat. There was a large paddock with a decrepit-looking pony in it. It was about seven o'clock when I got there; the rain had stopped and the clouds were clearing off before the sunset. The garden smelt wonderful after the rain.

I rang the bell and a maid came to the door. 'Can I see Miss Stevenson?' I said. 'It's about the car – I'm from the garage.'

The maid went in and a girl came to the door. She must have been in the hall.

'It's about the car?' she said. 'You've come from Weller's?'

That was the first time I met Joan Stevenson. I wish I could recall that first interview a little more clearly. She was a tall slim girl with grey eyes, by her complexion a country girl, rather plain and – which seemed strange to me – without a trace of powder or make-up. She had very soft brown hair, bobbed; she was wearing a brown jumper, a skirt that looked like corduroy, and brown brogues. She looked me straight in the eyes when she spoke, which worried me and made me nervous.

I produced a jet from my waistcoat pocket. 'It's about the carburettor on your car, Miss,' I said. 'The makers sent a letter round to us agents to say as some cars was issued from the factory wiv jets as gives trouble in the morning, starting from cold, like. They was to be replaced without charge. So as I was passing along this evening the manager told me to look in.'

'It's very good of him,' said the girl, 'but she's always been very easy to start. Beautiful.' I could see that she was puzzled.

27

'Could I just 'ave a look at her,' I said, 'if it won't be inconveniencing? 'Course, if she's going all right, I says leave well alone. There's a sight more damage done messing them about than what there is leaving them alone. But if I might look to see what number jet she has got in, an' then I can tell the boss.'

She took me round to the back of the house, and there was the car standing in the coach-house with the doors open. We went into the coach-house, but I didn't open the bonnet of the car. Instead, I straightened myself up.

'Miss Stevenson,' I said, 'I haven't come about the car. I've come about your cousin, Compton – I don't know his other name. He sent me here to see you. He wants help.'

She looked at me incredulously. 'He sent you here?' she repeated.

'I saw him this afternoon,' I said. 'I'm afraid he's in trouble. He broke prison apparently – he's been in prison, hasn't he? He's in the woods close here, and he wants help to get a change of clothes and get away.'

'Who are you?' she asked.

I could see that this interview wasn't going at all well. I didn't see what else I could do but to plough ahead and tell her exactly what had happened; if then she chose to disbelieve it I should have done my best. 'My name is Stenning,' I said. 'Philip Stenning.' I set out to tell her all that had happened to me that afternoon. When I got to the bit about Compton coming out of the wood and pulling me out of the machine she stopped me.

'I'm sorry, Mr Stenning,' she said, 'but I don't believe a word of all this. It's quite true that my cousin is in prison, but I don't believe a word of the rest of it. You shouldn't have brought in the aeroplane, you know; it's laying it on a bit too thick. As a matter of curiosity, what were you going to ask me to do?'

I laughed; it was the only thing to do. 'For one thing,' I said, 'I was going to ask you to believe me. I was going to ask you to put out food and clothes for your cousin in the morning-room at about eleven o'clock tonight after your people have gone to bed, and to leave the morning-room window open and to switch on the light in your bedroom when the coast was clear. But I'm afraid you'll find that as melodramatic as the aeroplane.'

She smiled gravely. 'I'm afraid I do, Mr Stenning. Much too sensational. Now I'm going to go down to the police station tomorrow morning and tell them all about you, so you'd better run away back to London tonight. It's an ingenious tale and for the moment you very nearly took me in, but you spoilt it by bringing in the aeroplane. You wouldn't have got very much out of this house, though. There's only the silver forks and things and I don't think they're worth very much. We shall have to put them in the dog-kennel or somewhere to-night, shan't we? Now you'd better go.'

'Right you are,' I said. 'You can go to the police station, and they'll probably tell you who I am. But, for God's sake don't tell them anything about your cousin being out in the woods, because he'll have to stay there for tomorrow till I can get him some clothes. So if you go telling the police where he is there'll be hell to pay.'

She wrinkled her forehead in perplexity, but before she could speak I stopped her.

'Look here, Miss Stevenson,' I said, 'I know you don't believe me. But walk down to the village after dinner and collect the local gossip. I promise you that you'll find that an aeroplane crashed this afternoon, and that I'm the pilot. If you find that's true you can take a chance on the rest of the yarn. If you leave the morning-room window open and hide behind the curtains with the morning-room poker you can hit him on the head as he comes in and examine him at your leisure. I promise you you'll find he's your cousin.'

She looked at me seriously. 'If I find that's true,' she said, 'we may owe you a great deal, Mr Stenning. But my cousin has only six months of his sentence left to run.'

29

'Then he must have a pretty good reason for wanting to be out,' I said. 'Well, we'll leave it at that, Miss Stevenson.'

I walked back through the lanes to the village. It was a wonderfully quiet evening; the clouds and the storm were rolling away towards the east and the sunset was clear. The birds had come out again, and I remember there was a thrush calling somewhere in the trees. It was a long time since I had been in the country. It was time I took a holiday. I thought of the aerodrome and the machines and Manchester and my flat in Maida Vale, and the more I thought of them the more I hated them. I thought what a fool I was to live that sort of life. I didn't want to go back.

When I got back to the pub I found the local constable waiting for me to give an account of myself; he seemed a little hurt that I had not come to do so of my own accord. I was a bit short with him till I remembered that this case was probably the most important that he had had to deal with for six months; then I loosened up and stood him a drink. By the time that had gone down the lorry had arrived with the breakdown gang.

I went out and had a chat with the foreman of the men; he clucked his tongue when he heard what had happened, and opined that I was lucky to have come off so lightly with nobody there to help me out of the machine. I passed that off without a blush and hoped that his practised eye would not betray me when we came to the wreck, and then, though it was after eight o'clock, we went off in the lorry to get the machine. We found her as I had left her, lying on her back by the wood surrounded by a crowd of yokels. The ground was hard, being summer, so that we could get the lorry right up to her; the foreman clucked his tongue some more and set the men to work. An aeroplane comes to pieces very easily. In twenty minutes the wings and the tail were off and we were loading the fuselage on to the lorry; in an hour and a half we were back in Stokenchurch just as it was getting dark.

We passed Joan Stevenson in the village street. I stopped

the lorry, jumped down clumsily in my heavy coat, and went to speak to her. I pointed to the wreckage.

'There it is,' I laughed. 'I was just bringing it along to show you.'

In the dusk I could see that her face was very white. I sent the lorry on, and it rumbled away into the distance with the mechanics all telling each other that the captain was a quick worker.

'It's terrible,' she whispered. 'I'm so sorry I didn't believe you when you told me this afternoon, Mr Stenning. What are we to do? Where is he now?'

'He's in the woods,' I said. 'I really don't know what we can do. He'll know what he wants to do, though.'

She nodded. 'He'll want clothes, won't he? I found some old clothes of father's that he'll never miss. They'll be a terrible fit. Father's so much fatter.'

'We must get him something that looks as if it belongs to him,' I muttered, 'or he'll be caught at once. He'd better have this suit of mine till we can fit him out properly. We're very much the same build.'

She looked me up and down. 'You're much broader across the shoulders than he is,' she said, 'but the height is about right. But what's it all for? Where's he going to go?'

'God knows,' I muttered.

'How do you think he got here from Dartmoor?'

I started. 'He was in Dartmoor? He must have had luck to get all this distance.' And then I remembered that I had seen a headline in the morning paper over my breakfast at Manchester – a meagre and a sour breakfast it had been that morning – that a prisoner had escaped and was still at large. I remembered that I had commented on it to the photographer, and had wished him luck. I almost wished now that I hadn't.

'I saw it in the paper this morning,' I said. 'We shall have to be careful.'

'I know,' she said. 'I'll have the window open tonight as

soon as it's safe. Mr Stenning – will you come too? I don't know anything about these things. Would it be frightfully inconvenient for you?'

I laughed. 'Not a bit,' I said. 'I should have been a stiff little corpse by now but for him – and nobody any the wiser.'

'It's awfully good of you,' she said. 'He'll have to get out of the country, won't he?'

'I don't know,' I said. 'He said he only wanted to be free for ten days. But I'll come up this evening and we can have a talk with him and find out what it is that he wants us to do. I'll be skulking round outside till I see him get in at the window, and then I'll come along. That way, you'll know I'm not playing any funny business on you. Right you are, Miss Stevenson – at about eleven o'clock.'

'It's awfully good of you,' she repeated mechanically. She hesitated for a moment. 'I don't want to tell my father or mother if we can help it,' she said. 'We mustn't bring them into this unless it's absolutely necessary.'

I went back to the pub. The men were in the commercial room, busy over the meal that I had ordered for them. They didn't wait long; they were anxious to get back with the machine to the aerodrome, and so to bed. They grumbled a good deal over the journey, but it appeared that Morris was eager to get the machine back into the works and start on the repair. I wished him joy of it.

I started with them on the lorry. The landlord showed some concern at my departure; I think he was counting on me to stay the night and fight my battles over again in the bar. However, we all crowded on to the lorry in the darkness and pushed off, not without a little song and dance from the men.

Half a mile from the village I stopped the lorry and got down, and the lorry drove on towards London without me. I never heard what the men thought about it, but I doubt if this proceeding did my reputation any harm. That was hardly possible.

It was then about half past ten, and quite dark. I fetched a compass round the outskirts of the village through the fields, and presently found myself on the road for Six Firs.

It was beginning to feel most frightfully rocky. During the early part of the evening I had been almost myself; I think the whisky I was drinking then had something to do with it. Now the cut in my forehead had stiffened up and was aching and throbbing till I could hardly bear it; it was the only thing that prevented me from sitting down under a hedge and going to sleep. I was most fearfully done. I walked up to the house and got there at about ten minutes to eleven; a hundred yards up the lane from the gate I found a gap in the hedge. I got through this into the field and, skirting along the hedge, reached a position where I could command a view of the whole front of the house.

I sat down on a hummock in the darkness and began drowsily to consider what would be the best thing to be done for Compton. All the little noises of a country night in June conspired to take my mind from the problem and to increase my drowsiness. Somewhere there was an owl hooting irregularly; the air was full of little rustlings and squeaks. I sat there till my head dropped forward and I awoke with a start; then I got up and began to walk up and down the field. The lights were still on in the house. Then as I looked again one of the lights in the downstairs rooms went out, and then all the others. A light appeared in an upstairs room; I interpreted that to mean that the old couple were going to bed.

I began to wonder what I should do if I were in Compton's place and had to cut the country without undue ostentation. I knew the answer to that at once. I would do it on a small yacht. For many years it has been my hobby to knock about the Channel whenever I had the chance; I owned a six-tonner of my own one season in partnership with another man, but for the most part my experience has been gained on charters.

I knew the Channel pretty well. I was convinced that one could slip quietly in and out of England in that way without anybody being any the wiser. Now that the coastguard has been practically abolished there is very little restraint or comment on the movements of small yachts. One goes over to France and cruises the French coast for a time; on one's return to England one may invite the local Customs officer on board by flying an ensign at the truck. Or one may simply join the throng of yachts cruising up and down the coast; it is nobody's business to discover in what country the anchor last bit the mud.

Yes, I decided, that is what I would do. It would need a little organization; one would have to have a suitable boat ready and, if possible, get someone to provision her. Then it struck me that there is little advantage to be gained in these days by escaping from one country to another unless it be to one where there is no extradition. Still, it would be a step in the right direction to get as far as France. And rather than begin on a ten-year sentence I would push off for South America in a decent ten-tonner, though I won't pretend that my seamanship is in the same street as that of Captain Joshua Slocum.

I moved up closer to the garden hedge and began to study the house intently. There were no lights showing now. I remember that I was very cold. I thought I could see that one of the windows of the morning-room was open; for what seemed an interminable time I stood leaning on the hedge, listening to the noises of the night, watching the house.

Presently a light flashed on in one of the upper windows, and almost at the same moment I saw Compton. He was standing on the lawn in the shadow of a clump of laurels; I saw him move silently across the grass and vanish into the shadow by the window.

I sighed with relief. The main part of my job was over; from now onwards I should be acting in a purely advisory capacity. I think I really believed that at the moment. As I have said, I was most frightfully tired.

I waited for a few minutes, then got through the hedge and crossed the lawn to the house. There was somebody standing at the unlighted window; as I drew near I saw it was Joan Stevenson.

'Mr Stenning,' she whispered.

I got into the house through the window. It was then about twenty minutes past eleven.

Chapter Two

AS SOON as I got into the morning-room I made straight for the anthracite stove; I was nearly perished with cold from hanging about outside, though it was June. For some reason connected with the old man's health a stove was kept burning in this room all through the summer; they had not turned on a light but had made up the stove to such an extent that it threw a warm glow all over the room. Compton was sitting on a chair in front of the stove clad only in a shirt, and pulling on a pair of very large grey flannel trousers. Miss Stevenson was moving quietly about the room in the semi-darkness collecting the materials for a meal. I stood warming myself by the fire, and for a time none of us spoke a word.

Compton finished his dressing, stood up, and turned to me. 'I'm so sorry,' he said quietly, 'but I never asked you your name. . . .'

'Stenning,' I said. 'Philip Stenning.'

He nodded. 'Yes. I don't think I need try and tell you how grateful I am to you for – for this?' He glanced at the table and the room.

'I don't think you need,' I said, and laughed. 'What comes next?'

He did not seem to have heard my question. He stood for a long time staring down at his own feet, warmly lit up in the glow from the stove.

'What comes next?' he said at last. 'If I could tell you that I don't suppose I should be – like this. Plato wanted to know that, didn't he? and Sophocles – certainly Sophocles. But I'm so rusty on all that stuff now.'

'Come and have some supper,' said the girl from behind the table. 'You must be frightfully hungry.'

He roused himself. 'I'm not very hungry. But thanks, Joan.

What's that you've got there – ham? I'd like a bit of ham. And then I must cut off again.'

'Don't be a fool,' I said. 'Where are you going to?'

He shook his head. 'God only knows,' he muttered. 'I must lie low for a bit.'

I saw the girl pause in the dim light behind the table, and stare at him. 'You must get out of the country somehow, Denis,' she said. 'You must get to France.'

He looked at me vaguely. 'I suppose that's the thing to do,' he said at last. 'But I've got to stay in England for the present.'

She looked at him in that uncomfortable, direct way that she had. 'What do you mean – you've got to?'

He pulled out a chair from the table and sat down. 'I don't know if you imagine that I cut out of prison for fun,' he said heavily. 'Anyway – I didn't.' He relapsed into silence again, and sat for a time brooding with his eyes on the table.

The girl looked at me helplessly.

I cleared my throat. 'I don't want to butt in on any private business,' I said. 'But isn't this going a bit slowly? I don't want you to tell me anything that you'd rather not talk about before a stranger. But I owe you a good bit for what you did this afternoon, and I'm ready to help in any way I can. I've come here prepared to do so.'

I hope that I may be forgiven for that lie. I thought for a minute, and then continued: 'I didn't quite realize from what you said this afternoon that you really mean to stay in the country. I've been thinking about getting you out. I'll even go so far as to say that I'm pretty sure I can get you to France within the week. I mean that. But if there's any other way in which I can help I hope you'll let me know.'

'I don't want to get you into trouble,' he said.

'It doesn't matter a damn about me,' I said. 'But it seems to me that by staying in England you run a great danger of being caught again – in fact, it's pretty long odds against you. But – from now onwards you've got to think about Miss Stevenson here. If they get you they'll pretty certainly be able to trace out everyone who's been in contact with you, and that may mean trouble. I understand that you got out of prison for some reason – and by the way, it would be interesting to learn how you did it. The point I want to make is that if you stay in England it's up to you to avoid being caught, and it seems to me that that's a far tougher proposition than getting you out of the country.'

'I see what you mean,' he said slowly. 'Yes, I see that.'

He turned from me to the table and began to eat. He had had no food for thirty-six hours, he said; at the same time, he had very little appetite and ate a surprisingly small meal. I mixed myself a stiff whisky and sat down by the fire, wondering what on earth was going to happen to this chap. Now that I had time to study him more closely, I liked the look of him. He was much my own build with very much the same hair and complexion, though his hair was short while mine was long and brushed back over my head.

The girl came and sat down opposite me, but we said very little till Compton had finished his meal. I sat drowsing in front of the fire, whisky in hand, and tried to think what was the best line to take if he insisted on staying in England. I wanted to help him. It wasn't only that he had saved my life; I knew as I sat there in the warm darkness that I should have helped him anyway. I looked round the room in the red light of the stove; it was a comfortable, decently furnished place. I could imagine from the room something of the nature of the owner of the house, the girl's father. He was a collector of mezzotints; they stared down from all the walls, some beautiful, more grotesque, all very old. He liked old blue china, did the owner of the house; he liked books more for their old calf and vellum bindings than to read. There were soldiers among his ancestors, for the walls were scattered here and there with swords and cases of medals, and over my head there was a framed scroll of honour.

I glanced again at the man at the table, and realized suddenly why it was that I should have helped him in any case. It was because he was so like myself; he was just such a man as I might have been if things had gone a little differently. I might have gone to Oxford too. My father was a naval officer, my mother was a lady of the chorus in a Portsmouth music-hall. It didn't last long. Soon after I was born there was trouble. I never learned what happened to my mother, but whatever it was my father died of it – of that and of malaria on the China Station. I was brought up all anyhow. That's what I mean when I say that I would have helped him in any case. It might have been me; it would have been me if I had been the son of Mary instead of the son of Martha. I was Martha all over; I laughed quietly to myself as I thought of the only poet I had ever read:

> *It is their care in all the ages to take the buffet and*
> *cushion the shock,*
> *It is their care that the gear engages, it is their care*
> *that the switches lock.*

Yes, I was certainly Martha. I had thought that I was coming into this thing in a purely advisory capacity. I was wrong.

I finished my whisky in one gulp and sat up briskly, most frightfully bucked with life. I knew what we were going to do.

The girl noticed the movement, and asked me what was the matter.

'Nothing,' I said. 'But I believe we can work this.'

Compton finished his meal and got up from the table. He turned to the girl. 'I'm sorry to have come here like this, Joan,' he said. 'It's a pretty rotten thing to have done, but I didn't dare to go anywhere where they'd look for me. I don't know if you believe I had that money or not. That isn't the point, though. I'm sorry to have come here like this.'

'I don't believe you took a penny of it,' she said. 'I never did.'

He smiled queerly. 'Well,' he said, 'I did. I took five pounds to tide me over the week-end because I'd forgotten to cash a cheque. I left the account open – I had to, you see, or I wouldn't have been able to put it back. I was away till the Thursday over that motor accident – as you know. But I never knew anything about the other three thousand; that went into the account on Monday and out again on Tuesday. I couldn't have laid myself more open to it. At the same time, he was a clever fellow.'

I gathered that he had been secretary to some sort of charitable association. Charity, it was evident, had not begun at home.

I heaved myself up out of my chair, crossed to the table, and took another whisky. 'We've not got too much time,' I said. 'Now look here. Is it quite definite that you've got to stay in England?'

He nodded. 'I can't leave England for the present,' he said. 'I've got one or two things that I must see to before I go.'

His manner of putting it made me smile; he might have been speaking of a business appointment. I think it must have been then that I began to realize that he really cared very little what happened to him. I think it was this very casualness that probably carried him through.

'All right,' I said. 'Now there's just one thing we have to think about, and that's this. If you get caught it means trouble for all of us. You've simply not got to get caught. How long will it be before you can leave the country?'

He thought for a minute. 'This is June 6th,' he said. 'The 15th. . . . I could leave England on the 18th. That's in twelve days' time, on Monday week.'

'Do you think they've tracked you to this part of the country?' I said.

He shook his head. 'It's very difficult to say,' he said. 'But I had the most extraordinary luck. I came here by road. I wasn't out an hour before I got into the back of a motor-lorry that was coming from the prison; I stayed there for about two hours, till it was dark. I don't think they saw me there. Then we stopped outside a pub; I waited till the coast was clear and got into a field. The pub was on the London road, I think, because presently a motor furniture van stopped for a drink and I heard them talking about London. They were driving all night. I got on top of that and stayed there till daylight; we weren't far away from here then, on the Henley road. I followed along across country till I got to earth in those woods this morning at about six o'clock. I don't think anyone saw me.'

I thought of the Stokenchurch constable and realized that if the country had been up in arms over an escaped convict in the neighbourhood I must surely have heard of it.

I drained my tumbler and slammed it down on to the mantelpiece with a sharp rap.

'Now look here,' I said curtly. 'You've not got a dog's chance, acting on your own. If you cut off now they'll have you back in prison again within two days. There's just one thing we can do for you that will give you a sporting chance. We've got to get the attention of the police off you and on to something else. We've got to lay a few red herrings. I think I'd better cut off tonight and start laying them.'

I don't know to this day what made me say that. It may have been a sudden flash from the whisky; I know that the moment I had said it I wished I hadn't. I wasn't fit; I was still feeling rotten from the crash and I was most frightfully tired. But even so I was glad at the way the girl took me up.

She looked me straight in the face in that embarrassing way of hers. 'What do you mean?' she said.

I laughed, not very merrily. 'Why, safety first. If he gets caught it's all up with us – all the lot of us. We're all in the same boat now. I don't know if it would mean quod, but there'd be the hell of a scandal. Now I'm pretty much the same build as Compton. Look at me. Think if I had my hair cut and walked with a limp and wore clothes that didn't fit me ... I don't say that anyone who had the photograph of Compton in his hand would mistake us for a minute. But for the others ... I could lay a pretty hot scent.'

'Oh ...' she said. 'You can't do that. It's not safe.'

41

I took my glass and helped myself to another whisky.

'It's not safe to sit here doing nothing,' I said shortly. 'I could work out that scheme all right. If anyone's got a better one, let's have it.'

'That might work all right for a day or two,' said Compton slowly. 'It doesn't appeal to me much. But you couldn't possibly keep it up; if you laid a strong enough trail to direct their attention to you they'd get you long before the 18th.'

I shot the whisky down and felt better. 'I can fix that all right,' I said. 'And incidentally, I'll get you over to France at the end of that time if you want to go.'

He eyed me steadily. 'How would you do that?'

I set down my glass, feeling more myself than I had since the crash. 'What I think of doing is this,' I said slowly. 'I start off from here and lay a trail to the coast – to Devonshire. I take two days getting down there, perhaps three. I can do that. I can fix it so that they're damn certain they're tracing you, and I can do it without being caught myself. In Devonshire I pick up a seven-ton yacht, the *Irene*, belonging to a pal of mine, and get away to sea on her.'

'Oh . . .' said Compton.

I thought for a little. 'That would be about the 9th,' I said. 'I'd have to leave a pretty clear trail to show which way I'd gone, and get away to sea. Then I'd simply have to keep at sea till the 18th; it's a long time to be single-handed in a small vessel, but I can do it all right. On the evening of the 18th I stand inshore, pick you up, and trot you over to France. Then I think I should cruise on up Channel for a bit to throw off the scent, and come back a week or so later.'

'It's possible,' said Compton. 'Where would you pick me up?'

'The best place would be the Helford River,' I said. 'That's near Falmouth, you know.'

We discussed the details of the business for half an hour or so. At last I got fed up.

'Well, there it is,' I said. 'It's a perfectly sound scheme and

42

it'll get you out of the country as soon as you've finished whatever it is you want to do.' I looked at my watch; it was a quarter to one. 'If I'm going to start off on this I must be well away from here by dawn,' I said. 'Now, what is it to be?'

Nobody spoke for a bit, and then Joan Stevenson said: 'I can't see why you should do all this for us, Mr Stenning.'

'Better to be doing this than to be dead,' I said. I turned to the telephone. 'That's settled then. Now, I've got one or two things to fix up before I go. May I use your phone?'

We tied a table napkin round the bell to prevent it from ringing and then I got down to it. First I rang up Dorman, the owner of the *Irene*. He lives in a residential club near Marble Arch; they told me on the phone that he was out dancing and wasn't back yet. I left a message for him to ring me up, and impressed its urgency on the porter.

Then I rang up Morris. It was no use trying the aerodrome at that time of night, of course, so I rang him at his home. The exchange said they couldn't get any answer, but I kept them at it and got him in the end. He sounded pretty sleepy.

'Hullo, Morris,' I said, 'having a good night? This is Stenning speaking – Stenning. Look here, I'm not coming back to work for a bit – I'm taking three weeks' holiday. What? No, I'm not coming back to London at all. I'm tired to death. I can't go on flying like this. I don't care a damn about that. I'm sending you a report of the crash that you can send on to the Ministry. If you think I'm coming up to Town simply to fill in one of your pink leave forms you're ruddy well mistaken. I'm taking this leave on medical grounds. I'm not fit to fly for a bit. I told you I wasn't fit. Now I'm going off for three weeks, as soon as I've sent you my report. No, I'm damned if I will.'

He asked where I was speaking from.

'Giggleswick,' I said at random, and rang off.

I turned to the girl. 'May I have some paper and a pen, please?' I said. 'To write that report.' I crossed to the table and took another whisky. 'Then I shall want you to cut my hair for me, if you will.'

43

She brought me the paper from another room and I settled down at the table to write my report, the glass at my elbow. Compton and the girl sat by the fire close together, talking earnestly in a low tone. I didn't pay much attention to them, but concentrated my attention on putting my report into official language for the benefit of the Ministry. Their conversation put me off; I never was very good at letter writing, and I don't suppose I was at my best that evening. I didn't try to follow what they were saying, but the name Mattani came up over and over again; it had a staccato ring that stood out clearly in their low murmurs. I finished my report at last, read it through, and was annoyed to find that I had said that the engine failed completely at a point about three miles south of Marazan. For a moment I stared at it blankly, wondering if Marazan was a place or a person. Then I struck it out, and wrote in Stokenchurch.

I put the report in an envelope, addressed it to Morris, and gave it to Joan Stevenson to post in the morning. Then I sat down in a chair and she cut my hair; for a first attempt she made a pretty good job of it. When she had finished I went and looked at myself in the glass.

'I believe this is going to work all right,' I said.

Then she got some warm water and bathed the cut over my eyebrow for me. It was a pretty deep cut, one that would serve to identify me for the remainder of my life, but it wasn't bleeding and it looked healthy enough. She washed it in something that stung me up all right; then she put a bit of clean lint on it and stuck it up with plaster again. Then I changed clothes with Compton. When that was done I went and had another look at myself in the glass.

I was surprised at the change. With my hair cropped and the clothes that Compton had been wearing I really wasn't at all a bad imitation of him. Joan Stevenson was busy with another meal; I sat down at the table, wrote out a cheque to her for thirty pounds, and gave it to her to cash in the morning. We agreed that she should post the money to 'Mr

E. C. Gullivant, The Post Office, Exeter – to await arrival.'
I had about eight pounds on me, which would carry me to
Exeter.

Then Dorman rang up.

'Is that Dorman?' I said. 'Stenning speaking – yes, Stenning. I say, I want to borrow the *Irene* for a bit. Yes. I'd like
to take her on charter if I may – I want her for about three
weeks. No, really, if you can spare her I'd rather have her that
way. I'll give you six guineas. You're sure you don't need her?
All right. Now, I want her at once; I want to start the day
after tomorrow if I can. She's at Salcombe? I know it's pretty
short notice. You'll telegraph to Stevens about her? Good
man. Look. Tell him to fill her up full of water, will you? And
about two stone of potatoes. The rest of the stuff I'll have to
get in Salcombe.'

Joan Stevenson touched me on the arm. 'Tell him that I'll
go down and provision her for you,' she said. 'You won't be
able to.'

I covered the transmitter and did some rapid thinking. It
would be very convenient to find the vessel already pro-
visioned and ready for sea; at the same time, the girl must be
kept out of it.

'You won't have time to get any food,' she said. 'They'll be
after you by that time. I'll go down tomorrow and fix up
everything, if you'll tell me what to do.'

'Then they'll get you.'

'No, they won't. I'll be back in London twelve hours before
you get to Salcombe.'

I uncovered the transmitter. 'I say, Dorman,' I said.
'There's a cousin of mine here, a Miss Fellowes, who's going
down to Salcombe to buy the stores for me and put them on
board. Tell Stevens to expect a lady with the stores tomorrow
or on Friday. Yes, old Stevens knows me. What? Oh, I'm
sorry to hear that. What did he die of? Really. I'm very sorry.
I don't think I know the son. Anyway, you'll tell him to expect
me the day after tomorrow and to expect a lady first with the

grub. It's all right – I'm not taking the lady on board. I won't do anything to sully the fair name of the *Irene*. Oh, just up and down the Channel – I've got a holiday sudden-like. You'll telegraph first thing in the morning? Right you are. Good night.'

I rang off and turned to Joan Stevenson. 'Bit of luck there,' I said. 'The boatman doesn't know me. Now look here. I said I'd be there the day after tomorrow – that's Friday. I probably shan't get there till the Saturday, but it will keep them up to the scratch if they think I'm coming earlier than I am. Can you go down there tomorrow?'

She nodded. 'I can say I'm going up to London for a night,' she said. 'I often do that. Then I can catch an express at Reading and be there by tomorrow night.'

'That's splendid,' I said. The whisky had killed my fatigue and my mind was in good form for once. I pulled a sheet of notepaper towards me and set to work with her to make a list of the things that she had to get in Salcombe and put on board the *Irene*.

Twenty minutes later I turned to her. 'Now you've got to get all that on board on Friday morning,' I said. 'You've got to catch an afternoon train back to Town. I want to make that pretty clear, please. Anything that you can't buy or that you haven't got time to get you must leave to the boatman, Stevens. I don't want there to be any mistake about that. You've got to be out of Salcombe and on your way back to London by two o'clock on Friday. That ought to give you a clear day in which to get away before things start to get warm there. On the other hand, I may be pressed and have to run for Salcombe ahead of my schedule. I may want to get to sea on Friday. If I get there and find you in the neighbourhood still I shall have to dodge back on my tracks. That may be unfortunate for me.'

She nodded. 'I'll be away by two o'clock,' she said.

'Right. Now there's one thing more. The *Irene* will be lying in the Bay probably – that's up the river. I want you to see her

46

brought down to her summer anchorage off the jetty. Tell the boatman that I want her there in order that I can get off at once. See that done yourself: it's important. And remember, your name is Miss Fellowes, and I'm your cousin.'

I made her repeat her instructions till I was sure she had them perfect, and then I sat down and had a meal. She offered to make me some coffee, but I refused that, had another whisky, and followed it down with a couple of plates of cold ham. One thing she got me, though, that went down well, and that was a little bottle of aspirin. I took four or five of them and they eased off my headache a bit, so that by the time I'd finished my meal I was very nearly fit.

I looked at my watch; it was a little after three. I lit a pipe and strolled to the window. It was a wonderful night. The clouds and the wind were all gone and there was a full moon dying down upon the horizon, big and red. Faint, earthy, flowery smells came in from the garden, and away in the field there was something squeaking plaintively, continuously, as it had been while I was waiting to enter the house. I leaned on the window-sill smoking and wondering what should be my first move; it was clear that I must begin operations at a considerable distance from Stokenchurch. It seemed to me that Abingdon, five miles south of Oxford, would be a good place to lay my first red herring; it was fully twenty-five miles away and on my road to Salcombe.

The curtain was pulled aside and Compton came and stood staring beside me. He didn't speak, but stood there staring moodily out over the garden, his hands in his pockets. And presently I heard him mutter to himself: 'The New Utopia. . . .'

'Eh?' said I. 'What's that?'

He didn't answer, but began to ask me how I was going to pick him up at the Helford River. I told him about a little beach that there is there close to the entrance; we fixed that I should be there from eleven o'clock till three on the night of the 18th–19th, and again, if he didn't turn up, on the night of the 19th–20th. If he weren't there then I would give it up and return to Salcombe.

He understood what he was to do all right, but for the rest he was distrait and moody. I knew all the time that I was talking to him that I held only a part of his attention; he seemed incapable of concentrating his mind on the measures that I was working out for his own safety. I am surprised that this didn't irritate me; as it is, I can only remember thinking how woefully unfitted he was for the business that he had taken on. I was sorry for him, I think.

He roused himself at last and turned from the window. 'I'd have done better on a pig farm,' he said, a little bitterly.

For the moment I didn't quite see what he was driving at. 'I've always thought myself that there was money in pigs if you go about it the right way,' I said. 'But it needs a good bit of capital. And they say there's a lot in the breed – more than you'd think. I was talking to a man at Amesbury about it last month.'

He looked at me curiously. 'I always had a great fancy to keep pigs,' he said. 'Live-stock of all sorts – but pigs in particular. I don't know why. My grandfather was the same. I used to look forward to it as a thing that I might do when I retired from business. I suppose I hadn't the courage to break off into it when I was young.'

He paused for a minute, and then he said: 'Shall I ever be able to come back to England?'

I knew that the girl was watching us; I could feel her looking at me for my reply. I couldn't see her, but I knew that she would be standing very straight, looking straight at me from her grave, deep eyes. I knew then what it was that embarrassed me whenever she spoke to me, something that I suppose I had never met in a girl before. Behind her were centuries of tradition, the traditions of a good college, of a good regiment, of a good club. She could have answered his question so much better than I could – but then, I don't suppose he'd have paid much attention to her.

I checked the emphatic negative, and turned to him. 'Man alive,' I said slowly, 'you've been a ruddy fool over this. What on earth made you break prison?'

He was going to speak, but I stopped him. 'I don't know what it is that you've got on hand,' I said, 'and I don't want to. If all goes well we can get you out of the country all right. But – is it worth it?'

He didn't speak, but stood staring out into the dim shadow of the woods. I went on:

'You'll never be able to come back to England now, you know, unless it's under a false name.' It was as if I had been speaking to a child. 'You've done with England. Your best line – the one that I should try if I were you – is to try and ship before the mast on a French vessel. Become a sailor for a year or two and see where that takes you to. Maybe you'll end up in America. But you've done with England.'

'Yes,' he said quietly, 'I've done with England.'

'There's the alternative,' I said.

'What's that?'

I knocked my pipe out sharply upon the window-sill. 'That you should go back and finish your sentence,' I said. 'When you've finished it, set up a piggery somewhere here in the south. There's money in that. In that case I'll borrow the car and run you up to Scotland Yard in the morning. Don't think that I'm suggesting this because I'm lazy.'

I turned round and saw the girl standing close behind us. 'Don't you think that would be the best thing to do?' she said.

He shook his head. 'I can't do that,' and from his tone I knew that that was final.

'Right you are,' I said. 'It's time that I was starting. I must be well away from here by daylight.'

The girl produced a rucksack from a cupboard; I had decided that I would pose as an art student or somebody of that sort on a walking tour. I chose an art student because I had knocked about a bit with them in their less artistic moments both in London and Paris, and I knew enough of the jargon to pass with anyone but an artist. The girl helped me to pack the bag with the convict suit and one or two things that she thought would come in handy, including an immense packet of ham sandwiches that she had been cutting all evening.

As she bent over the thing on the floor, tightening its straps, she leaned towards me. 'It was frightfully good of you to say that,' she muttered.

'I'm only sorry that he won't do it,' I said.

She tugged at a strap. 'You mustn't think it's going to be any easier for him this way,' she said. 'I do wish he could tell you about it. You've been such a good friend to us.'

We finished with the rucksack. Then we tidied up the room as well as we could, and made sure that there was no trace of Compton left behind us. We couldn't entirely do away with all evidence that the room had been occupied; the girl would have to see to that with the maids. Then we got out of the window, closed it quietly behind us, and went round to the garage. We had to be pretty quiet here to avoid waking the servants; for silence we pushed the car outside the gate and a hundred yards down the lane. There we started her up, got in, and trundled off for Oxford.

It was about half past four. The girl drove and I sat with Compton in the back seat. He was deep in his own thoughts; for a while he tried absently to make conversation, but soon relapsed into a silence that stretched unbroken through the miles. I remember he asked me if I had any ties in particular, if I was married or engaged.

'Lord, no,' I said. 'Nothing like that about me.'

I think he may have learned more from the tone in which I spoke than from my words, because he nodded slowly.

'There's safety in numbers,' he said. 'And it's really the happiest way, I suppose. Just take what you can get, and be thankful.' He relapsed into silence again, but something in the way he said that had given me a nasty start. It may have been that I was tired. It may have been that it was the sanest, most horrible hour of the twenty-four, when the cold grey dawn comes creeping up over the fields and means the beginning of another blasted day. I only know that my whole life was summed up in those words of his. I only know that they've come back to me time after time, and always with the same bitter ring in them. 'Take what you can get,' he said, 'and be thankful.'

A little later I said: 'It's getting quite light.'

He smiled. 'Hassan,' he said, and I wondered what on earth he was talking about.

Thy dawn, O Master of the world, thy dawn;
The hour of the lilies open on the lawn,
The hour the grey wings pass behind the mountains,
The hour of silence, when we hear the fountains,
The hour that dreams are brighter and winds colder,
The hour that young love wakes on a white shoulder —

He stopped short, it seemed to me in the middle of a sentence. I didn't remember all this stuff, of course, but long afterwards Joan built up the quotation from my garbled memories, and she wrote down a copy of the lines and gave it to me. I kept that carefully and I have it still – not for the poem, but for another reason.

It was very cold. The rush of cold air made my head sing and throb painfully; I wanted to concentrate on my plans, but couldn't focus my mind at all. Then I realized that I'd made a slip; I should have brought a flask of that whisky with me. I was sobering up. That meant that I should be no good at all until I had been to sleep; indeed, it was imperative that I should get some sleep soon. I was frightfully done. I had intended to lay my first red herring that very morning and clear off out of the neighbourhood; I saw now that that was impossible. I must lay my red herring after I had slept, or I should be an easy mark.

We went through Stokenchurch, down the Aston Rowant hill, and on over the plain through Tetsworth and finally by Wheatley. I should have gone on through Oxford, but the girl knew a trick worth two of that, and we turned off in Wheatley and for half an hour went wandering through lanes that seemed to lead to nowhere in particular. Presently she stopped the car by the side of the road and pointed to a spire about a couple of miles away.

'That's Abingdon,' she said.

I took my rucksack and got out of the car. She gave me the map that was kept in the pocket of the car; it was a fine large road map covering the whole of the south of England. We bent over it together and she showed me where I was, about two miles to the west of Abingdon.

'Right you are,' I said. 'Now you'd better get along back.' She was to drop Compton at a railway station; it was his business to lie low till the hue and cry was finally established after me. Then she was to get back to Stokenchurch before the servants got downstairs, and be ready to make an excuse and start for Salcombe after breakfast.

She turned to the car, and for a minute we stood together in the road, unwilling to separate. Then I shook hands with them and wished them luck. The girl got in and I started up the car for her, wondering if I should ever see either of them again. Then they drove off. The last I saw of them was Compton looking back at me, white and impassive as he had been all the time. It worried me, that look of his.

Well, there I was. It was about half past five in the morning, and to all appearance it was going to be as hot a day as the day before had been before the rain. I picked up my rucksack and trudged along the road, only half awake, looking for somewhere to sleep.

And then I saw the haystack. It stood by itself in the corner of a field; it was a fairly low one with a tarpaulin pitched over it like a tent. There was nobody about; I summoned up the last of my strength and climbed up on top of it. There was a space about two feet high beneath the tarpaulin. I took off my boots, dug myself a nest, made myself thoroughly comfortable, and fell fast asleep.

Chapter Three

IT MUST have been about midday when I awoke. I opened my eyes and lay blinking at the tarpaulin above me. It was getting very hot beneath the covering. I lay for a little collecting my thoughts; then I put on my boots, collected my things, and crawled to the edge of the stack.

It wasn't long before my troubles began. I looked round and didn't see anybody about, so I dropped the rucksack down on to the ground and half slid, half fell down after it. I reached the ground more or less inverted in a flurry of hay, and sat there for a bit trying to get it out of my ears.

At that point somebody shouted: 'Oy!'

I looked round, and there was a stocky-looking young man in breeches and gaiters striding up the field. From the first I disliked the look of him. He was one of those flamboyantly sharp young fellows that you sometimes find in the bar of a country pub; I suppose every village has one or two like him. He would be the local Don Juan, the crack billiard-player, the acknowledged authority on last year's musical comedy, the smart lad of the village. I looked at him with misgiving.

'Here comes trouble,' I thought. And I wasn't ready for trouble. I hadn't made any plans.

'Oy!' he said again. 'Coom on aht of that.'

I got to my feet and picked up my rucksack. By this time he was quite close.

'Coom on,' he said. 'You git on aht o' this. What the ruddy 'ell's the game? Hey? I seen you. You was up on top o' the stack. Hey?'

'Right you are,' I said. 'I'll move on.'

He stepped in front of me. 'No, you don't,' he said. 'You don't catch me like that.' He laughed. 'Not likely. What's the game? Hey?'

53

'All right,' I said. 'I've been sleeping here. That's all.'

He took me up at once. 'No, you wasn't,' he said. 'You was up on top o' that stack. I seen you slide down.'

'Damn it,' I said, 'I was sleeping on top of the stack.'

That seemed to amuse him. 'Oh,' he said. 'You was, was you. You can't come it over me like that.' Then, as luck would have it, he caught sight of the rucksack. 'What's that you've got there?' he said. 'Coom on. Let's 'ave a look.'

I stepped back a pace. 'You can leave that alone,' I said. 'It's no business of yours.' I didn't want him to see the convict clothes in the bag.

'Ho,' said he, 'so that's it. D'you reckon I don't know what you've got in that bag? Hey? D'you think I don't know the game. I'll tell you what you've got there. One o' my Plymouth cockerels. That's what you got there. One o' my Plymouth cockerels. The one as had his leg trapped, so's you got him easy. That's what you got there. Hey?'

It was absurd. To show that I was not responsible for the missing cockerel I had only to open my bag, and that was precisely what I could not do. It became evident to me that I was in a corner; that I could only get out of this absurd situation by laying a red herring. I must see that it was a good one.

I moved over to pick up my cap; as I did so it occurred to me to walk with a pronounced limp.

'Hey ...' he cried, and stopped short. I thought I could detect a note of uncertainty in that 'Hey', and smiled to myself. I crammed the cap on my head and turned to him again. He looked undecided and furtive; the colour was not so high in his beastly face as it had been. For a moment I felt quite sorry for him. Then I dropped my bag.

'What do you mean by that?' I said.

The stuffing seemed to have fallen out of him all of a sudden. 'I didn't mean nothing,' he said.

I moved a little closer to him. 'Oh yes, you did,' I said. 'Now suppose you think a bit, and tell me just what you did mean.' I eyed him carefully. He was a bigger man than I, but I could see that he wasn't going to give me much trouble.

He didn't answer, so I asked him again.

'I seen about you in the paper,' he muttered. 'I didn't mean you no harm.'

'That's as it may be,' I said very softly. 'But you weren't very hospitable, were you?'

Then I hit him. Looking back upon it now, I think that was the dirtiest thing I did in the whole business, if not in my life. He hadn't a notion what was coming to him. He was peering forward at me as they always do when you suddenly drop your voice. It's a trick I learned when I was a boy; I suppose that shows the sort of school I went to better than any words of my own. He was leaning forward; I caught him fairly on the point of the chin with the whole weight of my body behind it. His teeth came together with such a crack that for the moment I thought I must have broken his jaw, then he crumpled up at the knees and fell backwards in a heap at my feet.

As I say, I think it was about the dirtiest blow I ever struck. At the same time, I dare say I should do it again. I was four miles from a railway station; with this village Sherlock on my trail I'd never have got away. I owed it to Compton to make a better show than that.

There were a lot of tag-ends of bindings lying about on the ground, little thin bits of rope about the thickness of a pencil, but quite strong. Before he came to I had got him well trussed up, with his hands behind his back and his feet tied. Then I took him and laid him in the ditch by the haystack and covered him up with hay all except his face. I sat down beside him and waited for him to wake up, occupying my time and inventive capacity in devising a gag from his handkerchief and a bit of stick.

He came to himself presently, and when he was moderately clear I talked to him like a father.

'Now look here,' I said. 'You've got to stay here for the next five or six hours I'm afraid – and just to make sure that you do, I'm going to gag you. I don't suppose you'll be able to untie those knots. I see you know who I am; I'm Compton, the convict from Dartmoor. Nobody knows I'm in this part; if you hadn't come interfering with me I'd have let you alone. As it is, I've got to protect myself. Now, I'm going to gag you and leave you in this ditch covered over with hay; then I'm going up to London by train. When I get there I'll send a telegram to your home to tell them where you are.'

He began to swear in a perfectly dreadful manner, so I gagged him and nearly got my finger bitten off in the process.

'If you do that again,' I said angrily, 'I'll give you such a clip on the ear as'll send you to sleep again.' I got out my note-case and a bit of pencil and waited till he had done struggling. 'Now, what's your address? You'd better tell me quickly: it's your best chance of getting loose this evening.'

I untied the gag and he told me his name, Fred Grigger, and the name of his farm. I noted that down and gagged him again well and truly. Then I turned him over on his face and put another lashing on his hands for luck. Finally, I turned him right way up again, made him as comfortable as I could with a bundle of hay under his head, covered him over with hay, and left him to his own devices.

It was about half past one. I studied my map for a little and decided to make for Culham station, which I judged to be about four miles away. I picked up my rucksack, slung it over my shoulders, and set off down the road munching a sandwich as I went.

It took me some time to find the station and I had to ask more people than I liked. However, I was lucky in my train, which came along about ten minutes after I arrived. I booked a ticket to Reading, meaning to change there and get along down west after I had telegraphed about Grigger.

At Didcot an engine-driver got into my compartment with his mate. It struck me that I might get a little information out of them, and sounded them about trains for the west. It appeared that the next Exeter train was the 5.10 from Paddington, getting to Exeter at about half past eight. It stopped at Reading. I considered this information carefully. The train that I was in was due at Paddington at 3.34; it seemed to me that it would be wiser to go on up to Town and send my telegram from there rather than to risk identification by hanging about on Reading station for three hours.

We got to Paddington at about twenty minutes to four. I dived straight down into the Tube and took a ticket for Waterloo. At Waterloo I came up into the daylight again and plunged at random into a labyrinth of mean houses and squalid streets. After walking for five minutes I found a post office and sent the following telegram:

'Grigger will be found in a ditch by a haystack near the Dorchester Abingdon road tied up and covered over with hay.'

I put a false name and address on this and passed it across the counter; the girl looked at me curiously as she gave me the change, but didn't make any comment. I impressed myself on her memory by asking the way to St Pancras Station, and being so dense that she had to explain it all to me twice. Then I got away, found my way back to Waterloo and so to Paddington again. I had a quarter of an hour to spare, so I went out and bought a cheap suitcase into which I put the rucksack without unfastening it. It made me a little too conspicuous for my liking.

I got down to Exeter without any further incident, though I must say I was glad the train didn't stop at Didcot. It seemed to me that I shouldn't run much risk in going to a hotel for the night so long as it was one in keeping with my clothes and general appearance. I wasn't exactly tired, but I had the feeling that the chance of a good night in bed wasn't one that I could afford to despise.

I had stayed in the town once or twice when I had been flying in the neighbourhood, but I didn't want to go to the sort of hotel that I had stayed at then. For one thing, they might remember me, and that would tend to spoil any dramatic effects that I might want to produce when I left the town. I took my bag and walked from the station up to the High Street, and then down the hill towards the river. I crossed the bridge and a little farther on I saw exactly the sort of place I was looking for, a 'family and commercial' hotel of a definitely middle-class type. I went in there and booked a room, signing myself in the register as E. C. Gullivant.

I was afraid to stay in the hotel; it was becoming clear to me what a nerve-shaking thing it must be to be a genuine fugitive from justice. I didn't quite consider myself as that yet, though I must say the Abingdon affair had turned me into something remarkably like it. I went out again into the street, and up the town, and presently I turned in to a picture-house.

I like the pictures. It's the only place where I can enjoy myself when I'm at all tired. I never was one for reading much, and most theatres nowadays seem to require that one should be a little drunk to appreciate them properly. But the pictures are different; I turned in to this show with my pipe, sat down in the darkness behind a pair of couples and began to think what I was going to do next. I thought it pretty certain that I had thrown off any pursuit from Abingdon; at the same time I had managed to lay a good fat red herring there in the approved desperate character style. My next move must be calculated to bring discredit on the fair name of Gullivant.

This was Thursday evening. By this time Joan Stevenson would be in Salcombe fixing up the vessel for me – it seemed incredible that it was only that morning that I had left her and Compton. She would be clear of Salcombe by tomorrow afternoon; I could go down there tomorrow evening if I wished and get to sea at once. I knew that I could trust her to have everything ready for me.

There were two girls in front of me sitting together and flanked by their attendant swains. Suddenly one of them turned to the other:

'He's bitten me!' she said indignantly.

This sent me into a paroxysm of subdued laughter and put a stop to any further planning for the moment. I laughed so much that they heard me and broke away from the clinch; it was evident that I had spoiled their evening and presently they got up and went out, not without dignity. I was sorry then. It has always seemed to me that one should live and let live; after all, one never knows when one may want to bite a girl in the pictures oneself.

I stayed in there till the end of the show and then strolled back to my hotel. There was nobody about in the hall and I got up to my room without meeting a soul; a circumstance for which I was thankful. I was getting very nervous; I was half sorry that I hadn't spent the night in the fields somewhere. It was a warm night; I could have done so quite well.

I undressed slowly, pondering my plans. I came to the conclusion that I must lay two more red herrings before I got away to sea – good smelly ones. One I would leave next day in Exeter or the neighbourhood; the other I would lay in Salcombe itself on the Saturday morning, so that there should be no difficulty in connecting me with the departure of the *Irene*. I cannot remember that at any time I worried very much as to what would happen when eventually I brought the *Irene* back to Salcombe and took up my ordinary life again. That didn't worry me at all, oddly enough. I think that even then I must have realized that things were unlikely to go exactly to plan. For one thing, I thought that Compton would be caught by the police long before I landed to pick him up on the little beach at the entrance to the Helford River.

Still pondering deeply, I got into bed and snuggled down beneath the clothes. Then I swore, more in astonishment than in pain, because it was clear that somebody had been being damn funny with my bed. There was something in it, down at the foot. I lit my candle again and groped about at the bottom of the bed, and presently fished up a small china candlestick ornamented with a wreath of blue roses and the legend: 'A

Present from Plymouth.' And then I saw that it had a little china ring for a handle, and through this ring there was stuffed a piece of notepaper, rolled up into a little cylinder. On the paper was the direction, scrawled carefully in pencil:

'Mr Compton.'

'Good God!' I said weakly, and sat staring at it for a moment. Then I pulled myself together, took the paper from the candlestick, and unrolled it. It was quite a short note.

'The party you coshed at Abingdon got free at 4 and made hell you was a fool to tell him. Mattarney comes to England before the 15th and goes on with the boat. Write to RLT he can fix up for you to see him. You're OK now but move on tomorrow.'

Short, snappy, and probably very much to the point. It wasn't signed.

I must have lain in bed staring at the ceiling for fully half an hour, the paper in my hand and the candle guttering by my side. At last I roused myself, blew out the candle, and tried to summarize my conclusions before I went to sleep. The note I placed carefully in the pocket of my coat. I would have burned it there and then but for the reflection that if I did so I should think in the morning I had been under the influence of alcohol.

First of all, my unknown correspondent was in touch with a pretty efficient intelligence bureau of some sort. This bureau was evidently illicit or it would hardly be priming me with information of that sort. They knew all about Compton and were well disposed towards him. There was the information that Mattarney was to do something on the 15th, 'and goes on with the boat'. Compton's important day had been the 15th, and he had spoken about Mattani to the girl. I wondered who Mattani was and whether he was Irish or Italian. Lastly, it was evident that the bureau didn't know everything, because they hadn't tumbled to the fact that I had changed places with Compton.

I hoped most devoutly that the police would prove a shade slower at the uptake than this lot.

One thing was clear; that some organization was keeping a benevolent eye on me in the belief that I was Compton. Whether they would continue to do so when they learned the truth was another matter. I began to feel that I was not the important person that I thought I was; that I was a mere pawn in some game that Compton was playing which I knew nothing about. This worried me. It seemed to me that the best thing I could do was simply to carry on as I had intended, to lay my red herrings to the best of my ability, and to get away to sea as soon as possible. At the moment the only thing I could do was to go to sleep.

I turned over on my side and began to drowse. There was one point in the note that struck me then, and the drowsier I grew the more important it seemed, till it seemed to me that it contained the whole essence of the affair. Mattarney ... goes on with the boat. What boat was that? Surely not a liner; the phraseology seemed all wrong for that. A merchant vessel of his own? A yacht? And where was she going to?

Then, just before I went to sleep, my mind went off at a tangent. Private intelligence bureaux with a fatherly interest in criminals might be assumed to be criminal themselves. What grade of criminal was likely to need the services of such an organization? Secret societies have never had a very great vogue in England unless for definite purposes of gain. What sort of illicit gain? Coining? That didn't seem very likely. It would be something more easily concealed, some business in which the risk of detection was small, the profits large, and with a necessity for numerous agents. Possibly the boat was connected with it. Could it be some form of smuggling? That didn't seem to fit in with modern conditions.

And then, quite suddenly, I remembered what Compton had said when I asked him what he was imprisoned for. He had told me.

'Embezzlement,' I had said. 'Well, that's a nice clean sort of

61

crime. So long as it wasn't anything to do with dope or children.'

He had looked at me curiously and had asked rather a curious question considering that he was pressed for time.

'You don't like dope?' he had said. And I had cut him short. I wished now that I hadn't.

I slept well in spite of everything. I woke at about seven o'clock, got out the note, and read it again. Then I lay for a long time trying to make a plan. The essentials weren't difficult. I had registered in the hotel in the name of Gullivant. Gullivant had to be firmly identified with Compton, the convict, in such a way as to bring the police hot on the scent. I didn't think I ought to do that too early in the day. Salcombe was not so very far away from Exeter; I didn't want my Exeter reputation to follow me there before I was ready for it. I must have a bit of a start.

I dressed thoughtfully and went down to breakfast. It seemed that I was the only person in the hotel, which was very little more than a pub in point of fact. I ate my breakfast under the eye of the waiter, lit a pipe, and turned into the commercial room. Idly I picked up a paper, and there it was.

It shrieked at me in headlines on the front page:

OUTRAGE BY ESCAPED CONVICT ON OXFORD FARM
COMPTON IN LONDON?

Compton, the escaped convict from Dartmoor, was identified in Oxfordshire yesterday, where he was the author of a violent attack upon a young farmer, Frederick Grigger, in a field near Abingdon. The convict made good his escape, and at the time of going to press he is still at large. It is believed that he is making for London.

Our correspondent found Mr Grigger at his farm, where he is recovering from his injuries. 'I was walking along the hedge,' said Mr Grigger, 'when he dashed out and came at me like a mad bull.' Mr Grigger was severely handled. 'I am a strong man,' said Mr Grigger, 'having been runner-up in the South Oxfordshire Ploughing Championship two years ago, but he shook me as a terrier shakes a rat.' The motive of the outrage remains a mystery, though the disappearance of a cockerel from Mr Grigger's farm may supply a clue.

· · · · ·

There was a lot more of it; Grigger had evidently made the most of his opportunity. To every man, I suppose, there comes the chance of fame of one kind or another, and one would be a fool not to make the most of it. At the same time, it looked like being very awkward for me if it ever came out who I was. He had fairly let himself go. As I read the account I began to get a little indignant; he hadn't played fair. He said that I had struck him with a loaded stick. I hadn't; I struck him with my own strong right arm – as he knew perfectly well. My knuckles were still sore.

A waiter passed through the room and saw what I was reading. 'Shocking thing about this convict, sir,' he said.

'Perfectly appalling,' I said gravely. 'I can't think what the police are about, letting this sort of thing go on.' I was pleasantly conscious that I was providing him with the sensation of his life.

I finished my pipe and went out to the post office. My letter was there, an envelope with thirty pounds in notes in it. I looked for some letter with the notes; it seemed to me that it would have been an improvement if there had been a line or two of encouragement with the money. However, there wasn't. It was safer so, anyway.

I went back to the hotel and asked for a Bradshaw, asking at the same time if they knew anything about the trains for Liverpool. They didn't, so I settled myself down with the Bradshaw to map my route to Salcombe. There was a train to Kingsbridge, the station for Salcombe, at 3.30, changing at

Newton Abbot. I traced it back; it left Taunton at 2.45. There was a train from Exeter to Taunton at 1.56, arriving at 2.33, and this went on to the Midlands. I could get to Taunton and catch the train back again through Exeter to Kingsbridge with twelve minutes to spare at Taunton. The only thing I should have to be careful about was that nobody recognized me as I passed through Exeter again on my way west.

I got hold of a copy of *The Times* then, tore out that part of the shipping intelligence that covered the sailings from Liverpool, took the rest of the paper upstairs and left it in my bedroom; I could imagine the delight with which it would be greeted by some amateur detective later in the day. Then I went out into the town again and bought a long green raincoat and had it made up into a brown-paper parcel. In another shop I bought a deer-stalker hat; this I put in my pocket. Finally, I went back to the hotel and told them that I should be leaving after tea.

There was about a quarter of an hour before lunch. I went upstairs and opened my suitcase; there was the rucksack, the convict clothes, and one or two personal odds and ends of my own that I had stuffed into the pockets of my flying coat before leaving the aerodrome – a razor, shaving-brush, etc. I put these in my pockets. Then I took the convict underclothes, a rough grey shirt and vest with the initials of His Majesty splashed all over them with a stencil, and made them up into a parcel with the raincoat. The rest of the clothes I put back into the suitcase and left there, a handsome present for the owner of the hotel.

I went downstairs and lunched heavily; I didn't know exactly when my next meal would be. Then I took my parcel and walked out of the hotel without paying my bill, but leaving my suitcase in the bedroom. They would realize when I didn't turn up in the evening that all was not as it should be, and presumably would look inside the suitcase to make sure there was security for the debt. I wished them joy of it.

I walked to the station; at the booking office I asked the

price of a ticket to Liverpool. I retired without doing any business, came back again and asked the price of a ticket to Birmingham. The clerk looked at me askance this time, particularly when I questioned his information and asked if there was any way whereby I could get to Liverpool any cheaper. Having impressed myself sufficiently on his memory, I bought a ticket for Birmingham, asked the collector which was the train, and got in. From the train I was intensely gratified to see the clerk come out of his office and start gossiping with the ticket-collector, evidently about me.

Then we started. As soon as we were well under way I left the compartment I was in and walked along the corridor till I found an empty one. Here I unpacked my parcel and put on the raincoat and hat, making up the convict underclothes into a smaller parcel. Then I tore up my ticket for Birmingham and threw it out of the window. Presently a ticket inspector came down the train; I explained that I had had no time to book at Exeter, and took a ticket to Taunton.

At Taunton I went out into the town, made a rapid circuit round the station, and reached the down platform in time to book a ticket for Plymouth and to catch the train. Remembering the geography of the platform at Exeter I got into a compartment in the front of the train that would pull up well clear of the booking office, my chief hazard. But all went well. At Exeter I remained snuggled up in the far corner of the compartment, and after a five-minute halt the train pulled out of the station without any untoward incident having occurred to mar the even tenor of the afternoon.

I had tea on the station at Newton Abbot, booked again for Kingsbridge, and got there at about half past six. It was a clear warm evening and the air was sweet and fresh, with that indefinable salt tang that you only seem to get in the west. I had decided to sleep out. I still had the packet of ham sandwiches that Joan Stevenson had cut for me at Stokenchurch, and I had bought a bottle of Bass at Newton Abbot which protruded coyly from the pocket of my raincoat. It seemed to me that it would be safer to sleep out; Exeter was barely fifty miles away and I was pretty sure that my red herring would be tainting the breeze there before the evening was far gone – if indeed, it was not doing so already. I didn't want to be haled from my bed in the middle of the night to spend the remainder of it in the local police station. That would have been very distressing.

I turned out of the station and began to walk up the hill towards Salcombe, some six miles away. It seemed to me that it would be best if I found somewhere to sleep among the fields, not very far from Salcombe. Then I could walk into the town in the morning, find the boatman, and make all ready for my departure. I could then come ashore, lay my final red herring, and get away to sea.

I walked on up over the hill and through a village. Presently I came in sight of the sea, blue and smeared with currents like snail tracks beyond a stretch of yellow, gorse-covered headland. I was frightfully glad to see the sea, I remember; I hadn't been to sea for over a year. I needed a holiday and I wanted a cruise in a decent little boat almost more than anything. Moreover, I felt that it would mean an end to my responsibility for Compton – for the time at any rate. Once at sea I shouldn't be able to do any more for him.

When I had been walking for about an hour I came to a crossroads and a pub. I went in here and had a very satisfactory little meal of bread and cheese and beer; I explained that I had started to walk from Kingsbridge to my hotel at Salcombe, but found that I should arrive too late for dinner. I sat over the remains of the meal for a long time, smoking and pondering my last red herring. Abruptly, I made a change in my plans, paid my shot at the pub, and began to walk back towards Kingsbridge.

It was a perfect evening. The sun was setting brightly into the sea; there were no clouds about and hardly a breath of wind. I looked at the sun again and recalled the remnants of my weather lore; it seemed to me that everything spoke of calm weather and easterly winds. I thought that that would do me very well. I must confess that I didn't relish the idea of eight days single-handed in the Channel if the weather were at all tough.

I walked back almost as far as Kingsbridge. I must have had a divination for haystacks in those days, for I found another one to extend me its hospitality for the night. It stood about two fields away from the road. It was nearly dark when I chanced on it. The stack was half cut away and there was a pile of loose hay at the foot of it; I rolled myself up in this and made myself comfortable for the night. I was still carrying the parcel of convict underclothes; I made this a foundation for my pillow.

I lay for a little worrying about the note that I had had at Exeter, and finally fell asleep.

I woke up early and lay for a long time trying to go to sleep again. The sun was too strong, however, and a little before six o'clock I was sitting up and taking notice, ready for the day's play. First I got out the parcel of underclothes and examined the garments more closely. It seemed to be pretty obvious to whom they belonged; at the same time, it would be as well to take no chances. I got out my packet of ham sandwiches and ate all I could of them for breakfast; there were two and a half left when I had finished, the half being artistically munched at the edges. I got out the Exeter note, read it through carefully, put it with the underclothes and the remainder of the sandwiches, and made the lot up into an untidy parcel. My red herring was ready; it remained only to lay it.

They had told me at the inn that there was a bus from Kingsbridge to Salcombe at nine in the morning, connecting with the train arriving at 8.42. I hung about the outskirts of the town till I saw the smoke of the train, then strolled down the hill to the station and mingled with the little crowd in the station yard. The Salcombe bus was there and soon filled about half full with passengers. I noticed that the top of the bus was stacked high with supplies for the Salcombe shops;

groceries, Tate sugar-boxes, sides of bacon, and all the rest of it.

I bought a copy of the *Daily Mail* and got into the bus. I opened the paper and there I was again, in Exeter this time. There was a photograph of Compton on the back page and a description of him inside. There wasn't so much in the letter-press about me as there had been the day before; on the other hand, I had achieved the immortality of a ten-line editorial. This pleased me vastly. Grigger, I learned, was recovering from his injuries. I might have half killed him from the fuss he was making about it.

The bus started, and we went trundling out over the road that I had walked the night before. In half an hour we were running down the hill into Salcombe; I pulled myself together for the last lap. A great deal now depended on whether Joan Stevenson had done her part of the business all right. I didn't think that she would have let me down, but – a good deal depended on her.

We lumbered into sight of the harbour past the Yacht Club. Looking out over the low stone parapet of the road I saw the *Irene* lying at her summer moorings off the jetty, trim and smart, with the mainsail uncovered and the jib set and rolled. I remember registering a vow that one day I'd meet Joan Stevenson again to thank her. As things turned out, that vow wasn't necessary.

The bus drew up in the narrow street outside the door of the railway agency, completely blocking the road. The conductor got out first and began to busy himself with the stores on the roof; the bus was soon surrounded by a little crowd of the local shopkeepers, all talking nineteen to the dozen. I waited till the last of the passengers had got out of the bus, left my parcel on one of the seats in a corner of the bus, got out into the road, and mingled with the crowd. My red herring was well and truly laid; it only remained for me to get away before the drag began to run the scent.

I guessed that it would be ten minutes before the parcel was discovered and at least another twenty before it became clear to whom it had belonged. That gave me half an hour – with any luck – in which to get to sea. It would be sufficient if everything was ready – not unless.

I dodged down a side street that led to Stevens's yard. I found the yard without difficulty and a boy showed me which was Mr Stevens. When I had been here before it was with his father that I had dealt; the son was a stranger to me. I walked towards him, steadying my pace and trying to make believe that there was no hurry.

'Morning, Mr Stevens,' I said. 'My name's Stenning. You've heard about my charter of the *Irene* from Mr Dorman?'

He laid down his awl and rubbed his hands together slowly. He was a pleasant-looking bronzed man of about fifty, already a little stout. I knew him by reputation as the crack sailor of small craft in the estuary – or on the coast for that matter.

'Aye,' he said slowly. 'She's all ready for you. We looked for you yesterday. The young lady was down puttin' your stores aboard.' He mused a little. 'You'll have them two stone o' potatoes all sprouting in a week. I told the young lady, I said, "You don't want to buy all them potatoes." She would have it. She said you was to have two stone, and two stone you've got.'

He asked when I wanted to get away.

'At once,' I said. 'As soon as possible.'

He looked at me. 'Can't go afore one o'clock,' he said. 'Flood's still making.'

I nodded. 'She'll run out over the flood with the engine,' I said. 'I've got to get to Torquay either today or early tomorrow to pick up a friend. If I get away at once I'll take the last of the tide with me round the Start.'

He nodded sagaciously. 'You want to stand well in to Start Bay,' he said. 'You'll be on a foul tide all afternoon. Rackon you'll not do much good before six.'

He entered on a long string of admonitions as to pilotage,

and from that drifted into an account of the stores in the *Irene*. I didn't dare to hurry him very much, but presently I gently cut him short and suggested that he should put me off to the vessel.

We got into his dinghy and he rowed me off to where she lay at her moorings. I explained to him as we rowed out that my friend in Torquay was bringing with him all my luggage, one reason why I was anxious to get there that day. He shook his head. 'You'll not do it without your motor,' he said. 'You'll find the wind on the southeast outside, I rackon.'

The *Irene* was a little black cutter of about seven tons. She had the usual accommodation. Forward was the forecastle with a hatch to the deck. There was a folding berth in there, but mostly it was dedicated to cooking; one could sit upright to cook very comfortably. Aft of the mast there was the saloon with a folding berth on each side. Aft of the saloon one came on deck to the cockpit, and under the floor of the cockpit, accessible from the saloon, was her engine, a seven-horse-power Kelvin. Aft of the cockpit was a sail locker, in the counter.

I went all over her with Stevens. Everything was aboard; Joan Stevenson had done her bit wonderfully well. Stevens said dryly that she had been very particular. It was evident that he was making a considerable effort to restrain his curiosity; he commented more than once on the futility of lumbering up the cockpit with six cans of petrol when I could buy a can every time I went ashore.

In half an hour I had gone over everything and was only anxious to be off. He helped me to get the anchor short; then he went off in his dinghy and got the kedge for me, while I uncast the tyers to the main. He came back presently with the kedge and we stowed it in the cockpit with its warp. Then we hoisted the main together. Finally, we got the *Irene*'s dinghy on deck and lashed her down over the skylight.

'Anyone 'd say you were going to France,' he remarked cheerfully.

Then we got the motor going and eased her up to her anchor. I went forward and broke it out; then while I stowed it he held on slowly down the river. Finally, I came aft and took the helm. Stevens wished me luck, got into his dinghy, cast off, and dropped astern. I gingered up the engine a bit and stood on down the river. I was off.

Chapter Four

I STOOD away down the river under engine alone, heading dead into the wind with the main flapping idly above my head. Salcombe is one of the prettiest rivers in the west; I never drop down it without mentally thanking God that I'm alive. I suppose I was doing that this time, but all I can remember is the bright, hot sun that made the teak of the little cockpit warm to the touch, the faint tarry smell of the vessel and her gear, the white surf on the beaches that line the river, and the dark firs above. We stood on slowly down the river, stemming the tide. Slowly we drew up to King Charles's Castle; they used to stretch the chain from there in the old days. A little farther on a bit of a swell told me that I was crossing the Bar. Tennyson or somebody wrote a poem about that Bar; with the police hard on my heels I can only say that there was very little moaning at the Bar when I put out to sea.

I stood up to try and sniff the breeze. There was very little of it, but what there was seemed to be pretty well due south. I edged the vessel over to the west side of the entrance underneath Bolt Head, put her about, left the helm, and went forward and broke out the jib. It flapped lazily in the light airs; I decided to give her the balloon foresail and went aft to get it out of the sail locker. I busied myself in setting this for half an hour or so, the vessel ambling along gently through the water with an occasional touch on the helm from hand or foot.

I got the sail bent at last, ran it up the forestay, and had the satisfaction of seeing it fill and pull well. There may be a more satisfactory light sail to carry on a small vessel, but if there is I don't know it. When that was drawing to my satisfaction I went back to the helm, shed some clothes, sat down in the cockpit, and considered the position. It seemed to me that my best plan was to stand away out to sea till I was eight or ten miles off shore and well clear of the three-mile limit. I didn't really know if the police had the power to arrest me on the high seas, but I didn't think they had. I stood on for the three-mile limit with the engine thumping pleasantly below, and the calm water eddying away slowly beneath the counter. Presently it struck me to put out a mackerel line.

For a long time I let the vessel slip along on her course, still under engine. Then I lashed the helm and went below to get my lunch. I looked over the stores in the lockers and found everything ready for me, nothing forgotten. I put a kettle on the Primus for some coffee and opened a tin of bully. There were some tomatoes there that I hadn't ordered; I suppose she had thought of those herself. I made my coffee and set it aside to cool while I looked for the brown sugar. I found the sugar in one of those blue packets in an old biscuit-tin; one end of the packet seemed to have been unwrapped. I opened it, and there was a bit of white paper on top of the sugar, folded up into a little square. I knew what it was as soon as I saw it.

I went and stood in the hatchway with my head and shoulders on deck while I unfolded and read the note. It was quite short.

'DEAR MR STENNING,

'I do hope you'll find everything all right and as you wanted it. I think I've got everything. I hope you'll let me know how you got on when you get back, but I want to tell you now what a grand thing it's been of you to have done all this for us. I wanted to let you know how I feel about that, and to wish you the very best of luck.

'JOAN STEVENSON.'

After a time I went back to my lunch.

I washed up my plate and cup and came on deck. We were then some two miles off the Prawle and heading about south-east. The breeze was a little stronger than it had been before lunch and I stopped the engine; then, to my vast surprise, I found that I had caught a mackerel. I dispatched him and put

73

him in a bucket, and set to fishing in earnest. In half an hour I had caught six, and then, as if Providence realized that I had enough to be going on with, I caught no more for the rest of the day.

I spent the afternoon overhauling the gear. I didn't know what sort of a time I was going to have. If all went as it had gone so far, I should have a very pleasant little cruise, if a trifle solitary; on the other hand, if it blew up rough it would be damned unpleasant.

By the time I had come to an end of my little jobs we were a considerable distance off the land; I could see the whole run of the coast from Downend in the east to the low land behind Bolt Tail in the west. The sea was very calm and the wind light; we were hardly making any way through the water. At one time the Prawle had been abeam, but it was now clear that we were being carried down Channel on the tide; I decided to make the most of it and to put about, which I did with some difficulty in the light wind. Then I thought it was a pity to waste what might be the one calm day for a fortnight, and went below to commence an orgy of cooking.

I studied the fresh-water tank as I peeled potatoes. It was even smaller than I had thought it was; I didn't think that it would last more than a week with the greatest economy. In any case, in eight days' time I should be embarking Compton and remaining at sea for perhaps another three or four days with the two of us aboard before I could land him in France. It was pretty evident that I should have to land for water some time or other; it was equally evident that it must be before I picked up Compton. I didn't worry about it very much; it was no use making plans too far ahead.

Presently I had tea.

There was a gentle little wind after tea, pushing me slowly along down Channel. I came on deck and sat smoking at the helm, edging still a little farther out from the land. A black, dishevelled-looking steamer came bearing down on me from the east and passed me within a hundred yards; she was a collier, and as she passed on her way an untidy-looking gentle-man in a bowler hat waved a carrot at me in friendly salutation from the door of one of her deck-houses. After that the wind fell light, and I got out Joan's note and read it over again.

As the evening came on I began to snug the vessel down for the night. I took off the balloon foresail and ran up the staysail in its place; then I rolled down a reef in the main, more as a precaution than because I thought anything was coming. The glass was as steady as a rock, the wind was in the east and the sun setting with every promise of fine weather. When the reefing was done I began experimenting with various settings of the helm and sheets to find her best setting for lying quietly, though I had very little doubt that she would lie-to all right in a moderate wind. My trouble would come in heavy weather, when I could hardly leave the vessel to herself under sail while I slept. In that case my only course would be to take all sail off her and lie to a sea anchor. The one essential point was that I should have plenty of sea-room.

I got her to lie all right after a little adjustment and left her to it while I got my supper and made my bed on one of the folding berths. I made my bed on the weather side in order that any sudden list of the vessel beneath a strong puff of wind would wake me or tip me out of bed on to the floor. Then I got the side lights filled, lit them, brought them up on deck, and set them up on the shrouds. It was sunset, with the sun setting into a clear sea as it had been the evening before – a fine-weather sky if ever there was one. I was somewhere off Big-bury Bay and about eight or ten miles out; I tried to see the Eddystone lighthouse, but it was somewhere in the sunset and I couldn't pick it up. I picked up the light quite easily as soon as it grew dark, as well as the Start.

Scenic effects were by Vesper. I moved about the deck as it grew darker, tidying up the odds and ends and putting a lash-ing on to every movable object I could find. The wind was still light; it was freshening a little with the sunset and settling into the usual steady little night breeze. The vessel was still lying quietly; I went below and lit the cabin lamp. Then I came up again and relashed the helm. It was dark by this time but for a streak or two that lingered in the west.

I had never spent a night at sea alone béfore, and I found it lonely. I stayed up on deck till I grew cold, watching the blink of the Eddystone; I judged it to be about ten miles away, from the way in which the light shone down on the horizon. But the cabin looked bright and cheerful as the light streamed up through the hatch, and presently I left the deck and went below.

I slept pretty well, considering all things. I was up on deck at about half past one, and again at about four. Eddystone seemed much closer, not more than five miles away; I judged that the tide was carrying us down towards it. I was up again at dawn, but we were well clear of the rock – indeed, not very much closer to it than we had been before. I turned in again and went to sleep with an easy mind, and slept till nine.

There was more wind when I got up than there had been the day before, and the mill-pond calm was gone. I didn't think it was safe to let her sail herself, so I left her hove-to while I dressed and got my breakfast. Then I came up on deck with my pipe, made a tour of inspection, and finally got her on a course down Channel and settled down at the helm.

That was the first night of several that I spent at sea alone. That day was June 10th, and a Sunday. The wind freshened up a bit during the day and began to knock up a little sea, though it was nothing to worry about. I lay-to for the night somewhere off the Dodman, between Fowey and Falmouth and about ten miles off shore. I slept all night without waking. In the morning I woke to find another calm; I drifted about all day off Falmouth. I don't suppose I covered five miles between breakfast and five o'clock. It didn't worry me at the time; I was off Helford and all I had to do was to hang about there for a week or so till it was time to land to collect Compton.

Towards the evening I began to get uneasy. It seemed to me

that if I were to hang about off Falmouth for a week the fishing-boats or the pilots would be pretty sure to report me on shore; it was too public a place altogether to loiter about in. Before I knew where I was somebody would be coming off from Falmouth in a motor-launch to have a look at me. I chewed this over for a little, and came to the conclusion that my best plan would be to get out into the Atlantic past Land's End for a bit; the weather seemed set fair and I wasn't afraid of the open sea. It was obviously right to go that way and not back up Channel again. For one thing it was less public, and for another it would be better to go to the west of the place that I wanted to get to at a definite time, which was Helford. In the Channel an easterly wind seldom lasts very long, and this one had already held for several days. The probability was that it would soon go round into the southwest; if that were to catch me up Channel again I might have some difficulty in getting back to Helford to time. It was obviously best from all points of view to round the Lizard and stand out to sea for a bit.

It was obviously the right thing to do, but I must say that I had an attack of cold feet before I could bring myself to do it. I never was a proper sailor; the open sea always puts the wind up me, though of course one is safer there than anywhere else in a small vessel. I am by nature a coaster, I suppose. I only know that when a little breeze came up from the southeast again and I stood out past the Lizard into the Atlantic, I was about the loneliest creature on God's earth.

I stayed up late that night getting well off shore; it was about one o'clock when I hove-to and went below. There was a long swell coming in from the Atlantic, not very high, and the glass had gone down a little bit. I interpreted this with my vague weather lore to mean a strong wind out in the Atlantic, probably westerly. In anticipation of a change of wind I turned in without taking off too many clothes.

The change didn't come, but trouble of another sort did. Early in the morning, when it was just light, the jib sheet carried away. I was roused by the crack and the beating of the sail; at the same time the vessel began to wallow horribly as she fell away from the wind and came up into it again all standing. I tumbled out on deck; the wind had freshened up and was raising a cross sea against the swell that made her very lively. I had left her for the night with more stern canvas than was wise; I had to go forward and drop the peak before I could get her to lie-to against the staysail. She lay all right like that while I went forward and slacked off the jib halliards, putting the sail into the water. Then I got out on the stem and worked the overhaul of the jib till I had the sail on deck. She was dipping her nose into it in a perfectly disgusting manner, so that every time she dipped the water came over me green.

It took me an hour to get the mess cleared up. I was soaked to the skin and very cold; the only spare clothes on board were an old sweater and a pair of bags of Dorman's. I put these on and huddled into my blankets again to try and get warm. Presently I gave it up, and went into the little forecastle to hold the kettle on the Primus while I boiled it for a mug of Bovril. The vessel was riding nicely, but she was throwing herself about a good bit; I didn't dare to have the forecastle hatch open for fear of a sea, so that by the time I'd boiled my kettle the atmosphere in the forecastle was pretty ripe and I was too sick to drink the Bovril. I took it on deck for a breath of fresh air, but by the time I could face it it was cold.

It was quite light by this time, and I was somewhere off Mount's Bay. I went back to my blankets, and presently I fell asleep and didn't wake till ten. I cooked my breakfast in the cockpit rather than in the forecastle, and managed to enjoy it in a limited sort of way.

I got under way again soon after breakfast and spent the day at the helm wrapped in a cocoon of blankets, with my clothes spread out and drying in the sun. The easterly wind still held and we had a fine sail out of the mouth of the Channel. There was very little incident that day. I passed the Wolf lighthouse during the afternoon, going about three miles to the south of it in order to avoid the set of the tide into the Irish Sea.

That day was Tuesday. I got a sharp reminder about my water supply in the evening, when the tank was so empty that the water in it made a persistent thundering noise in the forecastle. I tried to plumb it to see how much there was left, but failed on account of the motion of the vessel; by banging on the outside I judged it to be about half full. I thought about this as I cooked my supper. Evidently I should have to land for water in the next day or two. It seemed to me that the only place on the mainland that was suitable for watering was the Helford River, where I was due to pick up Compton in a week's time. To land would mean that I must leave the vessel unattended; that meant anchoring. It would have to be carried out at night. The only places in the neighbourhood where I could safely run in at night and anchor the vessel were Falmouth Harbour and the Helford River.

I thought about this for a long time that evening, sitting in the hatchway after supper. The more I thought about it the less I liked the idea. I was to pick up Compton at Helford. I didn't want to draw attention to the place beforehand; however carefully I went about my watering, somebody was pretty sure to notice that a vessel had come into the river after dark and had slipped away before morning. If there was any hue and cry for me on the coast, that wouldn't do me any good when I wanted to use Helford for picking up Compton.

Besides, the only well I knew at Helford was in the middle of the village, too far up the river and too conspicuous for my purpose. I couldn't go wandering all round the countryside in the dark looking for water.

The bold course might be the best; to sail straight into Falmouth Harbour soon after dark with all lights and sailing lights displayed, anchor in the yacht anchorage off the town, and set a riding light in the normal manner. I could leave a light burning in the saloon, row ashore, and get my water at the fish quay. I didn't think anyone would dream of challenging me. The chief trouble would lie in getting away again. A yacht getting under way in the middle of the night would arouse suspicion at once, and once the cry was up a motor-boat could catch me three times over before I got to the Black Rock at the entrance. I shouldn't dare to wait in Falmouth till dawn.

I thought of France. I didn't know the coast of France very well, but I had very little doubt that I could smell my way by chart into some place where I could get water. The trouble there was that I hadn't a passport or papers of any sort either for myself or for the vessel. The Customs would probably compose the first bunker; I might get hung up under arrest while they made inquiries. And France was rather far away.

I thought it over for a long time and came to the conclusion that the safest place to water would be the Scillies. I had visited the Scillies several times before in small vessels. They were by no means a perfect haven when secrecy was essential. I shouldn't dare to attempt any of the entrances to the road-steads in darkness; it would have to be a daylight show, and that in itself made me hesitate. On the other hand, I did know one cove where I could lie safely and that wasn't overlooked by any house. And there was water close by.

The Scillies consist of a group of six large islands and a number of small rocks, all roughly grouped around a central lagoon that is open to the west. All of the six large islands are inhabited save one – White Island, that lies roughly parallel with Pendruan, the most northerly of the islands. White Island is about as large as Pendruan; it remains uninhabited because of the barren nature of the soil, being, in fact, very little but a rock of granite. Pendruan, a few hundred yards to the south, is rather more fertile and provides grazing for a few sheep; there are two cottages on the southern side. Between the two islands there is an anchorage that is entered from the northeast, un-buoyed, but not difficult to get into. I had been in it two or three times before; in westerly winds it makes a very calm anchorage, with the disadvantage that you have to row the dinghy three miles to St Mary's to get stores. Part of the anchorage is overlooked by Round Island lighthouse; I should have to take my chance of that.

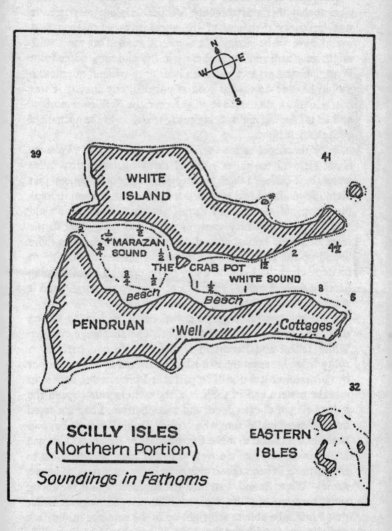

39

41

WHITE ISLAND

2

½

MARAZAN SOUND

½

¾ ½

2

4½

THE CRAB POT

1 2

WHITE SOUND

½ 1

Beach

1½

Beach

3

5

PENDRUAN

Well

Cottages

32

SCILLY ISLES
(Northern Portion)

EASTERN ISLES

Soundings in Fathoms

I thought about it for a long time, and came to the conclusion that that was the only practicable place to water. It was less risky than any of the alternatives, even though it would have to be a daylight show. It seemed to me that I might very well run in there early in the morning, water from Pendruan, and get away after an hour or so without question. I should have to do that as soon as possible, but already it was nearly dark. I should have to get near the Scillies tomorrow and lie off for the night, being ready to slip in to the anchorage with the first light.

I lay the vessel to for the night and went below. We were about eight or ten miles south of the Wolf, say thirty miles from the Scillies. I had a nasty fright about steamers that night. Soon after I had gone below I heard one of them thumping along quite close, and turned out on deck to see an old tramp pass within fifty yards of me. I was lying right in the track of vessels bound up and down Channel, as well as those bound up the Irish Sea from the south. There was nothing to be done about it; I couldn't stay up on deck all night burning flares at them. I had a bad attack of wind-up that night, and it was some time before I got to sleep.

I got my breakfast early next morning, and made a long study of the chart before I let draw. The anchorage between White Island and Pendruan is divided into two parts by a rocky ledge between the two islands, covered by only a foot or two of water at low tide. The part that I proposed to anchor in was the eastern end of the strait, the western side beyond the ledge being of uneven depth and rocky bottom. I had anchored in the eastern end before when cruising with Dorman, but had never had occasion to make a great study of the chart; Dorman had known the place too well to bother about charts. Now to my surprise I found that it was sufficiently important to have a name – White Sound. I studied the approaches to it for a long time, working out the various lighthouse bearings in order that I might be able to sail right up to the entrance in the dark and slip inside with the first light. There should be little difficulty, I thought, in doing that if the night were fine, though I knew that I should have strong and variable tides to contend with as I approached the islands.

I finished making my notes, but before putting the chart away ran my eye over the various features of the group, noticing particularly the course that would have to be taken by a motor-boat coming from St Mary's to intercept me. What I saw cheered me considerably. From the summit of Pendruan I should be able to see any boat approaching a good half-hour before it could get to me. That made me reasonably safe, the well being on the summit of the island. I thought that if I saw anyone coming while I was watering I should stand some chance of being able to get away to sea before they reached White Sound.

Then, in a final glance at the map before putting it away, I saw something that checked my breath for a moment and sent me straight back to the house at Stokenchurch. I have said that I was surprised to see that the eastern half of the straight between White Island and Pendruan had a name. I now saw that the western end of the strait, beyond the rocky ledge, was differently named.

The western part was called Marazan Sound.

I remember that I sat quite still and looked at that for a bit. Then I lit a pipe and looked at it again. There it was in print as plain as anything – Marazan Sound. I must have sat there for a long time, but presently I put the chart away, went on deck, and got the vessel on a course about northwest. I settled down at the helm and sat there all day; all day I puzzled the problem that had suddenly come upon me. I knew that Joan and Compton had been talking about Marazan while I was writing my report on the crash; I had even written the word down in my report by mistake. In the same connexion they had spoken of Mattani or Mattarney. Now with this evidence before me I was nearly sure that the word Marazan that I had overheard had been coupled with the word Sound.

I didn't give much weight to that impression, of course, but

I found the whole matter sufficiently disturbing as it was. I had actually written down the word in exactly the same spelling as it now appeared on the chart. Two possibilities that could not be overlooked suggested themselves. One was that I had seen the word on the chart some time before, and my ears had twisted some similar-sounding name to fit the name I knew. I thought that damned unlikely. The other possibility was that there might be more than one Marazan. One would expect names like that in Spain, along the borders of the Mediterranean, in Mexico, or anywhere in South America. I knew, too, that there was a Marazion in Cornwall.

I can't say that I thought very much of either of these possibilities. The note that I had had in Exeter definitely connected Mattani with the business that Compton had on the 15th. That business was in England – or in the British Isles. Marazan was connected with Mattani; it seemed reasonable to suppose that Compton's business was in some way connected with Marazan. It was too much to assume that there were two places in the British Isles with the same outlandish name.

I began to consider whether it was altogether wise of me to go to the Scillies. If this Marazan Sound was by any chance the place of Compton's business – the day after tomorrow – I should probably do much better to keep clear. Then, quite suddenly, I realized that I was on the wrong track altogether. I knew this Marazan Sound. It was a broad pool of enclosed water, entirely isolated, of such a rocky bottom and uneven depth that no vessel drawing more than two feet of water could enter it or lie in it except at high tide. There were two cottages on the far side of Pendruan, but nothing that could by any possible stretch of imagination hold any business interest for Compton. No, it was clear that I had gone wrong somewhere in my chain of deductions. I decided to put the matter out of my head and to carry on with my plan of watering in White Sound.

The wind changed in the afternoon and began to draw into the southwest. I didn't mind much about this; I had been very

lucky to have held the wind for so long and I had plenty of
time to get to the Scillies before dawn, even if it were to draw
dead ahead. I sailed on all day, and suddenly at about six
o'clock I saw the islands broad on my beam and at a distance
of about ten miles. I can remember that they looked very
beautiful in the evening light, very pink and hazy and low on
the horizon of a deep blue sea. Clearly the tide had carried me
off my course to the northward; I was too inexperienced in the
navigation of these waters to have made allowance for that. I
altered course more to the west and stood on towards the
northern extremity of the islands, which I took to be White
Island. I hove to presently and cooked some food in anticipation of an all-night watch, and when I came up on deck again,
the lighthouses were winking all around. It was a beautifully
clear night. I took my bearings carefully from the lights, in
consultation with the chart. I decided that the right position
for me to get into before dawn was with the Round Island
light northwest by half-north, and the Seven Stones northeast.

I'd never done that sort of jiggering about by compass in the
dark before, and I didn't like it a bit. I got the wind right up
as I drew closer to the islands, though I knew that the chart
showed clean ground to within half a mile of Pendruan. As we
closed the islands I had to force myself to stand inshore. Finally, at about two in the morning I got on my Seven Stones
bearing and beat down it in very short tacks till I brought
Round Island to west by south. Farther than that I could not
bring myself to go, being afraid of an error in the compass that
would bump me on to something sharp. Looking back on it,
I'm only surprised that I had the nerve to stand in as far as
that.

The day began to break at last after a most miserable night;
as soon as I could see a couple of hundred yards I started up
the engine and stood in towards the land. I saw as I drew close
that I wasn't lying badly for White Sound, though I was rather
farther out than I had intended. I think I must have had a tide
under me, for I drew up to the land remarkably quickly, and

the dawn was hardly grey when I was passing between the twin rocks at the entrance to the Sound.

I dropped anchor, as quietly as possible, at about half past four. The sun was not yet up; I made haste to roll the jib and lower down the mainsail. I shall always remember that anchorage as I saw it on that grey morning; I was hungry and very sleepy, I remember, and a little sick through working all night without proper food. There was a flat, grey calm over the anchorage; it was strange to me to feel the stillness of the vessel after so many days at sea. A few gulls were calling and wheeling about the rocks of White Island; I stood for a moment or two looking around the islands and the beaches. The place looked cold and ominous in the half light.

It struck me that I might have to get away in a hurry in an hour or two; so I didn't make much of a harbour furl of the main, but left it on the deck with only a tier on the gaff. Then I refilled the petrol tank of the engine in readiness for a quick getaway; finally, I got the dinghy over the side and put the canvas water-breaker in her.

By the time I had done this the sun was up. I was relieved to see that as I was lying now the hull of the vessel was hidden from the lighthouse, though I had no doubt that they could see her mast rising above the low-lying islands. They would probably report the presence of a vessel in White Sound to the harbour authorities during the day, but it was unlikely that they would connect the vessel with Compton, being unable to see the hull. That meant that I ought to be safe for several hours, and that I should be able to take my time over watering.

I went below and had breakfast, or as much of it as I could face. I must have been pretty confident that there was no need to hurry, because I remember that the cooking and eating of it took a long time. I was very sleepy. I must have been conscious of the necessity for getting water aboard without too much delay, though, for I went off to get the water and left my breakfast things unwashed all over the saloon. That was brought home to me later.

I had to make two journeys for the water. The spring was on top of the island; the water dripped from an overhanging rock on the south side and ran away in a little trickle to the sea. I had only one canvas water-breaker; that was a big one, too big for me to carry single-handed from the spring to the dinghy. I should only be able to fill it half full – say seven or eight gallons on each journey.

I tumbled into the dinghy, cast off, and rowed in to the beach. The north shore of Pendruan is a long beach of sand-hills petering out into the short turf and bracken of which the island is composed. This beach is only interrupted in the middle, where a rocky point juts out at the beginning of the shallow bridge of rocks that separates White and Marazan Sounds opposite to the little island that they call the Crab Pot. I rowed in to the beach, drew the dinghy up a little way on the sand, shouldered the water-breaker, and went ploughing up through the loose, dry sand till I got up on to the short turf above. Dozens of rabbits fled scurrying at my approach.

From the top of Pendruan I looked out southwards over all the islands of the group. The central lagoon, the Road, lay straight in front of me with the islands clustered round it on either side. There was a small sailing-dinghy crossing from Tresco to St Mary's three miles down the Road; apart from her I could see no vessels nor any signs of life upon the islands. There were houses, I knew, upon this island of Pendruan, but they were hidden from where I stood and I didn't propose to go in search of them.

I found the spring easily enough; indeed, the labour of watering a vessel in White Sound is well calculated to impress the position of the spring upon one's memory. I set my breaker down in the puddle and unlashed the mouth, and directed the stream into it with a bit of slate. It took an age to fill. It was well after half past seven when I tied up the mouth again, heaved it up on to my back, and set off for the dinghy.

I rowed off and emptied the water into the tank. I noted that the sailing lights were still in the shrouds; I took them down and put them in the forecastle, and that started me on a round of odd jobs. I thought about washing up my breakfast things, and decided that I would get the other load of water first. After half an hour or so of tidying up I set off again for the shore. I didn't hurry myself particularly, so that by the time I got to the top of the island again I suppose it was between nine and half past. I strolled up over the skyline with the breaker on my shoulder, and there I got the shock of my life. There was a small motor-boat on the beach not a quarter of a mile away, with a man sitting in the stern baling out her bilge with a tin.

I looked at him for a minute, then set down the breaker and began to fill it. There was only one thing to be done, to go on filling up with water in the hope that I should be taken for a *bona fide* yachtsman, not an escaped convict. While the water trickled into the bag I studied the man in the boat. His baling finished, he produced a bit of waste, and began swabbing about in the boat polishing the seats and the gunwale. It was pretty evident that he had brought somebody to the island on a visit, who had left the boat and gone ashore while the boat waited for him.

By now the visitor might be sitting in the cabin of the *Irene*. The thought made me feel rotten.

There was nothing to be done, I decided, but to try and brazen it out. After all, I'd done nothing wrong – or nothing that anyone was likely to discover. I owed it to Compton to keep up the pretence for as long as possible, to gain all the time for him that I could. More than that I could not do; if they arrested me I should be powerless to help him any more, and there would be an end of my part in his fortunes.

I stayed by the well till the breaker was as full as I could carry, then tied it up, slung it over my shoulder, and staggered back with it over the hill. I set it down when I came in view of White Sound and took a long look round. I was reassured. There was nobody in sight; the dinghy lay undisturbed upon the beach and the vessel at her anchor. It struck me that it was possible that the visit of the motor-boat had nothing to do with me after all. I might have been exaggerating my own importance.

I ploughed down through the soft sand to the beach and lowered the breaker into the dinghy. There was nothing else for me to do ashore, and the sooner I got away to sea again the better. At the same time, I was very loath to go. The anchorage is a delightful one; I would willingly have stayed there for a couple of days instead of beating about in the open sea with the wind up half the time. There was the matter of the butter, too; I was out of butter and very nearly out of margarine. There remained only a greasy and disgusting mass of lard. . . .

It was no good repining; it would have been asking for trouble to visit St Mary's to buy stores. I had enough lard to see me through, and it was time I got away to sea. I turned towards the dinghy, and then I pulled up short. There was a girl standing on the little point of rocks along the beach, about a couple of hundred yards away. She was looking in my direction.

Instantly my mind flew back to the motor-boat. I was tremendously relieved at the sight of the girl. The Scillies in the summer are full of visitors; clearly the motor-boat had brought no more significant cargo to the island than a party of holiday-makers on a picnic. This girl would be a straggler or an advance guard; somewhere in the background would be father carrying the lunch and the bathing things.

My fears had been groundless. Instantly I began to consider whether I couldn't afford a day on shore on this island – or half a day at any rate. I might walk round the island in the morning and get away to sea in the evening. It would be a change from sitting at the helm all day. I sat on the bow of the dinghy scrabbling the sand up into little heaps with my feet while I thought about it.

I kept an eye on the girl. She came down from the point after a little and began to walk along the beach towards me. I watched her as she came; I can remember noticing that she was very slim, and that she walked lightly.

I stared more intently at her as she drew closer . . . and then I knew that at all costs I should have kept clear of Marazan Sound.

She looked up as she came near. I didn't go to meet her, but waited her coming, sitting on the bow of the dinghy on the sand.

'Good morning, Miss Stevenson,' I said quietly. 'I'm afraid I've made a muck of this.'

Chapter Five

SHE DIDN'T speak at once. I remember that I sat watching her and waiting for her to say something, wondering what she would say, feeling a most almighty fool. I remember that there were kittiwakes crying and wheeling above us, and coloured butterflies flitting in and out of the speargrass of the sandhills, and a hot sun that made the water blue and sparkling, the sand white. I remember that she was wearing an old grey felt hat crammed down over her short hair, and a brightly coloured scarf, and the same brown jersey that I had seen her in at Stokenchurch. It had a little hole on one shoulder. I remember all that as if it had been yesterday; if I had the touch for painting I could sit down and paint her now as I saw her then, with the blue and white water running up behind her. I say that I could paint her as I saw her then, but the portrait would be painted better now.

At last she spoke. 'What are you doing here, Mr Stenning?' she inquired evenly. There was a note in her voice that stung me up a bit.

I raised my head and looked her straight in the eyes. 'I'm getting water for my cruise,' I said. 'Now I'm going to be rude. What are you?'

I guessed that that might be something of a home-thrust; she looked at me narrowly for a moment, but didn't speak. I got out my pipe and filled it slowly, while I thought things over a bit; by the time I threw the match down on the sand I had made up my mind – more or less.

'See here, Miss Stevenson,' I said. 'I'm going to speak pretty plainly. I'm getting mixed up in a lot of funny business that I don't understand and that I don't like. Don't mistake me. Compton pulled me out of a damned unpleasant crash, and I'm out to help him all I can. I've already broken the law for him in every position. If the police got me now they could plant about five sentences on me for various things I've done since I shot off on this trip. I don't care two hoots about those. What I do care about is that there's a lot going on behind the scenes that you know all about and that Compton knows all about, and that I know damn-all about. I mean Mattani, and Marazan, and all that.'

She started. 'Who told you about Mattani?'

'You did,' I said. 'At Stokenchurch. You were talking about it so loud that evening while I was writing my report that I couldn't help picking up bits of it. I told you then that I didn't want to know what you were up to. Well, I've changed my mind. I want to know what I'm in for. That is, if I'm to carry on. If you like I'll give up now and go home. I don't want to do that; I'd very much rather carry on and see Compton through this thing and out of the country. I mean that. But if I do that, then I've got to know what's going on. You see? You'll forgive me speaking straight to you about this. It seems to me that you've got something fishy going on here, something that's a thoroughly bad show. Something that's dangerous. I ran up against it in Exeter. Now if I'm to carry on I want to know what I'm in for.'

She was evidently puzzled. 'In Exeter?' she said.

I told her about the note that I had found in my bed addressed to Compton. 'That's the sort of thing that shakes a man,' I said. 'It put the wind up me properly.' Then I told her how I had been knocking about the Channel till I had run short of water. 'I didn't see how this particular Marazan Sound could possibly have any interest for you or Compton,' I said. 'I thought that there must be another one, or that I hadn't heard right. It seems that I was wrong.'

She nodded. 'This is the place,' she said. 'You know it well?'

'Not well,' I said. 'I've anchored here once or twice.'

She turned, and looked out over the blue, rippling water to

where the *Irene* was lying quietly at her anchor. 'Will you take me on board?' she said.

I pushed the dinghy down the sand, paddled out with her through the shallows till she floated, and rowed off to the vessel. The saloon was in a terrible state. I had used it as a lumber store during the days that I had been at sea; on the floor of the saloon was all the movable gear from the decks, the buckets, petrol cans, boom crutch, companion, and all the hundred and one oddments that are invariably falling over-board unless they are below. The remains of my breakfast lent a sordid appearance to the scene. I got the bucket and chucked the plates into it, and passed it through into the forecastle. Then I came back to the saloon and cleared a space on one of the settees for her to sit down.

'You won't mind if I do the lamps,' I said, and began to swab round one of the sidelights with a pad of waste.

There was a silence, so far as there is ever silence on a small vessel. A bee had invaded the cabin and was noisily investigating a jam-pot; I suppose he had come from distant Tresco. The vessel swung slowly on her heel with a faint grating and a scrunch from the anchor chain. A warm patch of sunlight slid across the floor and up my leg; away aft the rudder was cluck-ing gently in the pintles. Presently the girl spoke.

'Denis saw Mattani yesterday,' she said. 'I am expecting him in Hugh Town by this evening's boat.'

I grunted. 'And who may Mattani be?' I inquired.

She didn't answer; I could see that she hadn't got over my arrival in the Scillies yet. That seemed to have shaken her. She was suspicious, though what she suspected me of doing I couldn't make out.

'If I tell Denis that you are here,' she said, 'will you meet him this evening?'

I glanced up at her. 'Very glad to,' I remarked. 'But what if some inquisitive person comes and asks me who I am before this evening?'

'You mean if the police have followed you?'

I nodded.

'I think that would be the best thing that could happen now,' she said wearily – for everybody.'

I nearly dropped the lamp. 'I'm damn sure it wouldn't be the best thing that could happen to me,' I said indignantly. And then I stopped, because I saw that she was serious. I think it was then that I first realized that I was no longer playing a game of hide-and-seek that I could take up and throw down when I liked. I hadn't taken this business seriously up to date; to me it had been merely the excuse for a holiday of a novel and diverting kind. Now I was beginning to see it differently. The first thing I saw was that though I might not have been taking it very seriously, other people had; in this girl's face I could see that she was most miserably anxious. Whatever it was that she was afraid of, she had the wind right up. I was most awfully sorry for her.

I filled the little tank with paraffin from a can and set it in the lamp. 'See here, Miss Stevenson,' I said, 'I know you think I'm playing some funny business on you. Well, I'm not. I don't know what it is that you think I'm up to, but whatever it is, I'm not doing it. That's the first thing. The second thing is this. I'd better see Compton this evening. I suppose your trouble is that you can't tell me about Mattani till you've seen him. Is that it?'

'That's it,' she said.

'Well, don't let that worry you,' I remarked. 'I'll see him this evening and we'll have a chat about things.'

She hesitated. 'I think you ought to know, Mr Stenning,' she said, 'that he carries a pistol – as a precautionary measure.'

I laughed.

'Well,' I said. 'I hope he's got a licence for it.'

On deck one of the halliards was flapping merrily against the mast; through the planking of the hull I could hear the water tinkling along the topsides. I finished cleaning the second lamp and deposited them both in the forecastle.

'Cheer up, Miss Stevenson,' I said. 'Really, I'm only a

sheep in wolf's clothing, though I don't expect you to believe me.'

'I believe you now,' she said. 'At first I thought you must be one of Mattani's people.'

I laughed. 'Well, don't you go taking any chances,' I said. 'You say Compton arrives by the afternoon boat. I'll be on the look-out for him on the beach there any time after six o'clock. Then he can tell me what's happening if he wants to, or else – well, anyhow, he'll let me know what he wants to do. Will that be all right?'

'That will do, I think,' she said. 'He'll have to come here, anyway.'

'You might tell him to keep his finger off the trigger,' I observed. 'Nasty dangerous things – I never did hold with them. Though it would be almost worth while being punctured to find out what it is that you find so interesting about this place.'

She moved out of the saloon and went up on deck into the little cockpit. I followed her. On deck she stood for a moment looking over towards Marazan.

'It's quite shallow over there, isn't it?' she said.

'I think so,' I replied. 'A small boat can get about in it all right.'

'Not a steamer?'

'It depends how big she was.'

'Seven hundred tons.'

'Good Lord, no. I suppose a seven-tonner could get in at high tide, but she couldn't lie there when the tide fell. It's no earthly use as a harbour, if that's what you mean.'

'No,' she said wearily. 'That's what the boatman told me. I didn't believe him till I saw it. But we know that it has a use. Mattani uses it, because it's so quiet, I suppose, so desolate.'

I wrinkled my brows a bit over this. 'What does he use it for?' I said.

She shook her head. 'I don't know. But Denis may have found out by this time.'

I turned and looked out over the pool, mellow and rippling

95

in the morning light. 'He could have a pretty good bathe in it, anyway,' I remarked, 'if he's that way inclined. Fishing, too – I bet those rocks outside are full of conger. Birds ... study of wild life.' I knocked out my pipe upon the rail and turned to face her. 'I don't think we shall do much good discussing it till I've had a talk with your cousin. But I'd like you to know that whatever he has to say, you can count me in on this.'

She turned away. 'I don't see why we should drag you into our – our family dissensions,' she muttered.

I got the dinghy up and rowed her ashore to the beach. She walked up over the island towards her boat; I sat in the dinghy rocking gently in the shallows and watched her till she was out of sight. Then I put back to the vessel. She was lying quietly to her anchor; as a precautionary measure I let out a little more chain. After that I furled the mainsail. Then I sat down for a moment in the cockpit, and stared absently down into the saloon. Apparently the urgent necessity for me to lie low was over; I was beset by an uneasy feeling that there was a storm of some sort brewing that was going to burst before the police had time to get upon my track. I've never been a man to go about looking for trouble; I'm not like that. This time it seemed to me tolerably clear that I'd gone and got myself mixed up in some unpleasantly violent and illegal business that was intimately connected with my present anchorage. I didn't like it a bit.

Joan Stevenson had warned me that Compton was carrying arms. That worried me; half unconsciously I began to cast about for weapons of defence on the *Irene*. I only succeeded in unearthing a battered and unreliable-looking fire extinguisher. This I rejected.

It struck me that it would be a good plan if I were to go and have a look at Marazan for myself. There was no reason why I shouldn't go ashore during the afternoon and walk along the beach; if necessary I could explore the Sound in the dinghy. I thought I should see just as much from the shore, though, as from the dinghy. As it happened, I saw more.

I went ashore in the afternoon after washing up and left the dinghy on the sand opposite the vessel. The whole of the north side of Pendruan is a sandy beach on either side of the point of rocks that juts out opposite the Crab Pot. I climbed over this point and began to walk along the southern shore of Marazan. I saw nothing in any way out of the ordinary. The place was very desolate; a broad stretch of water, roughly circular, about three-quarters of a mile in diameter, lying between low islands almost destitute of vegetation. The sun was bright, and all over the lagoon I could see the pale green image of bare granite very close beneath the surface, or the glassy calm over a patch of weed. I judged that there was very little to hinder a boat that drew not more than three feet of water; for a larger craft the Sound seemed to me to be impossible.

I went on to the end of Pendruan and the little strait that separates Pendruan from White Island. I expected to find a heavy sea breaking up against the western side of the islands with the southwesterly wind, but to my surprise the swell was not heavy and it would have been easily possible to row an open boat out from the entrance to the Sound without shipping a drop. I learned later that the set of the tide round the islands renders the entrance relatively calm in the worst weathers, a point that would be more appreciated by the islanders if it were possible to anchor a boat in Marazan.

I came to the conclusion that there was nothing to be seen at the entrance and started to walk back along the beach, half with an idea to take the dinghy and row about the Sound. I was only a hundred yards or so from the entrance when I saw something on the beach that I took to be a dead bird. I don't know what impulse of curiosity it was that made me go and examine it – idleness, I suppose. I turned it over with my foot, and then I stooped to examine it more closely. It wasn't a dead bird at all. It was a mass of oily mutton cloth, such as mechanics use. It was heavy to lift; as I turned it over out fell a pair of engineer's pliers.

I spent a long time examining these. The cloth was covered

with blown sand upon the outside, but the fabric was good and undamaged by weather, delicate though it was. The oil on it was still moist and amber-coloured; I must say that puzzled me no end. I came to the conclusion that the rag could not have been there longer than two, or at the most three, months. It could not, for example, have been there all the winter. The pliers, too, were in quite good condition, a little rusty but by no means seriously so. I was turning these over when it struck me that there was something curious about the sand on which they had been lying. It was above high-water mark and the sand was loose and powdery, but where the rag had lain the sand was heavy and discoloured. I set to work and cleared off the loose sand to the depth of an inch or two over an area of about six feet square. And then it was obvious; indeed, I had already suspected as much. The sand immediately around the spot where I had found the rag had been soaked in oil.

That was all I found. The place was where the sand sloped gently down into the water. It seemed to me that they must have used the beach at some time for the purpose of repairing a motor-boat. It would be possible, I thought, to haul a small motor-boat out of the water there and slide her above high-water mark – if anyone wanted to carry out repairs in this outlandish spot. I even went so far as to climb up on to the bank above the beach to try to discover traces of any block and tackle with which they might have hauled her from the water.

Looking back upon that now, I am amazed that I could have been such a fool.

I walked back to the dinghy and rowed off to the vessel, taking the cloth and the pliers with me. I deposited them in a corner of the engine locker and began to overhaul the gear on deck. During the afternoon I cooked intermittently; that is to say, I put on things to boil and forgot about them while I was on deck. In this way I amassed a considerable quantity of boiled potatoes and a leathery and unappetizing suet pudding. The pudding turned my mind to matrimony. It is at sea, I thought, that a wife is really a necessity – and here I may say at once that I belong to that stern school of yachtsmen who hold that a woman's place is in the forecastle. I suppose almost any woman can make a suet pudding on dry land. A woman who can make a suet pudding over a Primus stove in the forecastle of a six-tonner on an ocean passage is worth marrying.

I supped upon bully and suet pudding garnished with treacle, smoked a pipe, washed up the supper things, and saw that the lamps were in order. There was still no sign of Compton. The light was failing fast; it was about half past nine. I made all square below and went up on deck and sat in the cockpit, waiting for something to happen. At about ten o'clock I heard the sound of a motor at the entrance to White Sound, and soon afterwards a small boat came into sight, the same that had brought Joan to Pendruan earlier in the day. There were two men in it, one in a heavy ulster and a soft hat that I knew was Compton.

I stood up as the boat came alongside and helped to fend her off. He had a small bag at his feet; it seemed that he was coming aboard for the night at least.

'Cheer-oh,' I said. 'I've been on the look-out for you since six.'

'Sorry,' he replied absently. 'I got hung up in Hugh Town.'

He spoke to the man in the boat, who touched his cap, pushed off, started his engine again, and headed away towards the entrance. Compton and I remained standing in the cockpit, and watched the boat as she drew towards the point, leaving a long smooth wash behind her, watched her till she vanished behind the land. Then I turned to him.

'Had any dinner?' I inquired.

I had only seen him at Stokenchurch before. I had thought then, if I had thought about it at all, that I had seen him in unfavourable circumstances, as a man who was a fugitive. One doesn't expect a man to look his best then. But now, meeting him again only a week later, I was shocked at the change that seemed to have come over him in that short time. I knew that he was about the same age as myself, if anything a little younger, but the man that stood with me in the cockpit was already old. His face was lined and grey. There was no spring about his carriage; he moved with the unsteadiness of age – I think with something of the dignity of age as well. I was suddenly most frightfully sorry for him. Whatever he'd been doing during the week, he'd had a pretty tough time of it.

He turned forward. 'I had dinner in Hugh Town with Joan,' he said. 'She told me that I should find you here. I didn't think about you having to call in for water. You couldn't have picked a better place.'

'It's very desolate,' I said.

He glanced at me, and nodded. 'Very,' he said quietly.

We went down into the saloon. I had no drink on board to offer him; the best I could do was to put on the Primus for some coffee. When I came back from the forecastle he had taken off his coat.

He refused a cigarette, but lit a pipe. 'Joan tells me,' he said, 'that you got a note that was meant for me – at Exeter, was it?'

I told him about it.

'What day was that?'

'Thursday evening – the evening of the day I started.'

He nodded. 'That was before I had seen Roddy,' he said.

I resented the intrusion of another character. 'I expect Miss Stevenson told you my position,' I said. 'I don't know where I am in this matter. There seems to be a lot more in it than I thought. I thought it was just a simple matter of getting you out of the country. Apparently it's not quite like that. Tell me, what are your plans now? I can put you in France the day after tomorrow if you like.'

He didn't answer directly; in the dim light of the cabin I thought I saw him looking at me curiously. 'I wonder what brought you into this?' he said at last. 'It might have been anyone.'

He roused himself. 'I've changed my mind. I'm not going to cut off abroad. I'm taking your advice.'

'My advice?' I said vaguely.

'I'm giving myself up to the police.'

It was nearly dark outside. Framed by the coaming of the hatch, I could see the stars beginning to show in a deep blue evening sky, without a cloud. There would be a moon presently, I thought.

'I'm damn glad to hear it,' I said. 'When are you going to do it?'

'The sooner the better,' he replied. 'Before they get me – they must be on my track by now. Perhaps tomorrow – or the day after. I've done all that I wanted to now – all except the one point that isn't clear. Anyway, I've got enough information now to break Roddy and his crowd if ever they try to run another cargo.'

I think I was very patient. All I said was: 'Who the hell may Roddy be?'

'Rodrigo Mattani,' he said quietly. 'My stepbrother.'

He leaned back into a corner of the settee and began to talk. I close my eyes and I can see him now through a haze of smoke against a background of charts, blankets, and flannel trousers, half seen in the dim light from the cabin lamp, pale, tired, and a little bitter. I don't know what I had expected to find at the bottom of this business – Romance, Adventure perhaps – I can't say. I only know that whatever I had expected, I was disappointed.

He told me that his mother had been a Fortescue, and had married a Baron Mattani. There was one child, Rodrigo, born in Milan about forty years ago. The Baron died a year or so later, and his wife went on living quietly in her palazzo in Milan till Antony Compton sought her out and married her. Then the trouble started. It had been the father's wish that his son should be brought up as an Italian and a Catholic; Compton was neither and the Baroness's Catholicism was nothing to write home about. What happened was inevitable. Rodrigo was left largely in the care of the Italian relations, paying occasional visits to his mother in England; the Baroness returned to the country that she never should have left. Compton himself was born, and a sister who was married. His father and mother were still alive and lived somewhere in Surrey, not very far from Guildford. He said that they were very old.

It was a common enough story of a mixed marriage. There was nothing romantic about it, nothing to stir one up, merely rather a pitiful story of misunderstandings with the foreign relatives, of irreconcilable points of view. Estrangements grew up as they were bound to do, till at the outbreak of war they were lucky if they heard of Rodrigo once in six months. He was a journalist in Milan.

'He carried a fiery cross all the war, Dago fashion,' said Compton, a little sardonically. 'You know the way they carry on. He was in the ranks, of course – the infantry. I believe he did damn well, as a matter of fact. But Lord – the stuff he used to write! He was the star turn of his paper and they gave him space for as much patriotic drivel as he could hock up. They made him editor while he was at the Front – the silly mutts. You never saw such drivel....'

He mused a little. 'It was all about Italia Irridenta, and Avanti – Bravissimo – all the rest of it. You know how they go on.'

Mattani, it appeared, had been with D'Annunzio in Fiume after the war, but it was under Il Duce that he found his destiny. He was useful to Il Duce and became a Ras. I wondered how he was useful, but Compton enlightened me only by his silence. Certainly, in Mattani Il Duce found a man of exceptional ability, considerable wealth, and peculiar resources. He was the owner of a little tramp steamer and used to run cargoes regularly from Genoa across the Atlantic, cargoes of wines and spirits for the consumption of our thirsty brethren across the way.

It would have been better if his enterprise had stopped at alcohol. A bootlegging organization, however, once set up, can deal with other commodities than alcohol; from the first Mattani found himself dealing with a considerable passenger traffic of those who were prepared to pay treble fare for the privilege of entering the United States by the back door. Moreover, very soon he found himself conducting an increasing and profitable trade in several varieties of dope.

I don't know what it is about dope, but it gets me just where I live. I don't know if it was always like that; I think I always had the wind up of the stuff even before I saw what it did. I dare say that's instinctive, but – there was a Flossie that I used to take about a good bit just after the war. A most awfully pretty kid. I'd never seen it in action before, and I had no idea that she was taking it till she tried to pass it on to me. That is an old story now, and one that I don't much care about remembering – and one, I dare say, that the Belgian doesn't care about remembering that I threw clean through the window of Les Trois Homards on to the roof of a taxi-cab out in the street, and his dope after him. If I'd known that it was going to kill her in the end I'd have – I don't know what I'd have done. But I never saw him again.

I don't know when it was that it occurred to Mattani that England wanted dope just as badly as America, but he had already run two cargoes into England when Compton got wind of the business. He told me that he had tumbled on it while he was in Genoa on business of his own, quite by chance. There was no secret in Genoa about the destination of the little tramp with the peculiar equipment of lifeboats and davits – two whacking great motor-boats each as big as a Navy pinnace, each with a couple of hundred horse-power in her. The Genoese were rather proud of the venture and used to stand about in a little crowd on the quay watching the cranes loading the stuff into her, perhaps in the faint hope that they might one day drop one of the crates and break it open. He learned in Genoa that the vessel sometimes made a detour from the true course for America, but it was left to Mattani himself, in an expansive moment, to let his stepbrother into a portion of the secret of the new enterprise. One of his golden rules, apparently, was never to tell the whole truth to anyone, and all that Compton really learned of any consequence was the name Marazan. There, Mattani told him, it was transhipped and taken to England in a way that was – oh, so clever. Just like that.

That was all he learned. He told me how he went back to England, to his home near Guildford, to tell his mother all the news of Roddy that he thought it was good for her to know. He digressed a little here, and talked for what seemed a long time about a bit of land behind their house that they wanted to buy in order to prevent their view of the Downs from being built up. And then he went rambling on, and told me how he took the car one Sunday morning and went off by himself over the Hog's Back towards the south, desperately worried about Roddy. It was a perfectly corking spring day, he said, one of those fresh sunny days with a pale sky when the country looks simply wonderful. He said he went on without bothering much about where he was going to till he found himself in Winchester, dropped into the Cathedral and out again, and had a very good lunch at one of the hotels. Then he went on and struck up over the Downs to the east, and so on till he got to Petersfield, where he had tea, and so home over Hindhead to Guildford in time for dinner. And so, he told me, after dinner, when his father and mother were playing piquet, it was easy for him to sit down and write to Roddy to tell him that he'd got to leave England alone for the future.

He said that after that drive it was easy, but he must have known at the time that it would mean – well, trouble of some sort. He said that at the time he didn't care, and I think that was true. But his letter was a threat. However courteously he may have put it, and I have no doubt that he was very tactful, it could hardly be interpreted as anything but a threat to lay information that would serve to locate a coastguard at Marazan. And – one did not threaten Mattani.

He never got an answer to that letter, but within three weeks he was in prison on a charge of embezzlement. He was very reticent about that; I think he thought that I disbelieved him, for he didn't even say that it was a put-up job. I went into that in some detail later, but I found out very little. He had been in the habit from time to time of borrowing money from his office till it was convenient for him to cash a cheque, an imprudent proceeding that put him well within the reach of the law. The sums involved had seldom exceeded ten pounds and had always been replaced within a few days, till the three thousand was found to be missing. They traced it through his account and produced his cheque drawing it out again. And that was that. It may be that his defence was hampered by some consideration for his mother – I don't know. They never put their hands on the money. I think myself it was a put-up job. I think he knew it was.

Quite abruptly, he began to tell me about his meeting with Mattani in Leeds. I think that even then he was a little suspicious of me, a little suspicious that if he were to tell me too much I might take matters into my own hands. I never learned how it was that he had heard in prison that Mattani was coming to England, or how it was that he got into touch with him in Leeds. It is certain that there was a far wider organization concerned in the distribution of the drugs than we ever managed to trace out. Compton had met Mattani in Leeds only two days before, while I had been beating about off the Lizard. I never managed to fill in the account of how he had spent the intervening days, but I know now that the meeting with his stepmother in Leeds was arranged through the medium of a retired butcher who lived in considerable comfort in Surbiton. We persuaded the butcher to tell us that later.

He met Mattani at dinner in the Station Hotel, Leeds.

I have often tried to picture this man Mattani to myself, tried to imagine what he was like to deal with. The one outstanding feature about him seems to have been his great personal charm of manner.

'If ever you have anything to do with Roddy,' said Compton, 'you'll find him very pleasant to deal with. Very pleasant ... very good company. I've tried him pretty far, I suppose, but he's always been the same. One can depend on Roddy in that way. It almost reconciles one to him. . . .'

Joan tells me much the same. She met him once or twice as a young man before the war when she was a child, and her childish memories give me a further clue to the man. She describes him as slight and pale, very pleasant but very dominating, so that she was always a little afraid of him. She remembers that he was intensely enthusiastic about Italy, and that he had an ingenious parlour trick of carving a swan out of a piece of cheese for her amusement. That is all that she can remember about him, and it is little enough to go upon. I met him once myself, but not to speak to.

I don't really know what Compton hoped to gain by meeting Mattani. It seems to me that he must have known the character of the man, have known that he was up against stronger forces than himself. I doubt if he really knew what he hoped to gain himself. I think perhaps he thought that he could induce his stepbrother to clear out of England – I think he may have been as foolish as that. I cannot think that he was so foolish as to threaten Mattani, but the threat was implied and he had sufficient information in his hand at that time to put it into execution. There is very little doubt of that. I think perhaps he may have spoken about their mother.

Mattani, he remarked, was very glad to see him. He was full of concern for his welfare, for his plight as an escaped convict. There must have been a quiet play of implied threats here, I think, for Mattani had only to speak to the waiters to see Compton arrested on the spot. However, he passed over any little incidents of the moment that might have caused unpleasantness between them, and busied himself with proposing plans for Compton's future.

One can see the way he worked. Compton was an escaped convict, Mattani one of the very few men in the world who could get him out of the country and start him again in life, under a secure protection. He was very genial, it seems, very optimistic. He said that there was a post in Italy that lay

106

within his gift, that really should be filled by an Englishman, that would suit Compton down to the ground. He was to be an Inspector of English in the Italian national schools. Mattani would see that any unpleasantness with the English police was safely laid to rest and Compton should be in Italy within a week, entering upon his new job in the Department of Instruction at a salary of twelve hundred a year sterling. He would live in Rome. For the time being he could camp out in a suite of rooms on one of Mattani's palazzi; that was, until he married. Italy was a pleasant country to live and work in, said Mattani – far pleasanter than Leeds. It was also a pleasanter country to marry in.

I expect it took Compton a little time to catch the drift of all this. However, it seems that when he realized what his stepbrother was proposing, his answer came bluntly to the point. He said that he didn't want to go to Italy and he wasn't going. As for the matter that he had come to Leeds to talk about, the dope smuggling, it would have to stop.

'You see, I told him straight out, we couldn't possibly have that sort of thing going on in England,' he remarked ingenuously.

I gathered that Mattani had laughed, and observed that it would certainly be very pleasant for one family to have two brothers in gaol at the same time.

I think by this time Compton must have realized that he was no match for his stepbrother in the battle of wits. And there, so far as I can make out, this curious interview came to an end, with nothing accomplished. There were no witnesses of the meeting save the waiters at the hotel; so far as I can make out Mattani told nobody what had occurred. I have to search my memory, as I have searched it so many times, to recall the words and phrases that Compton used that night as he told me this story in his queer, rambling way, digressing every now and then into irrelevant anecdotes, talking away the quiet hours of darkness.

That was all his tale. He had left Leeds firm in the intention to give evidence against his stepbrother and put a stop to this smuggling of drugs. He had come to the Scillies, not greatly caring whether he was detected, resolved to give himself up to the police as soon as the one link in the chain of evidence was established. He wanted to know what it was that happened at Marazan, and that he had been unable to find out. He had fixed upon that as the salient point of the scheme; until it was discovered how the stuff reached England he could not feel that he had anything but a case of suspicion against Mattani. It was important to find out that.

He told me that Joan had offered to go to the Scillies to see the place while he was in Leeds. That was how she had come to be there; her job had been to make such tactful inquiries as she was able, particularly among the lighthouse-keepers on Round Island. I gathered that she had discovered precisely nothing. To me it was pathetic to see the way in which these two had gone about this business, so different from anything that they had had to do before. They were so helpless, so unfitted for the job. I could see clearly that Mattani could make rings round them; I have no doubt that he knew their every movement, that they were closely watched. One can see now that that must have been the case.

I told Compton about the rag and pliers that I had found on the beach, and got them out and showed them to him. He sat for a long time fingering them, turning them over in his hands, evidently trying to link them up with anything that he had seen or heard about the place. I went through into the fore-castle and put on the kettle for a hot drink before turning in; it was about half past one in the morning. When I came back he had left the cabin, and I saw him standing in the cockpit. He was looking out over Marazan.

I went on deck. The vessel was lying very quietly; it was a bright moonlight night, not very cold. I had no riding-light up, and didn't intend to set one in such an anchorage as this. I moved round the deck for a little, making all square for the night; in the course of my orbit I returned to the cockpit.

'It's transhipment of some kind,' he said quietly. 'Motor-boats, of course, in one form or another. The oil shows that.'

I wasn't quite satisfied with this. 'They run a cargo to-morrow night?' I asked.

He nodded. 'I want to see what happens. I want to be on White Island tomorrow night. That would be the best place, wouldn't it?'

I thought for a moment. 'There's more cover on White Island,' I said, 'but it's probably farther away from the beach you want. They'll land on the Pendruan beach, where I found the rag.'

'They may not come at all,' he remarked. 'I may have given Roddy cold feet. But it's worth trying.'

'I reckon Pendruan would be our best place,' I said. 'But in that case we ought to get away tonight, I think. We can't leave the vessel here – obviously.'

It was a very still night. There was practically no wind; the water lapped continuously, gently against the topsides. The moon left a dappled trail upon the water like an oleograph. I had been listening while we talked, I suppose unconsciously, to the lapping of the water at hand and to the mutter of the sea on the rocks beyond the entrance to Marazan. And now there was something mingled with the mutter.

'Hullo,' I said. 'What's the row? Listen. . . .'

I knew what it was before I spoke. After all, it was my business to know that sort of row, and it was getting louder.

Compton turned towards the hatch. 'That's it,' he said, very quietly, as though he were answering some remark of mine. 'It's a motor-boat. And something pretty powerful.'

He slipped down into the cabin and turned out the lamp. In a minute he was back at my side. The vessel was now in darkness.

'I can't quite spot where she is,' I whispered. 'I think she's over there.' I pointed up-wind, in the direction of the entrance to Marazan.

He waited for a moment before replying. 'She's coming in

from the sea,' he said calmly. He looked at his watch, glowing faintly in the dark. 'Not quite full tide, as I make it. She can get through Marazan.'

'That isn't a marine engine,' I said. I strained my ears to analyse the rumble. 'It's something big. It sounds much more like an aero engine to me. But that's no aeroplane.'

I saw him smile at me in the moonlight. 'They have two hundred horse-power in them,' he said gently. 'I told you I saw them at Genoa. They use them for running the stuff ashore to America from beyond the twelve-mile limit.'

I stared at him blankly. 'You mean this is Mattani?'

He straightened himself up and gazed out in the direction of the rumble, much louder now and evidently coming over the still water through Marazan. I heard the note change as they throttled down.

'I'm so sorry about this,' he said simply. 'I didn't think it would come down to violence.'

I hadn't anything to say to that, but stood watching the Sound and the ridge of rocks between Pendruan and the tall rock under White Island that they call the Crab Pot. Compton sat down in the cockpit and began to fit a clip into a Colt automatic pistol that he had produced from his pocket. I looked at this thing incredulously.

'Do you really think that's necessary?' I inquired.

He looked up at me, quiet and reflective. 'Roddy was always a bit queer,' he said at last. 'Always dashing off and doing things that he'd be sorry for afterwards.'

I saw the launch for the first time then, crossing a moonlit patch of sea about a quarter of a mile away. I couldn't see very well what she was like; she was black against the moonlit water, and I could only say that she was a very large launch, one of the largest I had ever seen. I lost sight of her in a moment; we watched for her to reappear, but she came creeping along under the shadow of White Island so that we could not distinguish her against the land. Then we heard the engines reverse with a thrashing from her propellers; finally they stopped altogether. She was quite invisible, but I judged that she was lying in the shadow close under the Crab Pot.

There was silence for a little, and then somebody hailed us. The night was so still that though they must have been two hundred yards away, it was hardly necessary for the stranger to raise his voice.

'Ho – ah, the yacht!' he cried. At the first hail I knew that he wasn't English. The cry echoed round and died into the stillness. 'Ho – ah, the yacht!'

I answered. 'Launch ahoy. What launch is that?'

There was a pause. I fancied that I could hear them consulting one another in low tones; in my mind's eye I could see them. Then the same man hailed again.

'Ho – ah, the yacht! It is for Meester Compton. It is to Meester Compton that I have a message from his brother. It is allowed that I come alongside?'

'No, it ruddy well isn't,' I cried. 'Keep off.'

Compton touched me on the arm. 'They'll come if they want to,' he said. 'We can only keep them off by taking pot-shots at them, I'm afraid. I know these lads.'

There was another hail from the launch. 'It is necessary that we come alongside.'

I turned to Compton. 'Shall I say you're in St Mary's?'

'They'd come alongside just the same, to see.' He stood up in the cockpit and hailed. 'Hullo. This is Compton speaking. Keep away, and shout out your message.'

He drew the pistol from his pocket and laid it on the hatch at the head of the companion. There was another little silence, and then:

'It is more convenient that we come alongside.'

'No, it isn't,' I cried. 'Keep off.'

Our visitor seemed to resign himself to the inevitable.

'Very well. Meester Compton, I have a message to give to you from your brother. I am to say to you, to come to Italy, to Napoli. As he has told to you. I am to say to you to come in the manner of his guest, and to remind you that he will offer you the post of which he spoke to you. I am to beg of you to come.'

His voice died away over the stillness of the Sound. Compton roused himself and turned to me. 'Pressing, isn't it?' he said. He called across the water:

'What happens if I won't go with you?'

'Meester Compton, I am to beg of you to come.'

'I dare say. I'm not coming.'

There was a long pause then. I could imagine them crouched together in the darkness in the stern of the launch behind the engine, talking quickly together in low tones, perhaps making their preparations for what was now inevitable. Compton was staring out into the darkness beneath the Crab Pot; I stretched out my hand quietly and took his pistol from the hatch.

They hailed again. 'Meester Compton, I must beg of you to be wise. I have orders that you should come with me.'

'Now we're getting down to it,' said Compton quietly. He raised his voice:

'I'm not coming. What are you going to do about it?'

'Meester Compton. It will be better for all if you will come by your own will.'

Suddenly they started up their engine. She fired with a roar, and steadied into a low continuous rumble.

'See here,' I cried. The instant I spoke they stopped the engine again, I suppose to hear more distinctly. 'I don't know who you are in the launch. But you must keep away from here. You can go on down White Sound, or you can go back the way you came. If you come any closer to this vessel I shall open fire on you.'

There was a long silence, but when the reply came it was brief and to the point. I saw the flash from the darkness low down upon the water, and at the same moment the bullet whipped over our heads and splashed into the folds of the main. What struck me afterwards when we were huddled down on the floor of the cockpit and peering over the coaming was

112

that the report had been so slight. It struck me that they must be using a silencer on the rifle. I remember telling Compton that I'd like to get hold of that rifle and have a look at it.

I cocked the automatic. 'How many rounds have we got for this thing?' I asked.

He had two spare clips, about twenty rounds in all. I looked at my watch; it was a quarter past two. There were still two clear hours till dawn. One point was in our favour, I thought; our little cannon would make more row than forty of theirs put together. With any luck somebody would hear and come to see what it was all about – though I had to admit that the chance was pretty small.

I took a careful aim at the spot where I had seen the flash, and fired. Before the echo had died away we were lying flat on top of each other in the cockpit, listening to the bullets whipping over us or slapping into the topsides. I noticed something that put the wind up me properly. One of the bullets hit the boom above our heads and wrenched a great hunk out of it as big as my two fists, instead of penetrating. The sight gave me a nasty turn; I was on the point of calling Compton's attention to it, but thought better of it. It wouldn't do him any good, I thought, to know that they were shooting at us with soft-nosed bullets.

Presently the firing died away. I reckoned that they had hit us ten or a dozen times, mostly in the topsides. Neither Compton nor I were touched; the bullets did not seem to have the penetrating power to come through the cockpit. I couldn't see what sort of a mess they were making of the hull, but I remember thinking that I should have to sell out my Imperial Tobaccos to buy the vessel after this was over – always supposing she was still afloat and I were capable of instructing a broker in any more conventional manner than by planchette.

I stuck my head up over the coaming and fired again. They replied at their leisure with two that came unpleasantly close. I

113

didn't fire any more because I could see nothing to fire at, and for a long time there was silence. We could hear nothing from the launch.

'End of Part One,' said Compton bitterly. 'Part Two will follow immediately. I say, Stenning, I'm most frightfully sorry to have dragged you into this. I never thought that Roddy would go flying off the deep end in this way.'

We waited for some time, and presently he sat up. 'They seem to have a complex that I should go with them to Italy,' he said thoughtfully. 'It looks like one of those complexes that are dangerous to repress....'

He raised himself in the cockpit to hail the Italians. I took him by the shoulders and pressed him down again.

'No, you don't,' I said. 'You'll be cold meat ten minutes after you get aboard that launch.

In the dim light he looked at me wonderingly. 'I don't think Roddy would do a thing like that,' he said at last.

I laughed shortly. 'I do,' I said. 'When they'd done with you they'd come back and polish off me. I reckon we're better where we are.'

The vessel was lying about broadside on to the launch. 'I don't see why we shouldn't slip over the side and swim ashore,' I said. 'I believe we could do it in this light without being spotted. Can you swim quietly?'

He nodded. 'Would we be much better off on Pendruan?' he said. 'There's not much cover there.'

'There's a cottage somewhere on Pendruan,' I said. 'In any case, we'd be farther away from those lads in the launch for the moment. That strikes me as a considerable advantage. I don't think they're quite nice to know.'

It looked feasible enough. True, the vessel was lying in bright moonlight, and I had no doubt that they were watching us intently from the shadow. At the same time, I thought it could be done. They were a good two hundred yards away. One would have to move very slowly while one was exposed to view; a quick movement would be seen at once. I thought it would be possible to crawl very slowly over the coaming of the cockpit and to slip into the water silently on the far side of the vessel. Once in the water we should have to swim quietly to Pendruan, taking care to keep the vessel between ourselves and the launch. I didn't like this long silence. It seemed to me that they were up to some mischief on board the launch, and the sooner we were out of the *Irene* the better.

I took off my shoes and began to raise myself very slowly above the coaming by the upstanding hatchway. I don't know how long it was before I was lying face downwards on the deck – perhaps ten minutes in all. I only know that every muscle in my body was aching with the strain of holding intolerable positions as I climbed out of the cockpit, for fear of moving too quickly. On deck I was able to relax, and I lay face downwards for a little, resting myself before tackling the next effort of getting noiselessly down the curving side of the vessel into the water.

'Listen . . .' muttered Compton.

And then, as I lay resting on the deck, I first heard the motor-boat very faintly in the distance. I think she was on the far side of Pendruan then, because it was fully a quarter of an hour before she came round the point into the entrance to White Sound.

From the first it never occurred to us to doubt that she was on our side; that is, that she contained the police, the friendly, tolerant police. It could be nobody else. We lay and listened with the most intense relief to the steady thumping of the little single-cylinder engine, growing gradually louder as she approached the entrance. They must have heard it on the launch too, but there was no sound or sign from her. Apparently they were going to stay and see it out.

'I wonder if this is the end of Roddy,' muttered Compton. 'They're bound to see the launch.'

For my part, I was never so glad to see my sins come home to roost as I was then.

'I suppose this is the end of it,' I said. 'I can't say I shall be sorry to be arrested. I wonder if we'll be able to persuade them to go and have a look at the Dagoes.'

Compton shook his head. 'They'll be gone by the time this little boat gets here,' he said. 'They'll slip out back through Marazan, the way they came.'

But they didn't go. The puttering of the little engine grew clearer and clearer; even before I saw her I knew that she was the same little motor-boat that had brought Joan Stevenson and, later, Compton to Pendruan. The noise of her little engine dominated the situation. Long before she came in sight I was sitting upright upon the deck looking towards the entrance to White Sound for her appearance, a position that would have brought a dozen shots whistling about my ears ten minutes before.

She rounded the point at last and set a course straight for us. She carried a lantern in the bows and for a time this blinded us and prevented us from seeing by the moonlight how many men she had aboard. She came on straight down the middle of the sound, leaving a silvery trail behind her that spread till it lapped quietly upon the beaches on the Pendruan side. The Sound was as calm as that. I have often wondered what they thought of her on board the launch, how nearly they may have come to firing on her. She must have had a narrow escape, I think. I can only suppose that they knew what she was, and hoped to slip away unseen when she had departed with her prisoners.

Two or three hundred yards astern of us she altered course, and came up between us and Pendruan beach; I suppose, to put herself between us and the Pendruan shore in case we tried to swim for it. We could see then that she had four men aboard; the lantern glistened on a black oilskin that one of them was wearing who was seated in the bows, so that I judged them to be coastguards or lighthouse keepers enrolled for the occasion as guardians of the law. The boat came up between us and the land at a distance of perhaps fifty yards; in dealing with the motor-boat we had to turn our backs on the

116

launch. I didn't like that much, and resolved to keep an eye open in the direction of the Crab Pot.

They stopped their engine a little way astern of us, and the boat gradually lost way upon the water. I hailed them then, thinking it would be best to take what little advantage there was to be gained by assuming the offensive.

'Boat ahoy,' I cried. 'What boat's that?'

In the stern of the motor-boat a man stood up and coughed. 'Is that the yacht *Irene*, of Salcombe?' he said.

'This is the *Irene*,' I replied.

'Quite so. I'm afraid I must ask you to allow me to come aboard, sir. I am a police officer. I have a warrant here for the arrest of Philip Stenning, and instructions to arrest Denis Compton at sight.'

'You'd better come alongside, officer,' I said. 'I'm Stenning.'

They put out an oar and sculled her alongside. I watched the Crab Pot closely as they were doing this, but could detect no sign of life or movement from the shadow. They were playing a waiting game. One can see that clearly now.

The motor-boat bumped gently against the side. Standing in the cockpit of the *Irene* I was about on a level with the inspector standing in the boat. I leaned over the deck towards him.

'One moment officer,' I said. 'My name is Philip Stenning. This is Compton. We're giving ourselves up. Come aboard if you like, but be careful. There's a launch full of men in the shadow of those rocks – over there, just under the island. They came to kidnap Mr Compton. We've been firing at them, and they at us. Come aboard, but be careful.'

He clambered heavily into the cockpit and turned to me at once. One of the sailors followed him.

'Captain Philip Stenning, of Claremont, Simonstown Road, Maida Vale, London.'

'That's me,' I said.

117

'I have a warrant for your arrest under the Air Navigation Acts. I must ask you to come with me, sir.'

I blinked at him. 'Under *what*?' I said.

'The Air Navigation Acts,' he replied imperturbably. 'The warrant is issued in respect of offences arising out of an aeroplane accident at Stokenchurch on the 6th instant.'

'Good God!' I said weakly. That was how they got me. They had been unable to establish anything definite against me; they had such a strong case of suspicion, though, that they had raked up a string of technical offences connected with the crash upon which to issue a warrant. It seemed that I hadn't written up the log-book for the machine for three days. It seemed that I had 'committed material hurt or damage in landing' and had gone away without paying the farmer for digging a hole in his field with the machine. However, I have always held that the end justifies the means, and I've never managed to feel as much aggrieved over this proceeding as I should like to. Indeed, at the time it struck me as damn funny.

'All right, officer,' I said, 'I'll come quietly.'

He turned to Compton and produced a sheaf of papers from his pocket. For a moment he stood trying to sort them out in the dim light from the lantern in the bows of the motor-boat. Then he turned to one of the men. 'Pass me that lantern,' he said.

I interposed. 'One moment,' I said. 'Be careful of that lantern. There's a boat over there in the shadows. Don't show too much light about. Let's get down into the saloon.'

'Boat?' he said. 'What boat?'

I could have cursed his thick head, and did so under my breath. 'The boat I was telling you about,' I replied. 'She's lying over there in the shadow under the rocks. They've been firing at us.'

One of the men spoke up. 'I said I heard shots fired,' he remarked. 'Didn't I?'

The inspector turned his head and looked over the Sound to

the shadows beneath the Crab Pot. I think he must have thought that this was some trick of ours, some device to throw him off his guard and to prevent him examining Compton. At any rate, he turned back abruptly.

'I don't see any boat,' he said. 'We'll deal with the boat afterwards.'

He reached down to the motor-boat, took the lantern, and raised it above his head as he leaned forward to compare Compton with the photograph upon his papers. Compton grinned at him in the strong light from the lantern; I think he was going to say something funny. I like to think he was.

I glanced nervously towards the shadows across the water. I distinctly saw the two spurts of flame as they fired; there were two of them and they fired practically simultaneously. We learned later that their orders were explicit. They fired together. One of the shots missed and whipped through somewhere between us; the other went home with a sound that I wish I could forget.

For a moment I didn't see who it was that was hit. And then I saw that it was Compton that they'd got, as they had meant to all along. He was standing there quite motionless, a little bent over the tiller, gripping the coaming of the cockpit with one hand.

The inspector was still holding the lantern aloft. I pushed past him with an oath; as I jumped aft there was a roar from the shadows as they started up the engine in the launch.

I got to him as he collapsed. He turned to me with his face all puckered; for a moment I thought he was going to cry.

'I say ... that's torn it,' he muttered.

I had one look, gripped his arm close to his side, picked him up in my arms and carried him down the steps into the saloon. The inspector stood aside to let me pass; it had all happened so quickly that I think that it was only then that he realized that Compton had been hit. As I went I remember that I saw the launch slip out from the shadows, heading towards the entrance to the Sound. The men in the motor-boat saw her too; they say that she was a large, half-decked pinnace, painted grey. There was nobody visible aboard her. She tore down the Sound at a great pace, turned northward at the entrance, and vanished into the open sea.

I carried Compton below and laid him on the settee. For a long while I laboured over cutting away his clothes with a blunt penknife. I had a very small first-aid outfit on board; the tiny phials and bandages proved miserably inadequate. I don't think I need go into details. It was a chest and shoulder wound; with an ordinary bullet it would have been a comparatively slight affair.

One of the sailors kept his head and gave me a lot of help; for the rest, I was quite alone. The inspector, I suppose, was competent to put a broken arm into splints; wholesale surgery was evidently beyond him, and he was useless.

And so it came to an end. He died about twenty minutes later.

Chapter Six

THEY TOOK me back to Hugh Town in the motor-boat in
the early dawn; we left two men in the *Irene*. They were to
bring her round to Hugh Town later in the day, a sad, battered
little vessel; in the saloon a covered figure lay upon the soaked
cushions. They took me back to Hugh Town in the cold dawn;
the ebb was flowing strongly against us out of Crow Sound, so
that we were two hours on the way. All the way, nobody spoke
a word. It was the sanest, most horrible hour of the twenty-
four, the hour when nothing cloaks reality, the hour when one
sees things as they really are. I don't count myself a coward,
but I have always been afraid of the dawn.

They took me straight to the police station in the little grey
town and put me in a cell, not so much as a prisoner as for
privacy. I sat there miserably till they brought me some breakfast, and then asked to see the inspector. He came and I
had a short talk with him, a grizzled, unimaginative family
man of about fifty, desperately worried and entirely at sea over
the whole business. I told him about Joan, and sent him off to
break the news to her at her hotel. It was impossible to keep
her out of it any longer. Before he went he offered hopefully to
bring me writing materials if I would like to make a statement.
I said I wouldn't.

That was all that happened till we left by the afternoon
steamer for England; I slept a little, fitfully, throughout the
morning. They took me aboard the boat before the crowd came
and put me in a cabin below the bridge; from there I could see
the *Irene* lying off the end of the breakwater. There were one
or two ugly scars in her topsides, showing bright yellow wood.
I saw nothing of Joan, though I learned afterwards that she
travelled to England on the same boat.

We travelled up to London on the night train, and they lodged me in a room somewhere in Scotland Yard.

We got there about seven o'clock in the morning. I was tired and sick; a bath would have put me right, but there was no bath available. They allowed me to send out to my flat, though, to get some clean clothes, and in the meantime a barber came to shave me. I was more myself when I had shaved and changed. Then for some hours I was left to my own devices, till late in the afternoon they had me up for a sort of an examination.

They took me into a large room that was some sort of an office, of rather a menial variety. One knows the sort of place so well. The walls were distempered and peeling; the only furniture was two deal tables, ink-stained and loaded with files of dusty papers, and a few chairs. At one of the tables a sergeant was writing laboriously in a ledger, breathing heavily with the unwonted exercise. There was a large clock high up on one of the walls, stationary at eight minutes past twelve. The window was closed and dirty and there were a few dead flies lying on the sill inside – asphyxiated, I supposed.

The inspector who had arrested me was there, and two others. They opened a large ledger, and there I saw a photograph of myself, together with the Bertillon measurements that had been taken when I was in prison. They started off by taking another set of fingerprints. I was getting fed up with them already and asked them if the prints had altered much. I suppose that was a State secret, because I didn't get an answer.

I wasn't myself, I suppose, because quite suddenly I found myself beginning to lose my temper. I don't know now what it was that did it; I knew at the time that I was unreasonable, that these fellows were only doing their job in the way they were accustomed to. I think it was the room that did it, that and the off-hand way in which they treated me. There wasn't a man in the room who wouldn't have taken my tip if he had done me a service in the street or at a railway station, but I

122

was in Scotland Yard and arrested on a warrant. They modified their behaviour accordingly, and I found it galling. As I say, I don't think I was myself.

They finished their measurements at last and put away the ledger. Then they made me go and stand before the table; the sergeant, still breathing heavily, put away one book and opened another, and turned to a clean page. When he was quite ready, pen in hand, one of the inspectors addressed me.

He cleared his throat. 'Now, Mr Stenning,' he said weightily. 'I want you —'

'Captain Stenning,' I said curtly. I was all on edge.

'I want you to tell me when you first met the deceased, Denis Compton.'

For a moment the impudence of it staggered me. He had warned me before that my statement was to be noted and filed, as though that were not sufficiently obvious. The sergeant sat gaping at me, waiting for my reply. It was like some miserable farce. I realized then to the full the gulf that lay between these fellows and myself. To them 'the deceased, Denis Compton', was a case, and nothing more.

'My barrister will tell you that in court,' I said.

The sergeant wrote it down.

'You can give us a great deal of assistance by telling us now,' he said.

'I dare say,' I answered. 'I should prefer to see my solicitor first. I should like to write a note to him at once, please.'

'Time enough for that,' he said. 'Now, I want you to tell me when the deceased first came on board your yacht.'

I looked at my watch; it was nearly five o'clock. 'My solicitor's office closes at six,' I said. 'I want to write a note to him and have it delivered by hand at once.'

I turned to the sergeant. 'Please write that down.'

'That's enough of that,' said the inspector.

I moved towards the table. 'I should like to write that note.'

He hesitated and finally agreed, as a special concession.

123

'May I see the warrant upon which I was arrested?' I said, pen in hand. 'I haven't seen it yet.'

After a little consultation they showed it to me. It seemed that I had forgotten to sign the clearance certificate at the aerodrome, that I hadn't written up the machine log-book for several days, and that I hadn't apologized to the farmer for digging a hole in his field with my aeroplane. In addition, I had failed to appear before the Finchley Police Court to answer for these offences. I must say they had been pretty quick about it all.

I wrote Burgess a short note telling him that I was in trouble and asking him to come and see me, and gave it to the inspector, who sent it off by hand.

I got up from the table. 'Right you are,' I said. 'Now I'm ready to answer any questions arising out of this warrant.'

The inspector coughed. 'I want you to tell me when you first met the deceased, Denis Compton,' he said.

I lost my temper completely then.

'See here,' I said. 'I've answered that question already. My counsel will tell the court all about that when the time comes. As for me, I'm not going to make a statement of any sort now – not one ruddy word. I don't know under what authority you're making this examination. It seems to me that it ought to be made before a magistrate. In any case, it's time I came before a magistrate. I've been in custody now for thirty-six hours. I believe there's an Act called Habeas Corpus that has a word or two to say on that subject. I'm not going to make a statement now, but I'll see my solicitor as soon as he comes.'

Burgess arrived soon afterwards; they left him alone with me in my room and I told him everything. Burgess was the one link with respectability that I had at that time; he first dawned on my horizon when I came out of prison. He was a cousin of my father; I may say at once that he's the only one of my relations that I've ever been glad to meet. I wasn't long out of prison when he wrote me a pleasant little note asking me to dine with him; I went, and found him a widower, a cheerful old lad of about sixty with a shrewd judgement for alcohol. He expressed himself mildy surprised that I should have allowed myself to go to prison for being drunk in charge of a motor-car. I suppose I was bitter about it; I remember saying that it didn't seem to matter very much whether I went or not. At all events, there and then he constituted himself my solicitor; rather than appear discourteous I let him have his way. Later I found out that he was the head of one of the most conservative firms in London. The first thing he did was to put on one of his bright lads to unravel my affairs for me. They needed it.

I set to and told him everything from the beginning, down to the time when I arrived in Scotland Yard. I've often wondered what he thought of it. It wasn't quite in his usual line, for one thing. His line was litigation, land purchase, wills, death duties – the usual stock-in-trade of a respectable solici-tor. I was keenly aware of this while I was telling my story; I could feel that it was rather rotten of me to drag the old man into a criminal affair of this sort. Yet he was pretty well on the spot when he came to advise me. In the very short time before he came to me he had found out that I was to be brought up to answer the aeroplane charges the next morning; he promised to send one of his bright boys to represent me. He told me that all I had to do was to sit tight and say nothing for the moment; his bright boy would get me bail. He said he would find the surety himself. As for making a statement, I should have to do that some time, but I could take my time over it. In the mean-time he would find out by means of some legal backstairs in-telligence department exactly what was expected of me.

Finally, he surprised me vastly by saying that no court would dare to give me anything but a nominal sentence for helping Compton to get away. He seemed to consider it rather a creditable effort – not bad, I thought, for a lawyer of his generation.

He went away, and they brought me dinner, of a sort. I had nothing to do after dinner; I sat and smoked and read the morning paper that they had given me, till it was about ten o'clock. Then there was a bit of a bustle in the corridor outside my door, and a sergeant came in and told me to follow him.

I discovered that I was to see Sir David Carter.

They led me down a series of corridors and up a flight of stairs. They halted me there before an office door while one of the sergeants tapped respectfully and went inside. I was left to cool my heels for a little. I remember thinking that Sir David Carter was a tolerably late worker, and I remember the satisfaction of feeling that at last I was to be taken before the man who counted for something in the Yard.

I was shown into the office after a few minutes – a very different sort of place from the office in which they had examined me that afternoon. The sergeant who had shown me in backed out quietly, and I was left in the office with the two strangers.

One of them was sitting behind the desk facing the door. He was a grave, white-haired man, not very old; I shouldn't say that he was more than fifty, though he was quite white. When he spoke, he spoke very quietly, but I knew at once that he wasn't a man that one could play monkey tricks with. I got to know him quite well before I was through, but I never revised my opinion of Sir David Carter.

He bowed to me as I entered the room.

'Good evening, Captain Stenning,' he remarked. 'I am sorry that it has been necessary to disturb you at this late hour. My justification must be that I am, as you observe, working myself. As is Major Norman, Captain Stenning.' He motioned me to a chair. 'Will you sit down, Captain Stenning?'

I bowed to the man who was standing by the mantelpiece. He was a man of about my own age, and with one of the keenest expressions I had ever seen on a man. I began to sort out my ideas a bit. I had thought up till then that Scotland Yard was run entirely by a collection of superannuated police constables. It seemed that I was wrong.

I sat down in the easy-chair by the desk. I noticed with some amusement that they had put me in a strong light.

Sir David didn't waste any time on preamble. 'Now, Captain Stenning,' he said, 'I have asked you to come here because I want you to tell us what you know about the circumstances in which you were arrested. There is one point that I should like to make clear before you begin. That is that any statement that you may care to make to us is in no sense official. There is nobody taking down what you are saying – there is nobody within hearing but Major Norman and myself. I cannot say that nothing you may say will be used as evidence against you. I cannot say that, till I hear what your story is. At the same time, I cannot see at the moment any valid reason for bringing any charge against you other than the one upon which you were arrested – and which, I think, can be disposed of without any great difficulty.'

He paused for a moment. 'Our position simply is this. A murder has been committed, a murder at which you were present, the consequences of which, I am told, you did your utmost to avert. I should be failing in my duty to the State if I were to neglect any opportunity of bringing the murderer to stand his trial. It is for that reason, Captain Stenning, that I want you to tell me what you know about this matter.'

He stopped, and I took my time before replying. He put me in rather an awkward position. I had taken it for granted that, if any action were to be taken in the matter, I should be charged in open court with having assisted in the escape of a convict from custody. In those circumstances I should have allowed myself to be guided entirely by Burgess. Now the circumstances were very different. Apparently they didn't want to bring me into court; they wanted me to tell them all about it on my own. Well, I was willing enough to do that so long as I could avoid telling them about Joan. I didn't know how much they knew about her; I only knew that I wanted to keep her out of it as much as possible. After all, the part that she had played wasn't important.

I played for time. 'I know very little about the true facts of this murder,' I said.

They didn't speak, didn't hurry me, but let me take my time. Sir David sat quietly leaning back in his chair, his hands clasped before him on the desk, meditatively staring at the ceiling. I was suddenly aware that my remark had been fatuous. I certainly knew more of the facts than they did, and it was up to me to tell them. There was no need, however, to lay stress on Joan.

'I suppose you know that I helped Compton to get away,' I said slowly. 'I should do that again, of course. I was under an obligation to him.'

'In point of fact,' said Sir David Carter, without stirring or taking his eyes from the ceiling, 'he saved your life.'

'Exactly,' I said. 'After that, you would hardly expect me to give him up?'

'In law,' said Sir David imperturbably, 'I should certainly expect you to do so.'

He reached across his desk, picked up a paper with a few pencilled notes on it, and turned to me.

'I understand that after the accident to your aeroplane, Captain Stenning, you visited the house called Six Firs at the instigation of Compton. There you had an interview with Miss Joan Stevenson, who refused to believe that her cousin was at large in the woods and regarded you as an impostor. In some way you managed to convince her that your story was true, with the result that you visited the house with Compton late that night, where he obtained food and clothes. I understand that you then attempted – unsuccessfully – to persuade him to return to prison. You then decided to set off to lay a false trail in the hope of engaging the attention of the police for a few days while Compton made good his escape; in this you were assisted by Miss Stevenson, who visited Salcombe under the name of Miss Fellowes to prepare the yacht for you. You put to sea upon Saturday the 9th, from Salcombe. Perhaps you would take up the story from that point.'

It took me a minute or two to recover from this.

'There's one thing I should like to add to that,' I said at

128

last. 'Mr Stevenson, Miss Stevenson's father, had nothing to do with it at all, so far as I know. I don't know what happened after I left. But while I was there the matter was entirely between Miss Stevenson, Compton, and myself. Neither Mr nor Mrs Stevenson knew of what was going on.'

He nodded. 'That has already been made clear to us.'

I wondered who had made it clear, but refrained from asking. Whoever it was seemed to have told them all about Joan; there was now no reason for me to keep anything back. I started in and told them all I knew, from the time I left Salcombe till Compton was killed. They heard me without interruption and practically without any sign. I only caught one quick interchange of glances, when first I mentioned Mattani. It took me some time to finish my yarn, because I wanted to tell them everything, but at last I was through.

I stopped talking, and for a long time nobody said a word. Sir David sat leaning back in his chair, quite motionless, staring at the ceiling.

At last he spoke. 'That account tallies very closely with the one given to us this morning by Miss Stevenson,' he observed.

I was relieved. 'You have seen Miss Stevenson, then?' I said.

He glanced at me curiously. 'Miss Stevenson came to me this morning,' he said. 'She wished to make your position in this matter quite clear, Captain Stenning. Perhaps I may be forgiven for expressing the opinion that she came more in your interests than in the interests of justice.'

I couldn't think of anything to say to that, and didn't have much time to wonder exactly what he meant. Sir David nodded slightly to the man that he had called Norman, who took up the tale and proceeded to cross-examine me pretty thoroughly on the details of my story. He made me go over the account of Mattani that Compton had given to me; I searched my memory for details that I had already half forgotten in the stress of subsequent events. He was very anxious to find out in what way the stuff reached England, but I could give him very little information there. I told him about the rag and pliers that I had found on the beach, which seemed to point to transhipment to a smaller motor-boat. It was a theory that didn't bear close examination, but it was all we could think of at the moment.

He finished his questions at last. I plucked up my courage then, and asked one on my own account.

'I suppose you will want me to give evidence in court,' I remarked. 'Shall I be needed at the inquest?'

I saw Norman glance towards his chief, who sat motionless in his chair, staring straight ahead of him.

'The inquest will be adjourned,' said Sir David.

I felt that I was treading on thin ice, but I persisted. 'I see,' I said. 'I suppose you'll want me to give evidence some time, though? I take it that you are putting forward a case against Mattani?'

'That is a matter that will have to be considered rather carefully,' said Norman, with an air of polite finality.

I was silent. The room became very still; there were none of those sounds in the building to which one is accustomed. The absence of voices, of the sound of passing feet, and of the rumble of traffic seemed to leave a noticeable blank. I glanced at the clock, and was surprised to see that it was half past eleven. I was beginning to wonder irrelevantly for how long the sitting was to continue, when I was roused by Sir David.

'Captain Stenning,' he said. I turned towards him. 'I imagine that you must be feeling very curious about this unfortunate matter. So much is natural. I trust that when you leave this building you will not allow your curiosity to run away with you. I must ask you to be discreet.'

'I can hold my tongue, if that's what you mean,' I said.

He inclined his head gravely. 'Exactly. We expect you to hold your tongue. On our part, however, I feel that we are under some obligation to you for the part you have played in this affair. We should show a poor sense of that obligation if we were to conceal facts that may be of some importance to you. I think I need hardly dwell upon the fact, Captain Stenning, that I think that you may be in some danger for the present. I am sure that your experience of the world will tell you so much.'

I nodded. That was one of the conclusions that I had come to already; that Mattani, wherever he might be, would be feeling a little peeved with me. It was surprising that he had not made a greater effort to prevent me from giving evidence. I put that down to this: that when his men visited Marazan they had no orders regarding anyone but Compton. They must have expected to find him alone; it was probably beyond their calculations that he should have confided in anybody. They must have realized the position as soon as they found us together on the yacht; I have very little doubt that then they realized the importance of preventing my escape. The arrival of the police, however, had upset their plans; they had to stake everything on the chance of two good shots when the opportunity came. One had gone home, but mine had missed. It was certainly on the cards that they might try again.

'I can see that,' I said reflectively. 'I should think the best thing I can do is to make out a written statement, isn't it? You'll want that later, whether I'm in a condition to give evidence or not.'

He smiled. 'I should not put it quite like that, myself,' he said. 'However, I am inclined to think that there may be trouble, Captain Stenning. Briefly, I should anticipate an attempt to induce you to go to Italy, either with your own consent or without. I doubt if you are in any serious personal danger. I doubt if Baron Mattani would attempt another murder at this time; indeed, I should say that the murder of Compton was not entirely premeditated. However, I have no doubt that Mattani will be anxious to find out how much you know, how much you have been able to tell us. For this reason, I think he will be anxious to get hold of you.'

I did my best to look pleasant. 'That sounds jolly,' I said weakly. 'How long do you reckon this is going on for?

I take it that you will be bringing him to trial before so very long.'

He didn't answer for a moment, but then he said:

'That is a very difficult matter.'

I didn't follow him. 'Is it?' I inquired. 'Surely there's enough evidence for him to stand his trial on?'

He shook his head. 'I think that very doubtful,' he replied. 'You must remember, Captain Stenning, there is nothing to identify the launch that you saw with Baron Mattani – except your evidence. That makes a thin case, a case that needs further backing before it is brought into court. But even if the evidence were perfect, the difficulties would still be great.'

Norman nodded in corroboration. 'The Americans have been trying to get him for a year,' he remarked.

That startled me. 'What for?' I asked.

'The charge that they have been proceeding upon,' said Sir David, 'is one of wounding with intent to kill. There is very little doubt, I think, that other charges would be preferred against him if he were to arrive in America in custody. Unfortunately, that appears to be a most improbable event.'

'Good God!' I said bluntly. 'Do you mean he can't be extradited?'

'The difficulties are very great,' said Sir David quietly.

I began to realize then the significance of what Compton had told me in the *Irene*. He had said that Mattani was useful to Il Duce. He was a Ras, and I knew enough of Italy to know that one doesn't trifle with a Ras. He was editor of one of the Fascisti papers. I knew something of Fascismo through flying through the country, and through reading the *Corriere*. I could see that the difficulties of extraditing Mattani were likely enough to be – well, very great.

'I hadn't thought of that,' I muttered.

Sir David eyed me keenly. 'A charge of murder against Baron Mattani is a new thing,' he said quietly. 'The chain of evidence is not complete – at present. The charge of smuggling drugs into this country is also a new one.'

He paused. 'I can assure you, Captain Stenning, that if either of these charges can be upheld we shall see that he appears in England to stand his trial. In the meantime, I am sure you will be ... discreet.'

They sent me back to my room and I went to bed, a little overawed. Next day Burgess sent his bright boy along directly after breakfast, and I was driven out to Finchley in a taxi to answer my summons on the aeroplane charges. Morris was there on behalf of the firm; I managed to get in a word or two with him before the case came on. He was pretty terse about it all. The proceedings were purely formal. Burgess's bright boy stood up and explained that owing to my absence from land on a yachting tour I had not been served with the summons, and hinted gently at the illegality of issuing a warrant for my arrest in the circumstances. He had too much sense to dwell upon this point, but he so worried the court with his veiled allusions that they fined me two pounds and sent me away with a flea in my ear.

Immediately the case was over the inspector who had brought me out asked me to return with him to the Yard. I had only time for a word or two with Morris, but promised to turn up and give an account of myself during the afternoon. At the Yard I was shown into Sir David's office, who asked me to dictate a statement of the whole business. This took a considerable time, and it wasn't till three o'clock that I walked out of the place a free man – and fair game for Mattani.

The thought depressed me. A month before I wouldn't have cared two hoots about the chance of being shot at from round a corner; I should probably have welcomed such a diversion from the monotony of my daily round. But now – it was different. Compton's death had shaken me badly. One talks glibly of battle, murder, and sudden death; one takes the risk of all three with very little hesitation. But when one sees the results, it makes a difference.

I say that his death had shaken me. For one thing, Compton was a man that I could have hit it off with most awfully well.

133

One can't describe these things, but – I liked him. At that time I'd never had much to do with educated people, people of my father's sort; I can't say that I had felt the loss. Till I met Compton, I don't think I had ever dealt with a man of his sort quite on terms of equality, unless perhaps in the Service. It takes all sorts to make a world, and my way wasn't theirs. But Compton had been different. I walked up Regent Street and Oxford Street on my way to Maida Vale, and I was pretty miserable.

The sheer brutality of the murder came home to me then in a way that it hadn't before; I suppose because I had had my own affairs to think about. It was a blazing afternoon. I went striding on down the hot pavements without looking where I was going; once or twice I cannoned into people, but mostly they looked at me and got out of my way. I'm too old to have ideals. I had all that knocked out of me before I was fourteen. I'm not the sort of man that goes and puts his shirt on Truth or Justice or Purity, or any of those things with capital letters. That was the difference between Compton and myself; he was a man who lived for his ideals, whereas I hadn't any to live for.

The whole show formed itself into a series of pictures as I strode on down Oxford Street on that blazing afternoon. I saw Compton driving his car up over the Downs from Winchester to Petersfield, and returning to his home near Guildford to sit down and write to his brother that he really couldn't go doing that sort of thing in England. I saw him in the restaurant in Leeds, repeating the same vague threat. I saw him in the cockpit of the *Irene*, and then I saw him as I had seen him last, with that frightful wound in the chest that I could do so little for, that was hopeless from the start, smashed and broken. All these pictures shimmered and danced against a grey background of dope, grey, brutal, and depressing.

Presently I found myself in my flat. I was suddenly very tired, most utterly weary. I slung my hat into a corner and collapsed into a chair in the tiny sitting-room. I was out of it all now. I tried to get the whole business out of my mind; I didn't want to think about it any more. It had been a nightmare show; I didn't think that sort of thing ever happened in real life. I must get along back to my flying, I thought, and forget about it. It would be as well to avoid any trips to Italy for a month or two. I could do that all right; very likely there would be no occasion for me to go.

It had been a rotten business to get mixed up in.

It's curious how little a thing can turn the course of one's life. The old woman in the basement who came in every morning to make my bed had given me a calendar at the New Year, the sort of thing that tradesmen send round to their customers. It had some advertisement on it. I had kept it to avoid hurting her feelings, and because above the calendar there was rather a pleasant reproduction of a water-colour sketch. The picture was a wide landscape with fields and woods running down to a blue sea, all very bright and sunny. I had always thought of it as a bit of the North Devon coast. I suppose I must have seen it every day since it arrived. I looked at it again now, and for the first time I saw that there was a couplet below the picture, not very conspicuous. It was a bit of Kipling and it ran:

Our England is a garden, and such gardens are not made
By saying, 'Oh, how beautiful!' and sitting in the shade.

I remember I felt just as if somebody had hit me in the wind. I sat for a long time staring at that thing. Looking back upon it now after all these years, I don't think there's any argument that could have stung me up just like that calendar did. It got me just where I lived. I can't explain myself; I only know that I saw then that Compton had been right; we couldn't possibly have that sort of thing going on in England. I only know that when I got up out of my chair and moved over to have a better look at the thing, Richard was himself again.

The front door bell rang. I turned slowly away and went to open the door; as I went the words of the couplet were ringing through my head. Absently I opened the door. I was hardly surprised when I saw it was Joan Stevenson.

'Good afternoon, Miss Stevenson,' I said quietly. 'I want you to tell me what I ought to do about Mattani.'

She stood on the mat looking at me in that disconcerting, direct way of hers, as if she had been a man. I wasn't accustomed to it and it worried me; the girls I knew didn't look at one like that. This time I managed to meet her gaze. I don't think I shall forget that. I don't know how long we stood there; I only remember the shadows in her deep grey eyes, and the couplet that was running in my head:

Our England is a garden . . .

'Do?' she said. 'Haven't you done enough for us? It's in the hands of the police now.'

We moved in.to the sitting-room.

'I came to make sure that you were all right,' she said, 'and to hear what happened that night.'

'They told me at the Yard that you'd been there,' I said. 'Thanks for that.' I didn't say that they had told me that she went there to try and get me out of the mess, but I knew she understood.

'It seemed so rotten for you to have been dragged into all this,' she explained. 'And it was quite easy, because I was at school with Doris Carter, and she took me along to her father yesterday morning. He was so nice about it, and he said you'd be all right. Captain Stenning, I haven't really heard anything about this – this frightful thing. How did it all happen? Who killed him?'

'Mattani killed him,' I said shortly. 'Mattani, or his men.'

'It's horrible!' she muttered.

She sat down, and I told her the whole story so far as I knew it. I found that she couldn't tell me much that I didn't know already; we compared notes, but I learned very little more. She told me that they had had an inquest in the Scillies and had adjourned for a month; the funeral was to be held at Guildford on the following day. I don't know how much they had told his parents. Joan said that she thought his mother was

136

getting so feeble that she would hardly realize the details. It was an extraordinarily painful business.

Presently we had told each other everything we knew. I got up and opened a window, and stood looking out into the street. They had diverted a bus route down our road while the main road was being repaired, I remember; I stood and watched the scarlet buses as they passed below in the sunlight, their decks crowded.

As I stood there, it seemed to me that the man I ought to get in touch with was Giovanni da Leglia. He had been in my flight of Sopwith Camels during the war. Heaven knows what had brought him into the British Flying Corps; he was one of those freaks that turn up from time to time even in the best regulated squadrons. We used to call him Lillian, being the closest approximation to his name that we could manage. He was in my flight for six months, a long partnership in the Flying Corps. He was shot off back to Italy, as an instructor, then; I remember that we swore blue we'd meet in Paris when the war was over. I hadn't seen him since.

I had an idea he came from Florence. I tried hard to remember something of his characteristics. He had been a harebrained young man in those days, cool, keen as mustard on flying, and utterly irresponsible. We had a Bessoneau hangar on one 'drome that was open at each end, and served as a garage for cars. I remember the rowing I gave him for diving down at the end of a patrol and flying his Camel clean through this thing and out the other side, regardless as to whether there was anyone or anything inside. His speed was probably a hundred and fifty miles an hour or so, the clearance about two feet above and below the machine. It turned out later that there were two men in the hangar, who hurled themselves into corners as he came through. I made him give them credit for a quid each in the wet canteen when I'd done with him. I think he thought me very pernickety.

That was one side of him. The other point that I remembered was his fantastic pride of race. He was an aristocrat

137

of the aristocrats. He used to try and tell us all about the da Leglias. We used to throw things at him. Once, indeed, one guest night, we were too far gone to hit him, and he rambled on till he came to the bit about his descent from one of the Kings of Aragon on the wrong side of the bed. We began to sit up and take notice then; before we went rolling to our huts we had revised and improved upon his pedigree. It needed bowdlerizing by the time we'd done with it, but it proved a great attraction at subsequent guest nights.

That, however, is all by the way. The thing that really mattered, and the thing that had impressed me at the time, was his pride in his family. I began to wonder how that fitted in with Fascismo. For all I knew, he might be oneu of the most ardent of the lot. On the other hand, he might be sitting quietly at home in a dignified opposition. He had pots of money. But Fascist or not, I knew that I could depend on Leglia for advice. He was a stout lad; there would be no shaking hands with murder where he was concerned.

Joan got up from the chair where I had left her and came across to me at the window.

'Is there anything more for us to do?' she said. I think she must have guessed what I was thinking about.

I looked down at her reflectively. There was nothing more that she could do, and if there was I didn't want her to do it. Whatever turn this affair was to take; it was pretty sure to end in a vulgar brawl.

I temporized. 'The police are taking it up,' I said.

She nodded. 'They'll arrest Roddy?'

I laughed. 'If they get a chance,' I said. 'They'll have their work cut out to do it. He can't be extradited.'

She hadn't heard that, and I had to explain it. Something in what I said must have made her smell a rat, though, for her next question put me in a corner.

'Then there's nothing more that we can do, is there?' she said.

I shall always remember that, because the tone of relief that

138

she used startled me. It wasn't natural. I glanced down at her sharply, and I think perhaps I saw rather more than I was meant to. One remembers these things.

'I don't know,' I said. 'I had some idea of going to look up a pal of mine, a bloke called da Leglia. He lives in Florence.'

She caught her breath. 'Oh ...' she said. 'You can't go there. Sir David said that you would have to be careful.'

'I shall be,' I said. 'Damn careful.'

She turned away, and stood for a bit looking out at the strings of scarlet omnibuses that passed below, shaking the house. At last she said, without taking her eyes from the window:

'Don't you think it would be best to leave it to the police now?'

'They'll never get him, of course,' I remarked.

'Why not?'

'Look at it,' I said. 'They can't extradite him – for the present, anyhow. He simply refuses to be extradited, and that's that. As for getting at him any other way, they're so handicapped. They've got to play fair. They stand for England. If they could get to know that he was in England some day, I dare say they might be able to do something about it. They can't very well set about enticing him to come to England. At the same time, we know that he does come here from time to time. I've not had time to think about it much, but I fancy we might be able to work something on those lines if we went about it in the right way.'

She glanced sharply at me. 'You mean that you'd decoy him here and set a trap for him?' she said.

'That's about it.'

'They'd hang him, wouldn't they?'

'With any luck,' I said.

She turned back to the window. 'It would kill his mother,' she said quietly.

I had forgotten all about the old couple at Guildford. I've never had much to do with family matters, so that this remark

139

of hers put me all at sea. I tried to assimilate the idea for a bit. I tried to see it from her point of view, but I couldn't make it go. I really couldn't see in that any reason for letting Mattani go free. I was still worrying over this when she turned to me again.

'Leave him alone,' she said. 'It would be frightful for them if anything happened to Roddy – on top of this.' She stood fingering one of the buttonholes of my coat, and looking up at me.

And then, at long last, I knew what the trouble was.

'Look here, Joan,' I said gently. 'D'you think that's quite straight? Because I don't.'

I saw her flush up scarlet, but I went on before she had time to answer, and that gave her time to collect herself.

'It's not Compton that I'm thinking about altogether,' I said. 'I'd do my best to get Mattani hung for that, certainly, but if it was only that I'd leave it to the police. What worries me is the dope. We've got to stop that coming into England, you know, and the only real way to stop it is to get hold of Mattani. I don't know how many loads he's run in up to date – either two or three. I don't know how much he runs of it at a time or what the profits are; but I'm damn sure of this, the profits are something perfectly enormous. He'll go on doing it, you know. He may wait six months till the fuss has died down, but he'll begin again. We've simply got to stop that stuff getting into the country like that. So far as I can see, the only satisfactory way of stopping it is to hang Mattani.'

She flashed out at me. 'Don't talk about it like that.'

I was hardly listening to her. 'Sorry,' I said absently. I was thinking of the days just after the war, when I had been living at a fair rate, when it was all rose-coloured for us because we had not been killed. I was thinking of the girl that I had met then, and the fine times we had had, that first summer after the war. I was thinking of how it all came to an end.

'I don't suppose you've ever seen anyone that you cared for really well on in dope, have you?' I said. 'I did ... once.'

140

She looked at me in a troubled sort of way. 'It's their own fault if they take it,' she said uncertainly.

'I don't think so,' I said quietly. 'They take it – they take it because there's nobody to tell them any better. The sort of people who want looking after, only there's nobody to do it. The Wimps and Flossies, trailing about Shaftesbury Avenue in the evening, looking for a bit of fun. The ones that come from Golders Green and think they're seeing life when they dance all night in some damned cellar. They're mostly women. They take it because they think it makes them bright. Because they think it makes them pretty. They fairly lap it up. It's only because they haven't got anyone to look after them. They haven't a chance. It's not playing the game to put the damn stuff in their way. It's a Chink's game, Chinks and Dagoes.'

I might have added Belgians to the list, but I've never talked about that business. She didn't say anything to that rigmarole for a long time, but at last she looked up at me curiously.

'Do you really want to go to Italy for that, Philip,' she said – 'for those people?'

'I'm afraid so,' I replied.

'Why then,' she said quietly, 'you must go. And I must wish you luck.'

I looked at my watch; it was about half past four. I wanted to take her out to tea, but I couldn't think of anywhere to take her to except the Piccadilly Hotel, and that didn't seem to fit in somehow. She said she knew a place. We went down the road and got out my car from the garage, and drove to a place off Baker Street where I had the satisfaction of stuffing her with food. She confessed that she had dispensed with lunch.

Then we drove to Paddington and I put her in the train for Wycombe. I promised to keep in touch with her and let her know what happened in Italy; she made me promise to give her lunch when I had any news. At least, the lunch was my idea. In return, I made her promise to stay in Stokenchurch till she heard from me. Having made sure that there was some reasonable chance of our meeting again, I let her go, and the train steamed out of the station.

I got my car and drove out to the aerodrome. I found Morris in his office, and I found him pretty terse. It seemed that the police had been up at the aerodrome every day while I had been away. He said it was getting the place a bad name. He remarked that he was fed up with me. If I didn't like the job I could chuck it up, but while I remained in it I would behave myself, write up my log-books at the end of each flight, and keep out of reach of the law.

I gave him as good as I got, and for ten minutes we went at it hammer and tongs. It was quite homely; I had been missing my weekly bout with Morris. I pointed out to him that the whole business came from his infernal policy of taking orders for five times as many machines as were available, then waiting till a machine came in, turning it round, and pushing it off into the air again in ten minutes. For myself, I said, I'd had enough of it. If Morris wanted to carry on like that he could find some other ruddy fool to fly for him. Personally, I was lucky to be alive. In future I'd be a damn sight more careful how I risked my neck for the firm on their rotten machines. As for the engines, the whole lot were fit for nothing but the scrapheap.

He became personal then, and remarked that if I drank a little less I might fly a little better. Anyway, the Rawdon Aircraft Company wasn't a social club, and if my Dago friends wanted to find me they could go to my flat and not come hanging about the aerodrome. When Morris descended to personalities it usually meant the end of any bickering, and I wasn't surprised when he offered me a cigarette and telephoned for tea. We settled down then, and he told me the news. Collard was in the North, and his dog had produced a litter of puppies in the night watchman's hut. He was having my machine repaired that had been brought back from Stokenchurch.

'That's the way,' I said bitterly. 'Put a patch on it and it'll

142

be as good as new.' He didn't rise to that. 'By the way, what was that you said about my Dago friends?'

'Keep 'em off the aerodrome,' he grunted.

I lit another cigarette from the stump of the last. 'Haven't any Dago friends,' I said. 'What did they look like?'

'Dagoes,' he said lucidly. 'One tall and one short. The tall one did all the talking. He was all right, but the other looked as if he'd slit you up as soon as look at you. I thought they wanted a machine at first and had them shown in here, but what they wanted was to know all about you. I shot 'em out pretty soon. They were back again next day, but I didn't see them.'

'What day was that?' I asked.

He thought for a little. 'Tuesday was the first day,' he said. 'Tuesday and Wednesday they came.'

I nodded slowly. That would have been after Compton had seen Mattani in Leeds and before he had reached the Scillies. It seemed as though they had realized that I was working with him and were trying to get a line on me. They had been unsuccessful then, but they would be able to locate me now all right. I had an unpleasant feeling that that might be so much the worse for me.

Morris looked at me curiously. 'Friends of yours?' he inquired.

I shook my head. 'Dare say I owe them money,' I observed. I turned to him. 'Are we doing much work? I shall want a bit more holiday in a day or two.'

He looked pretty sour at that. 'How much?' he said.

'I don't really know. A week or so. Perhaps a fortnight. I've got to go abroad for a bit.'

He looked sourer than ever. 'It'll be very inconvenient,' he said. 'Where are you going to?'

I got out another cigarette and lit it before I answered him. He was a stout fellow at the bottom, was Morris.

'See here,' I said. 'If I tell you where I'm going, I don't want it to get out and round the town. If it does, I may be a stiff little corpse before I get back. I'd hate that. I'd like you to assimilate that idea first of all. I've been mixed up in some pretty funny business during the last few days – as you may have guessed.'

He nodded. 'I wish to hell you'd behave yourself,' he said fretfully. 'It was obvious that the police didn't want you for a little thing like that. I wish you wouldn't go dragging in the firm every time you get into trouble. The directors wanted to know all about you at the Board Meeting on Wednesday. It makes it damned awkward for me.'

I laughed. 'I'll resign, and go to Croydon, if you like.'

'I don't want you to do that,' he said. 'We only want a little peace and quiet.'

'I'll see what we can do about it,' I promised. 'Now look here. I don't expect you to believe me for a minute, but I'm on the side of the angels this time.'

He grunted sceptically. 'Don't bring them here,' he said. 'This is a business office.'

I disregarded that. 'It's been a long story,' I said slowly, ' – too long to go into now. But I'm serious over this. So far as I can see, I stand quite a good chance of a bullet in my guts before I'm through.' I saw him stiffen to attention. 'Now look here. I'm going to Italy, and I want to get there on the quiet. Can you fix it with the people at Croydon for me to take one of the regular Air Line machines over to Paris one day next week?'

He looked at me gravely. 'Not if you're wanted by the police in England.'

'I'll give you my word that I'm not.'

He still looked doubtful. 'If you'll promise not to bring the firm into it in any way? Right you are. I can fix that for you. Only the outward trip, I suppose?'

I nodded. 'That's it. That's damn good of you, Morris. The next thing is, it's just possible that I may have to get home pretty quick. If you hear from me any time in the next month, will you send a machine out? I want this to have priority over any other orders. It may be damned important. I'd like Collard to bring her out. I know it's a lot to ask, but can you fix that?'

'If you'll pay for it,' he said.

'How much?' I inquired cautiously.

'The usual rates.'

'Less the usual twenty per cent?'

'No,' he said. 'I'm damned if I will. I don't want to get the firm mixed up in any smutty business of yours. Besides, it's a priority order.'

We had the devil of an argument over that. Finally I made him see reason to the tune of seven and a half per cent; farther than that I couldn't get him to go. I wasn't sure that I should want a machine; I wasn't sure that I could pay for it if I did. It gave me a comfortable feeling to have it in readiness, though. It might be the means of getting the game into my own hands. And anyway, they say that one always plays a better game when one has had the forethought to fix an ace to the under side of the table with a bit of chewing-gum.

I went back to the flying for a week. Rather to my surprise nothing at all happened to me. For the first two or three days I went about in the panic of my life that somebody would throw something hard at me from round a corner, but nobody did. I avoided going out at night as much as possible; the daytime I spent almost entirely on the aerodrome. We were always pretty busy in the summer.

Then one day Openshaw, the chief pilot at Croydon, rang me up and asked me if I would mind taking a machine over to Paris on the following day. There was no hint that this was anything but a normal request, due to pressure of work. I wondered how Morris had worked it. I said that it would be rather inconvenient, but that I'd do it if he was really hard up for a pilot. Then I rang off, and went away and sat in my deck-chair on the aerodrome in the shade of one of the hangars to think about it.

Well, I was for it now.

145

I went over to Croydon early next morning. The machine was one of the single-engined ten-seaters that have done more than any other type, I think, to put civil aviation on its feet as a paying proposition. The load was a typical one. There were two American ladies, one of them with the inevitable Kodak, both very shrill. There was a honeymoon couple, as I judged, and the load was completed by three assorted business men, two of them foreigners, all with their little bags. I watched them bundled in and sorted out into their places in the cabin by the attendants, watched the door closed. Then, with a couple of men heaving on the tail in the blast from the propeller, I turned her and taxied out across the grass.

I took the whole length of the aerodrome to get off. It was some time since I had flown a Thirty-four, and unsticking was never her strong point at the best of times. Once off the ground she climbed well. I swung her round on to her course, climbed to about a thousand feet, and leaned forward behind the windscreen to light my cigarette.

It was an uneventful journey. There was a little loose cloud at about three thousand feet; I poked up through that on my way to the coast and came out above it. It was some months since I had flown on the Paris route; that gave the trip a little interest and saved me from boredom. I crossed the Channel near Folkestone at a height of about five thousand feet and trundled on on the familiar route through France till the haze over Paris showed up on the horizon, about two hours after leaving Croydon. I found Le Bourget and put her down gently on the grass, half sorry it was over.

I didn't stop in Paris, but caught one of the night trains on to Italy. I had brought a suitcase with me, and I left my flying kit at Le Bourget. By a little judicious bribery during the afternoon I managed to secure a corner seat on the train, and I spent a moderately comfortable night as we trailed down through France. It was a hot night. I slept fitfully; in the intervals I sat smoking and trying to remember what I could of Leglia. It was many years since I had seen him – not since

146

the war. He had never met me in Paris as he had said he would; on my part I had been a little shy of forcing myself on a man who was so much my superior socially, the war being over. If I had ever been in Florence I should have gone to look him up, but though I had flown to Italy many times, it had never happened that I had put down at Florence. It lies a little off the commercial track of modern Italy.

Dawn came as we were approaching the foothills of the Alps; in the early morning we began to wind our way slowly up to the Mont Cenis. It was most awfully pretty. I had never travelled much upon the Continent in the ordinary way, and in the air there is no scenery. Mountains become mere lumps of land, hazards, to be scrutinized for their physical features, compared anxiously with a hatched and contoured map, and ticked off as they are passed. These valleys were different. The little villages standing among the pine trees by the bed of the river tickled me immensely; it was something different, the sort of thing that I had never seen before. I leaned out of the window as the train went puffing up round the bends in the valley, and thought that it would be a good scheme to come out here one day, simply to walk about those hills and explore them. I remember that I thought it would be a good place to bring Joan to.

We got to Modane at about eight o'clock, and then on down the valley to Turin. All day we went meandering on through Italy, and it wasn't till dinnertime that the train drew into the station at Florence.

I had dined in the train. I didn't want to go to any hotel in Florence if I could possibly avoid it; to spend a night in a hotel meant registering, displaying my passport, and generally broadcasting my identity. I didn't want to do that. It struck me that there was a very fair sporting chance that I had reached Italy unobserved; it seemed to me that I might remain in the country for several days before Mattani and his crowd realized that I was there at all. On the other hand, it was quite on the cards that they knew all about me already. In either case it seemed that the best thing I could do was to go straight to Leglia.

I pushed my way through the crowd at the station, fending off the guides and porters who came clawing at my baggage, and found a carriage. My Italian is pretty rocky, but on this occasion I spoke it to some effect. The moment I mentioned the Palazzo Leglia the old ruffian on the box stopped leering at me, hopped down from his seat with a surprising display of agility, and opened the door for me to get into the carriage. I got in, a little bewildered at this unwonted servility; by the time I was fairly settled he had whipped up his horse and we were bowling along through the town at a smart trot.

The drive didn't take long. Not very far from the Piazza della Signoria the driver turned down a narrow side street, and stopped in front of a veritable barrack of a house.

It really was a most formidable-looking place. It was built of stone and filled the whole of one side of the narrow street, towering up into the sky. I don't know how old it was, but even in that clean air the stone was black with age. There were a few tall, dark windows looking out on to the street, all heavily barred with ornate steelwork that was rusty and eaten up with age. I could see no sign of life about the place. The door was a massive double gateway, as stained and old as the rest of the building. By the door there was a mounting-block, and there was a rusty torch extinguisher on the wall like a candle-snuffer.

Before I had time to get out, the driver tumbled down from his box and rang the bell. It went jangling mournfully somewhere inside the place. Almost immediately one half of the door swung open, and I was faced with a grave old gentleman in evening dress. He had white hair cropped very close to his head.

I mustered my wretched Italian to my aid. 'Il Signore Giovanni da Leglia, è a casa?' I said.

He said something that I didn't quite catch, with a rapid dignity; I think he was asking me my business. I got out my note-case and produced a card; he went fumbling in the tail pockets of his coat till he produced a pair of iron-rimmed spectacles with which to scrutinize it. That gave me a minute's grace, and in that time I concocted a wonderful sentence to the effect that my business was urgent and could not be delayed. I fired that off at him; he waited patiently till I had finished, and then gave utterance to that magic formula that pervades all Italy.

'Subito, subito,' he said gravely.

I made my driver understand that he was to wait for me, and passed in through the gates, which closed behind me. I found myself in an open courtyard with a cloister running round the walls; in the centre there was a fountain playing, with goldfish in the bowl below, and the place was bright with flowers. The major-domo rang a bell and presently a boy appeared; I was left in his care while the old retainer crossed the courtyard and disappeared from view, my card in his hand.

I thanked my stars that Leglia was at home. I put great faith in Leglia; though I hadn't seen him for all those years, I was positive that he would be able to help me. Looking back now, I am a little surprised at that. I'm too old to cherish illusions; I don't generally trust people so much as that. This time I did, and I wasn't let down.

After ten minutes or so the old man returned, and motioned to me to follow him. As we passed through the cloister I noticed an invalid chair standing in a corner. It was the sort of thing that can be manipulated up and down stairs; it had cushions in it and seemed to be in frequent use. I wondered idly which of Leglia's family was forced to adopt this means of locomotion. I thought that in all probability it was his mother. I knew nothing about his family or his private affairs at that time.

The journey through the house seemed endless. It was an immense place, full of the sort of furniture that makes a house look like a museum. We went through corridor after corridor, now and then up a flight of stairs, always mounting a little

149

higher till we were well above the level of the surrounding houses. I could see that much from occasional glimpses of the town as we passed windows. At last we came to a heavy door at the end of a wide stone passage. We were on the top floor then; so much was evident from the rafters that supported the roof, stained and carved like the roof beams of a church. The old man opened this door, stood aside for me to pass into the room, and closed it softly behind me.

It was a high, vaulted room, with a wide polished floor. There was a window at the far end opening on to a balcony; beyond that there was a fine view over the roofs of the city, the river, and the country beyond rising into hills. I looked round for Leglia. For a moment I could see nothing of him, and then I saw that he was lying on a couch just inside the window.

I went striding across the room towards him. As I went it was strange to me to see how old he looked. The years had made more difference to him than I could have dreamed.

He greeted me gaily.

'Stenning, Captain,' he cried. 'This will be magnificent, to meet again.'

'By Gad, Lillian,' I said. 'I'm damn glad to see you.'

And then I saw why he had not got up to meet me, why he had never met me in Paris as we had arranged, why the years had pressed so heavily upon him.

He was a cripple. Both legs had been amputated above the knee.

a country of born politicians. He never mentioned himself, but there was a personal note all through his story that I found it very hard to account for. For him the politicians were live men, men whose characters he knew, men with whom he had argued. He spoke as if he were reading extracts from a diary.

'You don't seem to miss much that goes on in Italy,' I remarked at last.

He laughed. 'But I see ... not very much of what goes on, is it not so?' he said. 'I go out only a little, only a little now and then. But sometimes my friends, they come to see me to talk about our country, so that I tell them what I think. They come to me to stay for a little in the country – from Milano, from Roma.' He mused a little. 'In England you have a proverb of the sport that sometimes I laugh about with my sister, because I think I am like that. The onlooker, he sees the most of the game. Non è vero?'

'It seems to be,' I said. 'You can knock spots off anyone else I've ever met on Italy.'

He smiled happily. 'Knock spots ...' he repeated. 'The English slang, that I have not heard not since we were together. Always I have wished to travel in England, to see again the little town where I learnt the flying, And – Andover. That will be the only visit that ever I have paid to England. Always I have wished to return, to see again your pretty country. But....' He glanced down at his legs. 'And I do not know any people....'

I put him right about that. Then I leaned back in my chair and thought a bit. It was almost dark.

'I say, Leglia,' I said slowly at last. 'I've not come to Italy for fun. I really came out to see if I could touch you for a bit of advice. I came to see if you could help me a bit. It's about one of your countrymen.'

He raised his hand with a smile. 'One moment,' he said. 'It is with pleasure that I am at your service of my countrymen, old bean. But for my countrywomen, I beg that you will remember that I am Giovanni da Leglia, and my people love me.'

153

That tickled me no end. 'It's all right,' I said. 'I wouldn't dream of coming to you about a girl. The man I want to find out something about is Baron Mattani.'

I saw him glance sharply at me. 'Ah,' he said quietly. 'He is half English, by his mother.'

It had become so dark that I could see very little in the room. Leglia lay silent on his couch in the gloom, quietly puffing a cigarette, waiting for me to go on.

'Does he cut much ice in Italy?' I asked.

He laughed suddenly. 'The argot!' he explained. 'I had not heard the word till I was with you, and I had forgotten.' He became serious again. 'He cuts much ice, very much. He is popular, as the papers say. He has the Press.'

'What do you think of him yourself?' I asked.

He flicked the ash from his cigarette. 'For myself,' he said evenly, 'the Leglias do not smuggle spirits. But in Italy it is not always that one will speak one's thoughts.' He turned to me. 'Now you shall tell me what you want to know of Baron Mattani. If it is that I cannot answer, yet you shall know to-morrow or the next day.'

'He murdered a pal of mine a few days ago,' I said bluntly. 'I want to see him extradited and hung.'

It was a long time before he spoke again.

'Murder ...' he said at last. 'That will be something new.'

I knocked out my pipe and filled it again. 'It's about that that I came to Italy,' I said. 'I can tell you about it if you like. But it's a long story.'

He lit a small reading-lamp that stood on the table by his couch; in the soft light I could see that he was very serious.

'Tell me, Capitano mio,' he said. 'Of Baron Mattani the littlest things are important to one who loves Italy. And murder is more still.'

For a moment I was at a loss as to where I should begin the tale. 'Did you know that Mattani had an English stepbrother?' I said. 'It was he who was killed.'

Leglia swore, very softly, in Italian. I glanced at him in

surprise; in the soft light of the lamp I could see that he was immensely shocked. In Italy there is a great sense of the family unity, far more so than in England. To us a murder is a murder, whoever it be. In Italy, I think, there are degrees of murder and fratricide is a very bad business.

I could see now that Leglia was intensely interested. He lay listening to me for the most part in silence; now and then he snapped out a question when I had not made myself clear, or when he had missed the meaning of the English. I told him the story straight ahead from the beginning, and left out nothing.

By the time I had finished it was nearly midnight. For a long time he sat smoking in silence, staring out over the quiet roofs of the city, bright in the moonlight. I knew what he was thinking about; his mind was running on the politics of his country. He was wondering what this would mean for Italy. I left him to it, and we sat like that for a quarter of an hour in silence. At last he threw away his cigarette.

'You will be tired from your journey,' he said, 'and it is late. We will go to bed, and tomorrow we will talk. As you have said, I do not think that Baron Mattani will have forgotten you. But for tonight you will be safe in my house. Tomorrow, when you have met my friends, you will be safe in the town. There is nobody in all Florence that will not see to a friend of Giovanni da Leglia.'

On this eloquent note we went to bed. He rang for his servant and I was shown to my room. For a hot-weather bedroom it was a pretty good spot. The floor was of stone with little rugs on it. Both the walls and the ceiling were panelled with dark cedar, with little patterns picked out upon the beams in blue and white paint.

I noticed these next morning as I was sitting up in bed over my breakfast. The valet who had brought the tray was quite a boy, with a rich crop of bright red hair. He referred to the meal proudly as a 'colazione Inglese', and it was certainly a noble effort for a household where breakfast was unknown. There was coffee, a sort of stuffed tomato with olives round it, a kidney aristocratically perched upon a bit of haddock, the cold leg of a small roast chicken, rolls, butter, and preserved ginger. I did pretty well by it, gratified at the thought that had evidently been spent over my comfort. Then I got up.

The red-haired boy came in in the middle and wanted to shave me, but I sent him away with a flea in his ear. He told me that Leglia was already up, and was sitting in the cloister. I had a bath, dressed, wished my suit was a little more respectable, and went downstairs.

It was a brilliant morning. After wandering about the house for a bit I found the cloister; Leglia was sitting in the invalid chair in a shady corner beside a table littered with papers. There was a girl sitting with him, his sister. We suffered a very proper introduction at his hands, after which he returned to his work and left us to amuse each other. She was a girl of the typical Italian type, small, with dark eyes, a lot of black hair, and a very clear complexion.

At the end of a quarter of an hour I had learned that she was an experienced charmer and that she liked her occasional visits to Milan, dancing at the magnificent balls given by the local nobility, officers from the Scuola Cavalliere across the river, and chocolates. After that I felt that I had learned all there was to know about her. She was a good sort in her own way.

Leglia asked me to excuse him while he finished his business. I sat down on the edge of the balustrade and told his sister what a corking breakfast I'd had. Her English was about on a par with my Italian; we tried each in turn with very similar results.

'Aha!' she laughed. 'La colazione Inglese!' She paused, and thought out a sentence. 'We have tried,' she said painfully, 'that it is made beautiful.'

'Squisita,' said Leglia, without looking up. 'Good to eat.'

'Si si si!' she said brightly. 'Squisita.'

I replied that it was a splendid breakfast and that I had enjoyed it very much, and got this through at the second attempt. For some time we conversed laboriously about England and the English, till at last we came to the point that was really exercising her mind; did I think the English girls were prettier than the Italians? I knew this gambit of old; I flatter myself that the delicate courtesy of my reply was well up to the high standard set by the officers of the School of Riding. At all events, it went down very well.

She glanced mischievously at her brother. 'For Giovanni,' she remarked, 'I must to find a bride English.'

He spoke very rapidly and tersely to her in Italian, and returned to his writing. She sighed and shook her head.

'Gli Inglesi,' she said. 'Always he talks of England and the English.'

She said that he was mad on England.

We went on gossiping till we were interrupted. The white-haired old man appeared round the corner of the arcade conducting the most gorgeously attired police official that I had ever seen. Leglia sat up as he came in sight.

'That is good,' he remarked to me. 'It is about you that he comes, old bean.'

He put his hands to the wheels of his chair and swivelled himself round to meet the official. He was very nimble in that chair of his. It was the usual motion of a host rising to meet his guest, but one that might well have been forgiven to an invalid. I think that must have been one of the many trifles that combined to build up his great influence in the town. I knew very little of Leglia; I had yet to realize what a popular idol he had become. It took me some time to adjust my ideas to the fact that his popularity was genuine. For centuries the Leglias had been nobles in the town, for centuries the townspeople had looked to them for a lead. Giovanni da Leglia before the war had been modern enough to please the youngest of them, a shade too modern for their elders. The war put the whole town at his feet. That one of the nobility should go and look at Jerry face to face in the British Flying Corps instead of going to Rome upon the Staff seemed to them a very strange thing, very modern and very wonderful. When he was crippled he became a hero. But when he came back to Florence and took up his hereditary position, when it became evident that his one care was for his people, he became a saint.

Leglia conversed in rapid Italian for a little while with the official, who seemed to be agreeing to everything he said. Presently he beckoned to me. I went up to them, and became aware that the official was scrutinizing me carefully. He bowed to me as I came up, and asked if His Excellency would have the egregious kindness to display his passport. I gave it to him; he stamped it with a stamp and pad that he introduced from the tail pocket of his coat, and returned it to me with a flourish. He made a little speech in Italian then, the burden of which was that in all my walks abroad the Civil Power would strew rosebuds in the way and would endeavour to restrain the populace from throwing things at me. I took this with a grain of salt, but it was a fact that for so long as I remained in Florence every carabinier saluted me.

I made a laboured little speech in reply, and presently he bowed himself away.

He was followed by a succession of visitors. To all of them I was introduced. Most of them came upon their lawful occasions to see Leglia at his hour of levée; some, I think, had been summoned only to be introduced to me. I could make nothing of the plan upon which they had been selected. Mostly they were of the black-coated bourgeois type, some evidently affluent, some less so. There were one or two that seemed to be peasants or small farmers in from the country; there was one that was a pure-blooded gipsy if ever I saw one. All at the conclusion of their business with Leglia turned and looked me up and down. Some of them even made a little speech assuring me of friendship should I be in need of it. I had a set answer which I gave them in reply to this sort of thing; to the others I bowed, and they went away in silence.

The whole show struck me as extremely curious. There was something in the way in which they had all offered their friendship that seemed to me too uniform to be altogether natural. It was as if they were accustomed to it, as if it was all in the day's work. And here I may say at once that I never found out any more about the conditions under which they offered me this friendship, nor did I inquire. Looking back upon it, I have become convinced in my own mind that it was to the members of some society that Leglia introduced me I know this much: that they were not Freemasons.

At last they stopped coming. Leglia turned to me.

'You have now many friends in Florence,' he said. 'I do not think that now you may come to any harm.'

I was very much impressed and said as much. 'It seems to me that you go one better than the law of the land.'

He smiled a little ruefully. 'The law of the land,' he said reflectively, 'he does not always work all of the time. In every country he will not work now and again.' He sighed. 'In my country I think he works not so well as he does in England. And the more so with the new Government.'

I began to see dimly what he was driving at. 'Do you get much trouble in that way?' I asked.

The girl had disappeared. Leglia motioned to me to sit down; he lay back in his chair and lit one of his innumerable cigarettes. 'I am Fascist, for myself,' he said.

He mused a little. 'Always with a Government of force there will be trouble now and again,' he said. 'It must be. And we have many troubles – very many troubles, so that sometimes one will doubt of Fascismo. But for myself, I am Fascist because the old Government was not – not so good, not sincere. Fascismo is for those that love Italy. And Il Duce is a man.'

He leaned towards me and tapped me on the arm. 'With some,' he said quietly, 'Fascismo is as a religion and Il Duce is a God. The people who think so, they are a danger to us all because they are so foolish, so led away. They are – what do you say? Mad. No. . . .'

'You mean they get fanatical about it,' I said.

He brightened. 'That is the word,' he said. 'They are fanatics, for whom the Opposition in Parliament is a heresy. They

159

are so foolish. For them the whole of the business of Government is to make a speech and to say "I am Fascist, I fought for Italia in the war."' The mimicry in his voice was wonderful. 'More still. They do not think. For them a Ras is as a God, and one above the law though he be smuggler and murderer.'

'I understand,' I muttered.

He laid his hand upon my arm again. 'Do not misjudge my people,' he said. He spoke royally, but somehow I didn't want to laugh. 'They are not as the English. They are as the Irish, I think, much as the Irish. They are so easily inflamed, so easy to lead away with talk, not very responsible. But they will settle; they settle now to the business of sound government of our great nation. Let only Il Duce live for ten years more, as we pray to the Mother of God daily.'

I glanced at him. 'And if he dies?'

He flicked the ash from his cigarette. 'My friend,' he said quietly, 'we pray that he will live.'

The sun was bright in the court, blazing down on the flowers in the shade of the arches of the cloister, and the queer dry-looking cactuses in the centre round about the fish-pond. I turned to Leglia.

'It's a Government that is open to abuse,' I said.

He inclined his head proudly. 'When I think of that, as sometimes I do, I tell you, old bean, I am most proud. The Government stands to be abused; in any other country it would be abused in fact. But in Italy the people are well governed. The people work more hard, and we balance on the Budget.'

'That's certainly a damn fine thing to be able to say of the country,' I remarked. 'At the same time, the Government is open to abuse. Mattani seems to get away with it here in a way he couldn't do in any other country.'

He nodded gravely. 'As you say, Mattani gets away with it.' He paused. 'It would be better for my country if he did not. It is the bad example, and makes many difficulties.'

I laughed shortly. 'It would be better for my country too,' I said.

He looked at me reflectively. 'That is so,' he said at last. 'Perhaps our interests will follow the same road. Is it not so?'

I knocked my pipe out sharply against the balustrade. 'My interests are pretty simple,' I said. 'I want to see him hung.'

He didn't answer that, but sat staring out over the court-yard; quite motionless. He seemed to have forgotten my presence; presently I heard him mutter, half to himself:

'It is but a tool that he makes of Fascismo. . . .'

I lay back in my chair and filled another pipe. I could see the position clearly now. Leglia wanted to get rid of Mattani, apparently from purely altruistic motives; he thought that he was a bad influence in the country. It seemed to me that Mattani had done him no personal injury, but for the sake of his ideals and for his country Leglia was willing to see him put out of the way – possibly at some danger to himself if his part in the affair should ever come to light. I turned in my chair and smiled a little. What a queer old cuss he was, so idealistic and so foreign!

At that moment England and the life I knew seemed incredibly remote.

'You think that he would be better hanged?' I said.

Leglia did not answer. He sat quite motionless in his chair, staring out over his little garden from the shadow of the cloister. I was suddenly ashamed of the bantering tone in which I had spoken. I had been speaking flippantly, but this was a matter of the life or death of a man whom I had never seen, who had done me no harm. God knows I had little enough cause to speak lightly of him. We were speaking of his death; it was just as likely that we were speaking of my own. I remembered with a start that for all the hospitality and good feeling with which I was surrounded, I was in a foreign country, a country in which Mattani's power was pretty nearly absolute. It would be time enough to laugh when I was back in

England again. I thought of England, and my mind travelled back to Stokenchurch, the crash, and the long night that we had spent in the smoking-room of Six Firs, Joan, Compton, and I, drinking and talking of what was the best thing to be done for him. And then I knew that it was up to me to see that his murderer was brought to stand a fair trial. If I could do that, I thought, my life would not have been entirely wasted.

Still Leglia was silent. I glanced at him, and my enthusiasm faded away. There was no personal bias about Leglia – of that I am positive. There was an air about Leglia; there had always been the same dignity about him even in his most irresponsible moments in the old days. I felt his dignity very strongly then. He sat there quite motionless, quite impassive, staring out on to his flowers. If ever I saw justice in a man's face, it was then.

And presently he spoke. 'Stenning, my friend,' he said, 'it is that my country stands at the parting of the ways. These years in Italy have been most difficult since the revolution, most upsetting of all order and moral behaviour. For my country when she is led rightly there stands a glorious future. Of that I am convinced. But the leading must be right, and in that there has been disappointment for us – much disappointment. I can speak, because sitting here and taking no part I have been able to watch the better. There are those of whom we had thought little before the revolution who have shown themselves of a great mind. And there are those on whom we had learned to trust, that have stood but to gain position for themselves and for their own purposes.'

He paused. 'We had hoped much of Mattani,' he said quietly. 'Of all men in Italy save only Il Duce he held the imagination of the people; in Italy that is to say much, though I know it is not quite like that in England. Moreover, he was a little English, and we hoped much from that. Of all men in Italy below Il Duce we had hoped the most of Mattani. And it was all for a disappointment. . . .'

I could find nothing to say to that.

He continued: 'Still he holds the imagination of the people

by the power of his papers, but his influence for long has been most bad. He holds himself – how do you say? – above the law. For Italy in these times that any man should hold himself above the law I think to be most dangerous, most probably to hinder the progress of our Government, the more so for such a man as Baron Mattani.'

He glanced at me. 'I am most happy that you should have come to see me,' he said, 'for I think it will be of value to my country that the law should be upheld. But the one thing I must press to you. If I can help you to secure Baron Mattani, that he shall stand a trial before the courts of your country; you shall not allow him to be killed before that. Only in that way will the example be of good to Italy.'

'I can promise that,' I said. 'Once we get him he shall have a fair trial.'

He threw away the cigarette and lit another. 'You shall tell me what you want to do,' he said.

I considered for a little. 'Is there any hope of extraditing him, do you think?' I said.

'It would be difficult,' he replied. 'Most difficult.'

He glanced at me. 'Is it a need to extradite him from Italy by force?' he said. 'It seems that you have but to wait a little time and he will come to you.'

'You mean he'll come to England?' I inquired.

He nodded. 'That there is much profit in his smuggling of drugs to England I do not doubt,' he said. 'That he will not give up, unless you will make it very dangerous for him.'

'I see,' I said. 'You mean if we leave him alone he'll carry on with the good work. If he really did that we might be able to do something about it. But I think it seems very unlikely. He'll drop that particular stunt now.'

'That will be possible,' admitted Leglia. 'At the same time, he will have much money in his organization in England – very much. Also he is very bold, a very bold man. I do not think that he will give up to smuggle into England, but he may change in the method.'

163

'We don't know what the method is yet,' I said glumly. 'We don't know how he does it.'

Leglia stared absently at the little fountain. 'That it should not be very difficult to find out,' he said softly.

'More than we've been able to do,' I remarked.

He laughed. 'It is because you have searched in England for the answer to your riddle,' he said. 'In England a plan to smuggle into England will not be easy to discover. But in Italy a plan to smuggle into England will not be quite of so great an importance, and may be more easy to be discovered. The more so by an Italian.'

I looked at him with an added respect. 'That's a pretty sound bit of reasoning,' I said.

'Where the murder took place,' he said, 'the harbour, what name —'

'Marazan Sound,' I replied.

'Marazan Sound,' he repeated. 'They guard it now, is it not so?'

'Put a guard on Marazan?' I said. 'I haven't heard of it being done. No, I don't suppose they do guard it. There's really not much evidence to show that it's ever going to be used again for smuggling. Not after what happened the last time.'

He seemed to reflect. 'He is a very bold man,' he said at last. 'It would be in his nature to go back there to smuggle again, being that one would think it incredible that he should do so.'

He relapsed into silence again. I left him to his thoughts and sat smoking and dozing in the warmth, till I was roused by the sudden tinkle of the bell on the table at his side. He rang again, and I saw his old retainer come hurrying from the gate.

He slackened speed as he drew near, and came and stood deferentially by Leglia, waiting for the order. No order came, but after a minute Leglia began to speak to him confidentially. He spoke in Italian, naturally, but I was able to follow the greater part of what they were saying.

'Nicolo,' he said. 'I am thinking of Luigi, the son of Elena with the goats at Estalebona. He is at home?'

'Excellency,' said the man, 'he is at sea, being a sailor by trade. In two months he may be home again.'

Leglia closed his eyes. 'A reliable man,' he said presently, 'and one who knows the sea and sailors, who is discreet, and who loves me.'

The old man bowed. 'Excellency, the cousin of Luigi, Benedetto, the son of Giacomo who lives by the gate, is also a sailor. They say that he is a silent man.'

'It is but to go to Genoa,' said Leglia carelessly, 'to the wine-shops, to get a little drunk, to make others a little drunk, to be silent, and to listen. Such a man would be of service to me.'

'Excellency,' said the old man, 'I will see Benedetto and I will bring him to you.'

He faded away down the cloister; Leglia sat in silence for a little, brooding with his head upon his chest. Presently he roused himself and began to talk of other things, of our old days in the Flying Corps when there was a war on.

Then came the summons to lunch, a very Italian meal, served in a long, dark hall. The sister was there with her chaperon; we made grave conversation for an hour. After lunch everybody went to bed. Leglia told me that he thought I should be quite safe if I wanted to go out and see the town; he hoped that he would be able to get some news for me in a day, or two days at the most. He knew that the English did not go to bed in the middle of the day; in summer he thought it was a mistake not to do so – but there! I should find fruit and wine in the cloister.

I found them.

Presently I got my hat and went out to see how the land lay. The old man stopped me in the gate, and in slow distinct Italian asked if I would mind if he were to send a boy to follow behind me. Il Signor Duca had not thought it neces-sary, but for himself he would like to send a boy with me. Things were, he said, 'molto turbato, molto turbato....'

165

His concern for me was so genuine that I agreed without a murmur, and the red-haired boy who had valeted me in the morning appeared in a plain suit of black. Wherever I wandered during the remainder of the afternoon the red-haired boy was always in the middle distance, never at hand, never quite out of sight. Every policeman saluted me. From time to time I passed people who took off their hats to me, but nobody stopped to speak. I recognized several as those to whom I had been introduced in the morning.

I went and looked at pictures all afternoon. I think at the back of my mind was the fear that one day I might be called upon to take an intelligent interest in things artistic. It was an occupation that I had never tried before; I can't say that I derived much benefit from it. I stuck to it conscientiously for two and a half hours by my watch, then wandered thankfully to a café, where I collapsed into a chair on the pavement and settled down to watch the people for an hour. My red-haired escort sat down a few tables away; I pretended not to see him, and paid for his drinks.

Presently I got up and went back to the Palazzo.

That afternoon was typical of my occupation for the next two days. Leglia told me that evening that he had seen his messenger and had sent him to Genoa; in a day or two he would return with what news he had been able to gather. Leglia said he was putting in hand certain other inquiries, but for the moment the only thing to do was to wait for the return of the sailor from the Genoese pubs. In that two days I saw more of the artistic side of life than I have ever seen before or since; I went at it with a grim determination that it was time I picked up a little education. Leglia and his sister were vastly amused; it turned out that they had never been to half the galleries that I plodded through. When I expressed surprise, Leglia asked shrewdly whether I had ever been into the National Gallery. He had me there.

After two days the messenger returned. He came in the middle of the night – heaven knows why. I was awakened by the red-haired boy, who tapped at my door a little after midnight, with a summons to Leglia's bedroom. I got up, put on a coat, and went with him through the dark, stone-floored passages of the Palazzo.

The night was very hot. Leglia was sitting up in bed when I entered, tastefully attired in striped pyjamas and a yellow, tasselled nightcap. His old servant was moving about in the shadows at the end of the room, and standing by the bed was the messenger. He was a tall, lean peasant, very tanned, with a straggling little moustache and with thin gold ear-rings. He was dressed as a sailor in a blue fisherman's jersey with a short coat over it. The room was lit by two tall candles by the bedside that were flickering and dancing in the draught.

Leglia nodded to me as I came in, and turned again to the messenger. The man was talking very quickly and earnestly, gesticulating freely with his gnarled and roughened hands. To my disappointment I could hardly understand a word of what he was saying; he spoke in some country dialect that was quite beyond me. I sat down on the end of the bed and waited.

Once Leglia turned to me and nodded gravely. 'Of all people,' he said, 'you might have thought of this.' He thought that I was following the story.

At last the tale was finished, and Leglia began asking questions. I hoped to learn something from these, but I could make nothing of the one-sided conversation that I could understand. At last the business seemed to be over. The man stood there in the wavering light as though awaiting his dismissal, a rough, queerly attractive figure, a man that one could depend on. Then he turned his head and glanced at the major-domo. Evidently there was more to come.

The old man moved softly forward from the shadows. 'Excellency,' he said, 'Caterina, the sister of this man, would by now be married to the son of the harness-maker in Estalebona, had not the harness-maker intervened. He objects that the settlement that she can bring is not sufficient....'

Leglia nodded comprehendingly. 'How much does she bring?'

'Excellency, she brings twelve hundred lire. But the father is a very vain man.'

Leglia seemed to consider for a little. Then he turned curiously to the messenger.

'The son,' he said. 'Is it that she loves him?'

The man shrugged his shoulders. 'Lord,' he said, 'it is necessary that my sister should marry to be happy, and this man has offered, and all would have been well but for the father.'

Leglia nodded slowly. 'I go very soon to Estalebona,' he said, 'as soon as this matter is decided. Then I will talk with the father, and they shall marry with my goodwill and with the blessing of the Church.'

The man knelt and kissed his hand.

Then the major-domo shepherded him to the door. They went out, and the door closed silently behind them. I was left alone with Leglia.

He stretched himself, and reached out for the cigarette-box by his bedside.

'Well, old bean,' he remarked, 'so that is that. You have understood what he has said?'

'Not one ruddy word,' I replied. 'It didn't even sound like Italian to me.'

He laughed and lit his cigarette. 'The dialect!' he said. He threw away the match.

'It is by aeroplane that they land the drugs in England,' he said quietly. 'Of all people, to you that will be familiar. He has said that it is by a flying boat, with the wheels, that can land on the earth or on the water.'

'Hell!' I said. 'I might have thought of that.'

The whole thing became obvious. I sat on the edge of his bed and stared into the great shadows of the room while the bits of the puzzle fell together into the pattern. That was the meaning of the rag and pliers that I had found on the beach at

Marazan. Where the sand was soaked in oil was where they had beached the machine to load her up; it was possible that they had refilled her tanks there. The pliers to undo some portion of the cowling round the engine, the rag to wipe up the spilt oil.

That was the only thing that Marazan Sound was any good for, for the operation of seaplanes. Drawing no more than a couple of feet of water, the machine could go anywhere in the Sound at any state of the tide. It would be easily possible to take off from the water in the Sound itself between White Island and Pendruan; in rough weather the Sound would always be calm enough to enable them to run the amphibian up on to the beach to load the cargo. The stuff would be brought to some point off the Scillies by the steamer. There it would be transferred to the motor-launch and taken to Marazan in the early part of the night, to meet the machine.

It was very silent in the room among the wavering shadows.

'Does the boat fly out from England?' I asked.

Leglia nodded. 'From England they fly in the early part of the night, to land at the islands in the darkness with the little lights. On the water they land, and to embark the goods – cargo. And then to fly inland into the middle of England, but never twice to the same place. Always it is many miles into the middle of the country that they will land with the cargo, where one would not think to smuggle.'

'The machine comes out from England?' I asked. 'Where does she come from?'

'An English machine – yes,' he said. 'But from where – I do not know. They are the sailors who have talked, and they have only seen that which happens in the islands.'

'I see,' I muttered. 'They load her up at Marazan, and then she flies back again – well inland somewhere.'

He nodded. 'That is so. Benedetto has told me that the load is not big, not more than two men can carry or that one man should carry on his back for a little way. That does not seem a great quantity.'

'Eighty or a hundred pounds,' I muttered. 'God knows how much that's worth. They mix it with some white powder generally before they sell it – to make it go farther. Boracic or something. The girl I used to know. . . . They sniff it up from the end of a spatula. You don't need much of it.'

'Benedetto has told to me that there is no guard upon the islands,' he said placidly. 'It is that they will recommence to smuggle on the next voyage.'

I sat up with a jerk. 'When's that?'

He shook his head. 'It is not yet known. By the crew it is not known at all that they return to the Scillies, but by the – the officer below the mate. I do not know the name. He has told to Benedetto in the *osteria* that the crew would not voyage if it was that they knew that it was to England that they go again. The officer has said that there was trouble the last trip, with shooting. The crew of the ship have been frightened for prison, and for himself he is a little frightened and would like not to go back. But it is not yet known when they will sail. Perhaps in a week, perhaps a fortnight. Benedetto returns to Genoa tomorrow. In a few days we shall know more.'

'By God,' I said, 'we'll make it hot for them next time!'

I went back to bed. The next three days passed uneventfully; I didn't see that I could do anything but sit still and wait for news. If it was really true that an attempt was to be made to run another cargo, the Scotland Yard people ought to know about it. Oddly enough, my mind kept running on the man that Sir David Carter had called Norman; a useful sort of chap, I thought, and one that I could work in with pretty well if it came to anything of a rough-house. I didn't see how I could communicate with the Yard. Anything I did might give the game away; it was even possible that a letter might be intercepted. In any case, a letter could not put the urgency of the case as I could put it to them myself. I didn't see that the preparations to give them a warm reception need take very long to fix up. Even if we had no word of the departure of the vessel till the day she cleared from Genoa, I could still be in

London four or five days before she reached the Scillies. I decided that the only thing to do was to wait.

I was much puzzled over the aeroplane. An aeroplane is a most conspicuous thing; all sorts of regulations hedge it round about, so that in England there is not the slightest possibility of concealing one's ownership of a machine. I didn't know of a single privately owned amphibian machine in England. An amphibian is a flying-boat or seaplane that is fitted with landing wheels to enable it to put down on land or water. I knew of two privately owned seaplanes and about a dozen privately owned aeroplanes of various denominations and vintages, but no amphibians. There are plenty of amphibians in the Air Force, but it didn't seem likely that anyone could get hold of a Service machine for a job of this sort. No doubt one or two firms that specialized in building them would have a machine on hand for experimental purposes. It might be one of those.

We waited for three days. Then came the news that Benedetto had been killed.

I don't think Leglia had suspected that the man was in any danger or he would have gone about the matter differently. We heard about it early one morning. I was sitting with Leglia in the cloister when his old servant came hurrying from the gate. In a minute we had the whole story. Caterina, the sister of Benedetto, was at the gate. She had been visited by a priest that morning, who had broken to her the news of her brother's death in Genoa. It seemed that he had been killed in a tavern brawl.

Leglia asked me to go away while he saw the girl. I left him to say what he could to her, not envying him the job. I went up to the top room where we used to sit in the evenings and dropped into a chair to think what this meant for us.

I didn't get far. It was murder – of that there could be little doubt. I sat there and remembered the man as I had seen him in Leglia's bedroom, 'the silent man who loved him'. The thought that we had been sending him to his death fairly made

171

me sick. This man was dead, murdered in our service. I was pretty sick about it, but for Leglia it was hell.

I went down after an hour or so. He was sitting where I had left him, brooding in his chair. He refused to discuss the matter then.

However, he wasted no time. 'When one has had defeat in the front attack,' he observed, 'one will send out to the flank, both sides at once.' That was all he told me, but that afternoon his flankers left for Genoa.

I saw them before they went. It seemed that he was attacking from above and from below. One was the gipsy that I had seen before, the other was a puffy little bourgeois, a traveller in a line of cheap celluloid novelties. I don't know what their instructions were, or why he chose them. I saw them passing the gate as they left the Palazzo after a long interview with Leglia. Then they vanished into the blue, and we were left to await their news.

We had a long talk about it that evening sitting in the top room looking out over the river to the hills. Leglia hardly mentioned the dead man. He said briefly and conclusively that it was certainly murder, and laughed at the idea of the murderer being brought to stand his trial. The real point of interest was – how much did Mattani know? This we had no means of estimating till the return of the two flankers.

I shall always remember the dreariness of that second period of waiting. Leglia was worried and uncommunicative; for myself, I roamed restlessly about the Palazzo and the town, wondering how much of my movements was known, wondering every time I went out if I should get a knife in my ribs, too restless to remain in the Palazzo, wishing most desperately that I could be up and doing. The evenings we spent in the top room, smoking and drinking the Madeira. During this time I saw very little of the sister or her aunt. I think they kept out of our way purposely. I don't blame them for that; we must have been pretty poor company during that time of waiting.

My mind kept turning to Mattani. To me he was an abstraction, a force in this matter without a personality. It was like blindfold boxing. It worried me very much, I remember, that I could only conjure up the vaguest idea as to the personality that I was up against. I had to rely on Leglia's descriptions of the man; he told me that he was short and thickset, with a very bland manner. That tallied more or less with what Compton had told me. 'If you ever have anything to do with Roddy,' he had said, 'you'll find him very pleasant to deal with. Very good company....' There was something about this description of the man that simply terrified me. I say that in all seriousness. I did my best to hide it from Leglia, but during those days of waiting I was miserable. I had the wind right up.

The gipsy was the first to return. He came in the morning at the usual hour of levée; Leglia saw him in the cloister. He brought with him indisputable evidence that the murder had been committed at the instigation of Mattani, but he thought that it was not known that Leglia was concerned. He had heard no mention of me. The affair had happened in some pretty low pub in Genoa. Benedetto had entered the place and sat down with a drink at one of the tables, probably to wait for some sailor from the ship. It was a put-up job. One fellow went lurching across the room swearing that that was the man who had seduced his sister in some little inland village; two or three others had taken up the cry, shouting that that was the man. It was all over in a minute. There was a short scuffle, and in a moment the crowd were pouring out of the inn, so that by the time the keeper of the house and his daughter got to him they were the only people in the place. He died very soon.

The innkeeper had denied all knowledge of the men, and it seemed that the police had not exerted themselves more than was necessary for the sake of appearances. As Leglia observed, it was in Genoa that it happened, and in Genoa Baron Mattani 'had the Press'. The murderer had not been identified.

173

According to the gipsy he was one of three men, all of whom had been present, all of whom were Fascists of the lower type and strong partisans of Mattani.

Suspicion was certainly aroused, but the indications were that Benedetto had been considered to be an agent of the Americans, anxious to discover the date of the next appearance of the vessel in Rum Row. He had drawn suspicion on himself by his eager curiosity; I think he had probably been very careless. He must have found out something of importance, or they would hardly have flown to extremities to secure his silence.

There was no information about the departure of the vessel to be gleaned from the gipsy. He had been able to discover nothing of that, judging it wiser, I suppose, to let things simmer down a bit.

That was all he knew. He stood by while we talked it over in English, leaning against the balustrade in the sun, a picturesque, rather a dirty figure. Presently, tiring of a conversation that he could not understand, he began to whistle a little tune between his teeth, very softly, over and over again. It had a plaintive, eerie sort of lilt to it; I never think of that day but I recall that little tune. I could whistle it now.

Presently it drew Leglia's attention.

He glanced at the man. 'That is a sad song,' he said in Italian.

The man smiled broadly, expansively. 'Lord,' he replied in his vile dialect, 'it is one of the songs of my people.' Then he began to sing, very softly and distinctly, to the tune that he had been whistling:

> '*I am not of this earth,*
> *Nor born of mortal mother,*
> *But Fortune, with her turning, turning wheel,*
> *Hath brought me hither.*'

Leglia eyed him keenly. 'My friend,' he said in Italian, 'you shall tell me the meaning of your song.'

The man laughed cheerfully. 'Lord,' he said, 'there is no

174

meaning. My father sang that song to me, and my father's father. Many of our songs are such.'

He stopped laughing and glanced slyly at Leglia. 'Yet, Lord, there are other songs? ...'

He began to whistle some air that I had never heard before. He stopped after the first bar or two; there may have been something in Leglia's eye, I think, that told him it would be unhealthy to proceed.

'That is a song that one does not sing aloud,' said Leglia sharply.

The man looked abashed. 'Lord,' he said, 'I am thinking of Benedetto.'

For a minute Leglia was silent. Then, 'I, too, am thinking of Benedetto,' he said quietly, and dismissed the man.

Finally, after two more days, the little black-coated commercial traveller returned.

His story was quite explicit. The date when he came to us was July 8th. His information was to the effect that there was certainly no guard on Marazan, and that a cargo was to be transhipped there on the night of the 16th–17th. He told us, beaming, that while primarily engaged upon obtaining this information he had been successful in obtaining an order for some incredible number of celluloid serviette-rings. One thing, he said placidly, always led to another.

That evening I left for England. The Leglias bad me farewell each in their own way.

'For Giovanni,' said his sister, 'you will search diligently for a bride English, is it not so? I do not think that he will want for her to be very pretty, because already I have brought to him all the most pretty girls of Florence and he is – pah! Not at all interested. Like suet.'

'Captain, old thing,' said Leglia, 'next year I come to England for a certain, and I shall enter you to fly me in a two-seater in the King's Cup race, and we will have the perfectly marvellous time.'

Chapter Eight

I GOT to Paris at midday on the 9th and went out to Le Bourget. My luck was in here; a machine was leaving for Croydon in half an hour's time. A touch of blarney with Kerret in the aerodrome office secured me the mechanic's seat, and I crossed with Bluden as pilot in a little under two and a half hours. We were telling each other stories most of the way. It wasn't until we landed that we realized that he had given the passengers palpitations by switching off the engine while we were over the Channel in order that he might listen the better to one of mine. At the time it never struck either of us, but we heard later that there was a fine to-do in the cabin when the engine stopped.

It was about half past four when we put down at Croydon. I had some tea, and was in Whitehall by six. It was a Saturday afternoon and Scotland Yard looked pretty barren, inhabited solely by unintelligent and asthmatic sergeants recruited from the more remote parts of the country. One of them received my inquiry for Norman with an air of polite finality. It was, he said, Saturday afternoon.

'Do you expect him back here today or tomorrow?' I asked.

The sergeant ruminated, grunted, and rubbed his chin. 'Well,' he rumbled benevolently, 'Monday morning. He might be in Monday morning, and then again he mightn't. It's like that, you see, sir.' He beamed at me.

'Is Sir David Carter here?' I asked.

He looked troubled at that. 'Strangers 'ave to 'ave an appointment to see Sir David,' he said. 'If you'll just put down your business on this form I'll lay it on Major Norman's desk. That's what I'll do. I'll lay it on his desk, and then he'll see it first thing Monday morning.'

'Sir David will see me,' I said. 'Here's my card.'

He laughed pleasantly. 'Not this afternoon, he won't,' he remarked. 'He's not here.'

My patience began to wear a little thin. He stopped laughing when he caught my eye.

'My business is urgent,' I said. 'If you can give me Major Norman's private address I'll go and see him there.'

He stiffened at once. 'All business to be passed through the proper channels,' he said. 'We don't give no private addresses at the Yard. If you'll tell me what it is you wants done I'll see to it myself.'

He had my card on the table before him. 'See here,' I said. 'You see who I am?'

He took up the card in an enormous hand and spelled it out. 'P. H. Stenning,' he said. It didn't seem to convey much to him.

'Right,' I said. 'You remember the Marazan murder. I'm the man who was on board the yacht when Compton, the convict, was shot. I've got some urgent information about that to tell Major Norman. That's my business.'

He looked terribly worried. 'I don't rightly know what to do about that,' he said. 'Did you want to make a statement?'

'I can tell you what you're going to do,' I said tersely. 'You're going to give me Major Norman's address. If you don't I shall go and see Sir David Carter. I can get his address out of *Who's Who*. I tell you, this matter is urgent.'

He moved ponderously to the door. 'What you want to do, sir,' he said definitely, 'is to make a statement.' I realized that he was about to summon witnesses.

I stopped him. 'I'm going to do nothing of the sort,' I said. 'I've got valuable information about the murder of Mr Compton. If you'll give me Major Norman's address I'll go and see him now. Otherwise I shall walk straight out and go to Sir David Carter's house. I must see one or other of them today.'

He capitulated, and in five minutes I was on my way to Charing Cross, bound for Chislehurst. I reached the house at about half past seven. It stood back a little from the road, a

177

small house with a large garden. I asked for Major Norman at the door, and was shown into a morning-room to wait.

The room opened on to the lawn. It was getting on for dinnertime, but there was a game of tennis going on on the lawn, two men and two girls. I saw the maid go out and speak to one of the girls.

She turned to the others. 'We'll have to chuck it,' she cried. 'There's a bloke come to see Reggie.' I learned later that she was his wife.

They gathered together on the court; I recognized Norman as he was putting on his coat. 'About time we stopped, any-way,' said the other man. 'I could do with a bath, and the odd spot of dinner.'

'Bags I first go at the bath,' said the other girl.

I had to pinch myself to realize that I was awake. It all seemed incredibly remote from the violent business that I had come upon. It seemed a shame to break in on Norman in this quiet suburban atmosphere with a talk of dope and murder. I could see Norman whispering with his wife, and as he broke away from the group she called after him that there was plenty of supper. He came up to the window and entered the room.

'Good evening, Captain Stenning,' he said. 'I hope this doesn't mean that you've been having trouble with the Italians.'

I laughed shortly. 'No,' I said. 'It means they're going to have trouble with me.'

He slipped into a chair, and it was half an hour before we stirred. I told him everything that had happened in Italy, and I told him as much as I could remember about Leglia's talk about Fascismo. He listened attentively, making very little comment till I had done.

At the end he remained staring into the sunlit garden. 'Marazan again,' he muttered. 'On the 16th.' He turned to me. 'You surprise me very much, Captain Stenning,' he said.

I nodded. 'I know. At the same time, it seems quite likely that he should try it again. It means that the place is an in-tegral part of the whole scheme, that the success of running a

178

cargo depends on the use of Marazan. I take it that it's true that there is no guard there?'

He nodded absently. 'There is no guard. I didn't mean that when I said that you surprised me. By going to Italy you ran a very grave risk.'

He eyed me steadily for a moment, and then laughed. 'As you know.'

'I was well protected,' I remarked.

'That's obvious,' he said drily. 'This friend of yours, the Duke of Estalebona, did you say? . . .'

I nodded. 'You'd better make some inquiries about him, to satisfy yourself,' I said. 'But you'll find him all right.'

He sat drumming with his fingers on the arm of his chair for a minute. Then he got up.

'If you'll stay and have dinner with us,' he said, 'I'll come up to Town with you afterwards. Good.' He stood in the window for a moment rubbing his chin thoughtfully.

'It's a better line than we've been able to strike,' he said at last. 'We've not been able to do much up to date.'

We went up to Town together after dinner; I parted from him at Charing Cross with an appointment to meet him and Sir David Carter at the Yard at eleven o'clock next morning – Sunday. I got back to my flat in Maida Vale at about half past ten, and I must say I wasn't sorry to be back. I was relieved that I had managed to see Norman. At the back of my mind had been the disturbing thought that if Mattani had got to hear that I had been in Italy, it was to his interest to prevent me getting to Norman with my news. It had not been altogether a sincere devotion to duty that had made me eager to see Norman at the first possible moment. Till my tale was told I could only regard myself as a possible target for people to shoot at, or to hit on the head with something blunt. Now that anxiety was removed. If Mattani was clever enough to find out that I had been to Italy, he was probably clever enough to find out that I had already seen Norman – in which case there was no longer any point in hitting me on the head.

In the morning I went to the Yard again.

I never felt quite at my ease with Sir David Carter. He was one of those men like Morris, keen and efficient, but with an air that rather kept one at a distance. I could see from his manner that the old man must have a bitter tongue when he was roused, and it was pretty evident that Norman had had some of it in his time. And yet there was some stuff in Norman – as we saw later.

Sir David greeted me with a sort of old-fashioned courtesy that made me rather ill at ease. 'Major Norman tells me that you have been in Italy, Captain Stenning. I should be greatly interested in your account.'

He turned to Norman. 'It would be better if Captain Stenning told us his story again from the beginning,' he said. 'You had better make a few notes.'

Norman sat down at a table with a writing-pad, and I started in and told my story again, from the time I left Scotland Yard till I returned to England. Sir David sat as he had sat before, his chair tilted back behind the desk, staring motionless at the ceiling. It was very quiet in the office. It was a Sunday morning and there was no traffic in the streets outside to disturb us; for what seemed a long time my voice was the only sound in the room. I had no interruptions from Norman. Now and again I was aware that he was writing rapidly; then for a time he would sit still. At last I had finished. Norman glanced at his chief, took up his notes and asked me half a dozen questions – dates, times, and names of people.

At the end, Sir David stirred and sat up. 'A most capable piece of work,' he said gravely. 'One point. This friend of yours, da Leglia —'

Norman got up from the table and passed his chief a slip of paper. 'I think this covers him, sir.'

Sir David ran an eye down it. 'The Earl of Rennel,' he muttered. 'The Italian Embassy. . . . You are in touch with the Consul?'

'There has been hardly time for a reply yet, sir.'

Sir David laid the paper on his desk. When next he spoke it was to me.

'As you see,' he said slowly, 'this matter of Baron Mattani is extending into a wider field than the extradition of a suspected murderer. I am sure, Captain Stenning, that you will see the necessity for the greatest discretion?'

I said that I quite understood that.

There was a long silence, till suddenly he sat up in his chair and began to ask me questions about the note that I had found in my bed at Exeter. I had to go over the whole of that incident again, and at the end there was another pause.

Presently he laid off on another tack. It was rather like watching the hounds working a covert.

'Major Norman,' he said, 'from your memory of the dangerous drug cases, can you locate any steady and considerable source of supply other than through Asiatics?'

Norman wrinkled his brows. 'There are always a number of cases where the origin is evident,' he said slowly. 'Cases in which a Lascar brings over a parcel of the drug in the forepeak of his ship. Of the cases where the origin is obscure, I can remember very few where the origin has been non-Asiatic. That is to say, the stuff is generally traceable to some Chinaman who cannot be identified. I can remember very few obscure European cases.'

'Verify that,' said Sir David. 'It is possible that the Chinaman takes rather more blame than he deserves.'

'They would have to have a clearing-house,' said Norman. 'It would be reasonable for that to be Chinese.'

Sir David glanced at him. 'There has been no indication of that up to date?'

'Not that I am aware of.'

'There must be a clearing-house for the division and distribution of the drug. There may be two or three.'

There was a long silence. An omnibus or two went rumbling down Whitehall. In a side street near at hand, close below the window of the office, some wandering violinist struck up the *Caprice Viennoise*. The prologue over, he launched into the melody; it rose and swelled about us till it drowned my thoughts, till I could recall nothing but the details of that stage tragedy that had been set to the music by a great actor. I glanced at the others. Norman was worried by it; I saw him glancing irritably at the window. The Chief sat as he had sat before, motionless, leaning back in his chair and staring at the ceiling. Presently the air drew to its sobbing, tremulous end. Sir David sat up.

'At one time,' he said, half to himself and half, I think, to me, 'I considered Kreisler's reputation to be misplaced.'

He leaned forward upon his desk and began to talk. In a moment I saw how far ahead of ours his mind had been working. 'With the information supplied by Captain Stenning,' he said, 'we stand a very fair chance of detaining the vessel that brings the drug to the Scillies – unless, of course, she lies-to to dispatch her launch at a point beyond the three-mile limit. We should be able to detain the launch with tolerable certainty. We might even be able to secure the aeroplane, and so to solve the problem of her identity. From all these sources it should be possible to obtain sufficient convictions to prevent the possibility of any further cargoes being smuggled in this way. At the same time, it seems to me to be extremely doubtful whether we should be able to break up the organization in England – the clearing-house. Frankly, I do not consider it likely that we should secure either the ship or the aeroplane. There remains the motor-launch. Is the launch alone worth securing?'

He shifted his position. 'It might be. The possession of the launch would certainly strengthen our demand for the extradition of Baron Mattani from Italy. It might or might not lead to further evidence with regard to the murder of Compton. It would be unlikely to lead to evidence concerning the clearing-house. Consider. The men taken in the launch in all probability will be entirely Italians – Fascists, no doubt. For them to give information would mean that their return to Italy would be impossible, considering the position held by Mattani. I doubt if we could get much evidence from the capture of the launch.'

I cleared my throat. 'The aeroplane would probably tell us something, if we could get hold of that.'

Sir David stared straight ahead of him at the desk. 'Would it tell us very much about the clearing-house?' he inquired. 'I rather doubt it. Suppose we were to capture the aeroplane at the same moment as the launch. We should then have the launch, the launch's crew, the aeroplane, and the pilot of the aeroplane. I think the only one of those who would be capable of giving us any information about the clearing-house would be the pilot of the aeroplane.'

'Very likely the pilot would know nothing about the clearing-house,' said Norman, 'unless he had a financial interest in the cargo. His business would be to fly the machine. In any case, it's not likely that he would give evidence.'

Sir David was pursuing his own line of thought. 'I put the dispersal of the clearing-house as our primary object,' he said at last. 'It is not going to be very difficult, I think, to put an end to this particular mode of smuggling. The capture of the launch, for example, would give such diplomatic leverage to the Foreign Office that I doubt if Mattani would be in a position to carry on – for the moment. But if the organization in this country remains untouched, then in three or four months' time we shall have the whole trouble repeating, with a different method of introducing the drug into the country.'

He paused. 'I should consider no scheme of operations satisfactory that left out the clearing-house.'

I turned to Norman. 'I don't know how you work these things. But do you see much chance of getting a line on to the clearing-house before the 16th?'

He shook his head. 'There's only a week to do it in,' he protested. 'Frankly, I know nothing about them yet. It's possible that one of the men here may have information that will put us on the right track, or we might have a bit of sheer luck – such as a conviction for disposal. Failing that, I should begin working it on the elimination and inquiry lines. We might get on to them within the week, but I shouldn't say it's hopeful.'

'I see,' I said slowly. 'Then the only other line to them is through the aeroplane.'

Sir David nodded. 'The aeroplane might be the means of putting us in touch with the clearing-house,' he said. 'Wherever it lands, it must be met by the agents.'

'They meet it in cars,' I said. 'The landing-place is changed from trip to trip.'

'That makes it rather difficult,' said Norman quietly.

It certainly did. For a moment it seemed as if we had run up against a brick wall. We just sat for a bit, looking helpless.

'There'd be one way of doing it,' I said at last. 'Let the aeroplane get away with its load, and follow it in another machine. That seems to be about the only way of getting in touch with the clearing-house – unless you can do it by your usual methods.'

The Chief eyed me for a moment. 'I know very little about aeroplanes,' he said, 'but I imagine that there would be considerable practical difficulties in doing that, Captain Stenning.'

I considered for a moment. 'It would be damn hard,' I said. 'I think it might be done.' I was thinking rapidly. 'We should have the hell of a job to get in touch with the seaplane without being spotted. That's the first thing. But if we could do that – assume that we can do that ... I think we can limit her possible landing-places to one or two definite areas, and I think we can make a pretty good shot as to how she gets there.'

I paused to collect my ideas. 'You see, we know this much. We know that she leaves the Scillies an hour or so before dawn, and we know that she flies well inland, and lands her cargo in the early morning. We don't know where she lands. Well, first of all, as regards her range. I don't believe she cruises at a greater speed than eighty-five—she'd be an exceptional amphibian if she did. I don't suppose she refuels at the Scillies; it would complicate things and keep her there too long. It's the hell of a job filling up a seaplane, you know. I don't suppose she carries more than five hours' fuel at the outside. And so I think we can put down the extreme range from the Scillies as two hundred miles, or more likely a hundred and fifty – to allow for head-winds.'

They were listening to me intently now. I asked for a map and they produced a large atlas; I opened it at a plate of Devon, Cornwall, and the Scillies.

'First of all, about the possible landing grounds,' I said. 'We want a place fairly remote from the sea. It must provide a really long run – at least half a mile of smooth, level grass for an amphibian with a heavy load. It must be in a very desolate neighbourhood. I don't know if you've ever made a forced landing in ordinary country? No – of course you haven't. But the excitement it causes is tremendous; the whole countryside seems to hear of it in an hour or two. It's the children that do it, of course. Even at that hour in the morning, a landing in ordinary farmland would be bound to attract notice.'

I stared at the map. 'Anyway,' I said, 'there's nowhere in Cornwall. It might be possible to work it all right on Dartmoor or Exmoor.'

'They'd go farther inland,' said Norman. 'What about Salisbury Plain?'

I turned up another map. 'It's a bit far,' I said. 'But it would be quite possible, and much more central for the disposal of the stuff. But anyway, the point that I'm making now is that they've got to fly beyond Cornwall – probably a long way beyond. Now . . . I'll tell you what I should do if I was making that flight.'

I paused again. 'Starting, say, one hour before dawn, I'd make the shortest sea passage possible. I'd have the wind up of my engine conking miles out at sea. That is, I'd make straight for Land's End. That's about thirty miles or so. It would still be dark when I got there. I'd fly along the coast then – no

185

matter where I was going to. It's easy to follow the coastline in the dark, for one thing, and at night – on the whole – I'd rather risk a forced landing on sea than on land. I should have to fly pretty low to see where I was – probably under two thousand feet.'

'If you could be sure of that,' said Norman, 'it certainly might be possible to get in touch with the machine.'

'You can't be sure about it,' I said. 'But that's what I should do if I had the job. Whether I should go up the north coast or the south depends on where I was heading for. Whichever coast I went by, I should leave it as soon as it became light enough to see my way, and head straight inland for wherever I was going. I should fly higher then if I wanted to keep out of sight.'

Sir David interposed a question. 'Suppose that you could pick up the seaplane and follow it, and saw it land. It would still be very difficult to effect any arrests. I imagine that it would be out of the question to carry any considerable force of police in the following machine?'

'One or two at the most,' I said. 'No, the arrest would have to be carried out from the ground. The part of the following machine could only be to keep in touch with the ground by wireless telephony, to tell the police where the landing is taking place and to keep an eye on any of the cars that got away.'

'The difficulties would be enormous,' muttered Norman.

I fully agreed with him there. At the most there would be perhaps twenty minutes in which to make the arrest from the time of landing till the agents were well away from the landing ground in their cars. If there were only one car the aeroplane could follow it and keep it in sight; if there were more than one, all but one would have to be let go.

'Of course we might be able to get some help there with additional machines from the Air Force,' said Norman.

We wrangled over the details of the scheme for a bit. At last Sir David pulled out his watch.

'Get it worked out,' he said to Norman. 'If it comes to the

worst we may have to try something of the sort. But push ahead with the elimination and inquiry for the clearing-house.' He turned to me. 'I am afraid, Captain Stenning, that I am sufficiently old-fashioned to prefer the conventional methods. . . .'

He rose to go.

'Anyway,' I said, 'we seem to stand a pretty fair chance of getting at Mattani, one way or another.'

For a moment a wintry smile chased across his features. 'I could view that prospect with more enthusiasm, Captain Stenning,' he said, 'if the House were not in session.'

With that he took up his hat from the table, bowed to us, and went out.

I lunched with Norman, and after lunch we returned to the Yard and settled down to the aeroplane scheme in earnest. When we came to put it down in black and white it didn't seem to be so impossible after all. I discovered that the resources of the Yard are simply enormous. The chief difficulty that I could see was that of getting into touch with the seaplane at all in the early dawn. It seemed to me that the following machine would have to wait in the air on patrol somewhere about the middle of Devonshire, waiting for news by wireless from ground observation stations along the coast.

From Norman's point of view, the chief difficulty would come after the seaplane had landed. Assuming that from the following machine I could wireless the point of landing directly I saw the seaplane put down, there would be an incredibly short space of time in which to effect the arrest. The place of landing would be quite unknown. Though I could keep in wireless touch with the ground during the flight and tell them in which direction the chase was heading, the most that could be done would be to concentrate a few police in various towns and trust to luck in being able to rush them to the spot before the cars meeting the seaplane had time to disperse. If, however, the cars dispersed before the arrival of the police, they must be followed as well as possible from the air; it was here that Norman was counting on the co-operation of the Air Force. It should be possible, I thought, for one or two aeroplanes to join in the pursuit, keeping well astern of me.

I didn't think that there was much danger of the pilot of the amphibian getting to know that he was followed.

'But the whole thing depends upon our having decent weather,' I said.

I went back to my flat and rang up Joan at Stokenchurch.

'Good afternoon, Miss Stevenson,' I said. 'Stenning speaking.'

There was a sort of bumble on the line. I shook the receiver.

'I'm so glad you're back all right,' she said. 'I've been – I mean – how did you get on? Did you find out anything?'

'A certain amount,' I said. 'I had quite a good time, really – a very easy trip. But what I rang up for was to find out if you'd care to come and have lunch with me one day. Are you doing anything tomorrow?'

'I'd love to,' she said. 'I'll come up to Town. Where shall we meet?'

'Not in Town,' I said. 'Don't like London – too many Dagoes in the restaurants. Give me cold feet. Let's have lunch in the country somewhere. I say – you know the Hornblower? That pub at the bottom of Aston Rowant hill. They give you a corking good lunch there.'

I heard her laugh. 'That'll be splendid,' she said. 'I can drive over there in the Cowley.'

'Right you are,' I said. 'I'll drive down from Town. I'll probably be there at about half past twelve.'

I drove down there on the following morning and lunched with her at the pub. I didn't like to talk about the Mattani business at table; I remember that I was mortally afraid of anything getting out. They gave us a rattling good lunch – the sort of thing one dreams about. It was a bright, sunny day with a little wind that rustled the flowers on our table by the window. I remember that we talked about flowers and beechwoods and red squirrels and things, and when I remember that I cannot help wondering a little. Queer subjects for me in those days.

We walked out a little way on to the hills after lunch, at my suggestion. I wanted to get away from the waiters and people at the hotel before launching out on my story. We walked slowly – she because it would have been rude to outwalk me, and I because I had lunched too well to hurry. And as we went I told her all about Italy and da Leglia.

There was a gate at the top of the hill leading into a spinney. We didn't go in, but sat on the gate and looked out into the blue hazes over Oxfordshire. I finished my yarn there, and told her about the scheme for following the amphibian that we'd been getting out.

'Will you be flying that machine?' she asked.

'With any luck,' I said. 'It would be a pity not to be in at the death.'

'It all turns on the smuggling now, then,' she said a little later. 'There's no question of arresting Roddy for the present, is there?'

'Not much,' I said ruefully. 'He's rather faded into the background. You see, it's going to be most frightfully hard to make out a case of murder against him. We may get some decent evidence if we succeed in capturing the ship or the launch, but at present we haven't got a case against him that will hold water – on the murder charge.'

'I'm rather glad of that,' she said quietly. 'It would be a dreadful thing for him to stand his trial in England.'

I knocked my pipe out sharply on the top rail of the gate. 'It was a dreadful thing when Compton got it,' I said curtly. 'He's going to stand his trial for that, one of these days. We'll see to that.'

She sighed. 'I don't believe he meant it,' she said. 'I never did. He – oh, he was different. Roddy wasn't like that. He couldn't have done a thing like that.

'I went down and saw his mother,' she said, 'the day after I met you. She's too old to understand.'

I glanced at her. 'This is a pretty miserable show for you,' I said.

'It's like the sort of thing one reads about in the papers,' she said vaguely, 'the sort of thing that happens to other people.' She turned and looked up at me. 'Why do you say it's miserable for me?' she asked. 'You've had as much to do with it as I have – much more.'

I didn't know what to say to that. 'They're your people, for one thing,' I said. 'You know Mattani, and you knew Compton.'

She nodded slowly. 'I don't know what we should have done without you – by ourselves, just me and Denis,' she said unexpectedly. She was silent then for a bit. I remember that I sat looking at her, at the soft lights in her hair, at her slim grace. She reminded me of the drawings of a man who used to do things in *Punch*, a man called Shepperson or some such name. She was just like that.

She continued: 'I can't think what we should have done by ourselves. You don't know what a help you were – in every way. You braced up Denis so.' She laughed. 'You know, we were both dreadfully afraid of you. You looked dreadful with that cut over your eye, all bandaged and dirty. And your coat made you so big.... Did you know you drank nearly a bottle of whisky that night? Denis was awfully afraid you were getting drunk, and it didn't have the least effect. I don't know what we should have done without you. You came along, sort of grim and efficient, and took everything on your shoulders.'

'I suppose I'm more used to this sort of thing,' I said at last. I looked down, and saw her grey eyes fixed on me.

'How do you mean?' she said.

I laughed, and then wished I hadn't. I didn't like the sound of it.

'Birth, education, and upbringing,' I said, a little bitterly. 'I was much better fitted for it than either of you.'

She looked at me queerly, and I went on to tell her all about myself, about my father who died on the China Station and my mother that I never remember to have seen. I didn't dwell very much on my life before I was sixteen because I don't very often think of it myself; to me it now seems inconceivable that any well-meaning people could have given a boy such a rotten time. But I told her how I cut away from such relations as I had – about the wisest thing I ever did – and how I got a job as odd boy in a motor garage, years before the war. After that I was a chauffeur for a bit, at a place in Herefordshire. And then I told her how Pat Reilly and I started a garage on our own with a capital of forty-one pounds, and how we produced a cycle-car that was the hottest thing in its class for six months – the Stenning-Reilly car. I told her what a corking little car it was, and how proud we were of it, and how it was going to make our fortunes. I still think we could have done it. Then came the war, and I told her how we had chucked it at the beginning of 1915 and joined up. I told her something of what that had meant to us, just as we had got the capital promised for setting up a little factory, just as we were beginning to book orders for the car.

Then I went on to tell her how we had both got commissions before very long, and I told her the story of how Pat was surrounded in his tank in 1917, and killed. I told her how I had gone on flying all through the war with hardly a scratch. I told her about the life in France, too, where between the patrols I learnt golf from one of the St Andrews caddies and boxing from an ex-welter-weight champion; and I told her of the hectic, miserable leaves from France, when a dozen of us used to come over and plant ourselves at the Regent Palace – never entirely sober from one day to the next. Then I told her how I was sent home early in 1918 as an instructor, and how for me that proved to be the end of the war. I went on and told her about my life after the war – my piloting, my golf, and my little speculations.

I got tired of the sound of my own voice at last, and we stood leaning against the gate for a bit looking out into the fields. Below us the road to Oxford ran down the hill, the road that we had driven on that first morning of all, when she was

191

driving me to Abingdon on the first stage of my run. I was about to remind her of this when she spoke again.

'You've had a very full life,' she said quietly. 'You don't regret that, do you?'

I thought for a minute. I'd never looked at it like that.

'No,' I said at last, 'I don't. I've had a pretty good time, taking it all round, and I don't know that I'd change it. But if it has been a full life, it has been because I hadn't the wit to make it otherwise.'

'How do you mean?'

I glanced at her. 'Did you know that I had been in prison?'

She looked up at me, and smiled.

'Yes,' she said simply.

I didn't expect that, and it put me badly out of gear. 'Who told you that?' I asked.

For a moment I thought that she was going to laugh outright. 'Sir David Carter,' she said.

I tried to adjust my ideas a bit.

'Did he tell you anything else about me?' I asked weakly.

She nodded. 'Lots of things that you've left out – all the really interesting things.'

I looked at her steadily for a moment, and then towards the path that led down to the hotel. It was what a man like me had to expect, I thought – and I can't say I found the reflection sweet. It was natural that they should have found out all about me at the Yard. It was natural that Sir David should have told his daughter's friend something about me when he saw the way the wind was blowing, but – it was bad luck.

I looked at my watch. 'I'm afraid we ought to be getting back,' I said evenly. 'I've got to meet a man in Town at six.'

'Oh ...' She remarked. 'Sir David didn't tell me anything as bad as that.'

I swung round, and saw her still sitting on the gate and laughing at me. That stung me up a bit.

'I don't suppose he did,' I said. 'There's nothing to tell. He probably told you that I've been thrown out of half the theatres in London in my time. He may have told you about that business at the Metropole, and I dare say he told you about the row I had at les Trois Homards. If he told you about that he probably told you about the girl, and how she died.'

'Yes,' she said quietly. 'He told me about that.'

I turned away.

'Well, there you've got it,' I said bitterly. 'There's nothing sensational – I don't go in for chicken butchery. I've never had anyone to think about except myself. If you like, it's a record of a mean life, meanly lived. You know how I started. Did you expect any more?'

I knew that I had hurt her. She slipped down from the gate and came and stood beside me.

'Philip,' she said, 'you mustn't be so sensitive. You know I didn't mean all those silly little things. You know they don't matter two hoots.'

'I'm sorry,' I said. 'What did you mean?'

She glanced up into my face. 'The other things,' she said. 'The things you haven't told me about even yet. About your DSO, and why they gave you the Military Cross.'

I turned and faced her. 'You mustn't think about those things,' I said evenly. 'That was in the war – nearly ten years ago. But this is peacetime, and those things don't count for anything now. Or they oughtn't to. You mustn't let them.'

'It may have been years ago,' she said. 'But they haven't forgotten about them at the Yard.'

'It's their business to remember things,' I said.

She came very close to me. It was bright sunlight on the down. I remember noticing a rabbit that came out from behind a patch of furze about fifty yards away and looked at us.

'Philip,' she said quietly, 'you mustn't talk like that. You know Sir David Carter thinks a frightful lot of you.'

I took her by the shoulders. 'I don't care a damn about Sir David,' I said. 'But you – what do you think of me?'

She looked up at me gravely. 'Philip dear,' she said, 'I think that you're the best and truest man I've ever met.'

Chapter Nine

I WAS pretty busy in the next few days that remained
before the 16th. They sent out a chap from the Yard to watch
things in Italy, but by the time he got out there the steamer
had already left – we presumed for England. I spent most of
my time running backwards and forwards between the Yard
and the aerodrome.

We had a little trouble with Morris at first, who refused
point-blank to charter us a machine for the job. Civil aviation,
he said, was a sober and a serious business, and stunts of the
sort that we proposed would only serve to hinder progress by
frightening away the man in the street, who very naturally
regarded flying as the special province of warriors, criminals,
and the like.

I made him see reason at last. Then he wanted to make a
little money out of us, arguing that the machine was to be
utilized against the King's enemies and so the insurance policy
was void. We argued him off this, and finally won his grudging
consent. He stipulated :

(a) for the utmost publicity if the affair were a success,
and

(b) for complete secrecy if, in his opinion, publicity would
cast a slur upon the firm.

I remember this amused Sir David. We could have got a
machine from Croydon without all this fuss, but I wanted to
have my own mechanic on the job. And I knew perfectly well
that if Morris once took it on he'd do his utmost to make a
success of it.

I chose one of our light touring machines. She had a turn of
speed of about a hundred and twenty miles an hour, and she
handled like a fighting scout. She had a cabin to seat four; I

decided to fill up a part of the cabin space with extra fuel tanks, and in this way I provided sufficient fuel for seven hours in the air. For a long time I hesitated over the question of taking a passenger as an observer, and finally decided against it. The view from the cabin was very much restricted, and communication with him wouldn't have been easy. The extra weight would have taken a little off the performance of the machine. It meant letting someone else into the secret, and we didn't want to do that till the last moment, when, of course, the signallers would have to be instructed in their part of the business.

I had the machine fitted with the standard wireless telephone set. I knew all about that and had used it regularly when I was flying from Croydon on the cross-Channel service. The fitting up of the machine in this way raised very little comment in the works. Morris gave out that I was taking the machine abroad on a journalistic stunt, to rush back the photographs and cinema films of the wedding of an archduke. We often had those jobs to do.

So the days passed in preparing the machine. If what I had heard in Florence was correct, the cargo was to be landed in the Scillies on the night of Saturday–Sunday. On the Thursday afternoon I went to the Yard for a final conference. They had kept me rather in the dark till then, but now they produced all their plans and arrangements and showed me everything.

Norman's part of the business put the wind up me properly – I wouldn't have taken on a job like that for quids. He was to be the observer at Marazan. He had had a telephone line run unostentatiously from St Mary's to White Island, the rocky and uninhabited island to the north of Marazan Sound. He proposed to take up his position there under cover of darkness on the previous night, and to lie out there for the whole of Saturday to avoid the possibility of being seen on the way to his observation post.

Under the cover of darkness a destroyer and a sloop were to

close the islands from the direction of the southeast. During the early part of the night these were to work round and lie off to the north of the islands, showing no lights. Norman, in telephonic communication with Hugh Town and so with the mainland, would watch events in the Sound. Immediately after the departure of the amphibian he was to send up a rocket. On that the sloop and the destroyer were to open up their searchlights and arrest every vessel in the vicinity.

It seemed to me a pretty little plan, and quite likely to go through all right. I must say I didn't care much for Norman's job. It struck me that he'd stand precious little chance if the Dagoes happened to find out that he was there.

My part of the business was not so difficult; for one thing, I had plenty of help. My job was to stand by with the machine at a point not very far from Taunton. I had chosen a large pasture there that the machine could operate from, and in one corner of it the Sappers had set up a field wireless station. This was in telephonic communication with half a dozen observation stations up the north and south coasts of Devon and Cornwall. I should wait on the ground till we had some news of the amphibian travelling up the coast; then I should get into the air and trust to luck to be able to pick her up in the dim light of the dawn, keeping in touch with the Sappers by wireless telephony.

At Fowey and at Padstow the Anti-Aircraft lads were setting up sound-ranging stations.

I had only one modification to suggest to these arrangements, but that was one that saved our bacon later. I suggested that a line of posts should be strung out along the Exeter-Barnstaple road that runs straight across Devon from north to south. The Sappers laid a field cable along the whole length of this road on the Saturday morning, and dropped a man every three miles with a telephone that he could tap into the wire. All through they did their part of the business extraordinarily well.

I flew down to Taunton on the Saturday afternoon, taking

my mechanic with me. The field that we had picked to fly from was a couple of miles to the west of the town, not very far from the village of Grant Haddon. It was a fine, sunny afternoon. We got down there at about six o'clock after an uneventful flight. I found the field without difficulty, circled round once for a look-see, and put her down gently on the grass.

There was a bell tent in one corner of the field with one or two soldiers beside it, watching the machine. I taxied over to the tent, swung the machine round into the wind, and stopped the engine. As I was slowly unfastening my helmet one of the men came up to the machine.

'Captain Stenning?' he said.

I heaved myself up out of the cockpit and dropped down on to the grass beside him. 'Right you are,' I said. 'That's me.'

I followed him into the tent. He had a vast amount of electrical gear there that he said was a wireless station; I took his word for it. He showed me the land telephone line that connected him up with all the other stations, and then he showed me the petrol that had been provided for filling up my machine. I left the mechanic to deal with this, and went with an orderly to meet the officer in charge.

I dined alone that night, in a little hotel that I found in the village. It was half full of summer residents, a couple of elderly maiden ladies, an old man who looked as if he'd been missing his Kruschens, and a honeymoon couple. I had nothing to do that evening till ten o'clock or so, and was too restless to spend it in the tent gossiping with the subaltern in charge. I wandered off to the village and found this little place, and ordered a dinner that brought the proprietor hurrying to me in respect.

It was a warm summer evening. I lingered for a long time over my dinner, grateful for the quiet of the moment. I knew that I had a pretty tough night before me; I think that even then I had a dim idea that when the cold dawn came up over the fields I should be fighting for my life. Certainly I made the most of that dinner. They served me well. They had put me at a small table by an open window that looked over a croquet lawn to a little wood; I sat there musing between the courses, my chin upon my hands, staring out of the window, thinking about my engagement, thinking about my golf handicap, thinking what a perfectly corking country England was.

I shall always remember that evening that I spent alone in that little pub, the night before I met Mattani. I had a straightforward job ahead of me, a job that I knew I could do well. I had no worries. I remember that I was most frightfully happy, in a quiet sort of way.

It came to an end, of course. I had my coffee out on the mossy lawn, and then it was time for me to go. I paid my shot in the dusk of the little hall, and strode out of the hotel. I passed the window of the drawing-room as I went by outside; the lights were on and the window open; I paused for a minute in the darkness and looked in. There they all were. The two maiden ladies were sitting together in a corner, one of them knitting, the other writing a letter on her knee. The old gentleman was reading an old book, his spectacles insecurely mounted on the extreme end of his nose. The honeymoon couple were sitting very close together on a settee, reading the same book. It was like a bit of Jane Austen.

I laughed, and swung away to my own life, the life that I knew, and as I went I thought of that same old line of Kipling:

> It is their care that the gear engages, it is their care
> that the switches lock.

I laughed again, and swung down the drive towards my work. I was still smiling over this when I arrived at the field and saw the machine looming darkly behind the bell tent.

I had a curious experience then. I found the officer in charge talking into the telephone; he was a subaltern, and rather a good sort. He turned as I entered the tent and nodded to me.

'Half a minute,' he said into the telephone. 'Here is Captain Stenning.'

He was talking to Norman in his look-out station on White Island. I took the instrument and spoke to Norman, and told him the detail of the arrangements I had made. There was very little to discuss. I remember it made a deep impression on me to be talking to Norman as he lay stretched in a crevice of the rocks overlooking Marazan Sound. It made me feel that things were beginning to happen. Norman had little to say. It appeared that he had been very bored all day, and had attempted to pass the time by a telephonic game of draughts with the coastguard at St Mary's, sketching the position of the pieces on the back of an envelope. He remarked that he had suffered much from gulls and guano.

After that I went and sat with the subaltern at the mouth of the tent, gossiping in a desultory manner. The night seemed interminable. Every half-hour or so we rang up Norman, always with the same result; there was nothing yet in sight. Always after that we rang up the round of the patrols to make sure that everyone was awake. There were over twenty of those calls; we left them to the corporal, so that by the time he had finished with them it was time for us to speak to Norman again.

At about two in the morning one of the patrols a mile or so south of Barnstaple rang up and said he heard an aeroplane.

When the subaltern heard this he gave a terse, monosyllabic comment that expressed my opinion of the observer very well. He took the telephone from the corporal and was about to speak to the man to tell him not to imagine things, but I caught him by the arm.

'Steady a moment,' I said. 'That'll be the seaplane going down.'

It hadn't struck me before – so far as I know, it hadn't occurred to anyone – that we should hear the machine on its way to the Scillies. It's the sort of detail that one is apt to forget. But there it was; the man was quite sure it was an aeroplane. He thought from the sound that it was a mile or two to the north of him, and travelling westwards. We rang up Norman to let him know about this, and then we rang up the rest of the patrols to tell them to keep an eye open.

It was really quite interesting. The man at Hartland seems to have missed it, and the next we heard was from the sound-ranging station on the headland above Padstow. They put the machine about a mile out to sea; they waited for five minutes and gave us a second observation, showing by the comparison of the bearings that the machine was travelling down the coast. They gave it as their opinion that the engine was a Rolls Eagle or Falcon, probably an Eagle.

That was the last we heard of her. We never got a report from Land's End; we rang up half an hour later, but nothing had been heard there. We came to the conclusion that the machine had left the coast for the Scillies somewhere between Land's End and Padstow.

Then we sat and waited to hear from Norman. I went to the door of the tent and had a look at the night. It was pretty clear by that time that I should have a job of work to do before many hours were out. It was a fine night with a bright moon, a little obscured by cloud. I remember thinking how quiet it was. I strolled over to the machine and mooned about it for a little, drumming with my fingers on the taut fabric of the lower plane. The lamplight in the tent streamed from the open flap and threw a broad belt of colour on the grass; over the tent the aerial loomed mysteriously against a deep blue sky.

I ran over in my mind the various civilian aircraft that I knew were fitted with a single Rolls engine. The information about the engine narrowed the field considerably, but I was still quite unable to identify the machine. I knew of seven machines fitted with one or other of those engines that might conceivably be used for the job, but none of them was a sea-plane or amphibian.

Then Norman rang through. They called me from the tent;

I went back and spoke to him on the telephone in his lonely crevice on White Island. He spoke as quietly as if he were in the room with me. I remember wondering at his nerve.

'Is that you, Stenning?' he said. 'All right – this is Norman speaking. I can hear the machine quite close now. Yes, it's bright moonlight here; I've got quite a good view of the Sound. There's a launch in the Sound with her bows run up upon the beach. She came in about a quarter of an hour ago. Yes, on the Pendruan beach about halfway down Marazan. Wait a minute – the aeroplane's shut off her engine.'

'Where's she putting down?' I asked. 'In the sea or in the Sound?'

There was a silence. Away in the darkness I could hear a mouse or something chittering in the field. At last Norman spoke again. 'They've lit a lantern in the stern of the launch,' he said, 'and two more that they've placed upon the shore down by the water, near the entrance to the Sound. Do you think those are the landing-lights?'

'That's it,' I said. 'She'll probably put down beside the one in the launch, heading towards the two fixed ones. They point into the wind, I suppose?'

He didn't answer, but a little later he said: 'I can hear the machine again now. Not the engine – I can hear the squealing of the wires in the wind.'

'She must be very close to you,' I said.

Then he saw her. 'Right. She's coming in to land now, gliding down on to the water. Stenning! She's a float seaplane with two floats on the undercarriage – but I don't see anything under the tail. She's a single-bay machine – one lot of struts in the wings. She's quite a normal design, but I don't know what type she is. She's painted some dark colour on the wings and white or silver on the fuselage. I can't see any registration letters. Are you there? Can you hear what I'm saying? All right – you've got that. She's just landed on the water of the Sound – she's lost way, and they're turning her in to the beach with the engine throttled right down. You've got all that?

Right you are. Now get off the line while I speak to the Yard. I'll ring you again in a minute or two.'

I laid down the receiver and turned to the subaltern. 'My God, they've got a nerve!' I muttered absently. 'Fancy trying it again in the same place after last time.'

He looked at me curiously. 'What happened then?' he asked.

I hadn't realized that he had been told so little. 'The odd spot of murder,' I said shortly. 'They've got the nerve of the devil.' I said no more, because I didn't quite know how much he knew. I had been pretty taciturn all the evening, so that I think he may have been a little in awe of me. He didn't ask any more questions.

In a minute or two Norman was on the line again. 'They've got the machine up against the beach,' he said, 'but the engine is still running. I can't see what they're doing down there.'

'She won't stay long,' I said. 'If the engine's still running it means that she'll be off again quite soon.' I looked at my watch; it was about half past three. 'If she starts now,' I said, 'it'll be touch and go whether I shall be able to pick her up, you know. It'll be damn dark still by the time she passes here.'

'I don't think she'll be long,' he said. 'I don't think she's aground on the beach – she seemed to move a little then. I think there are people standing in the water, holding her. They've still got the engine running.'

'No reason why they should stop it if they aren't going to refuel,' I said. 'It won't take them long to load up the cargo. It's only about a hundred pounds' weight, you know.' I could see the subaltern out of the corner of my eye, half crazy with curiosity at the one-sided conversation.

'I hope to God the destroyer's in her station,' muttered Norman. 'Hullo. They're turning the seaplane round. I can see the men wading in the water now.'

'She'll be off in a minute,' I said.

There was a pause. 'She's going off,' he said. 'They're

202

taxi-ing towards this shore, towards the Crab Pot, astern of the launch.'

'Damn it,' I said. 'She'll be here too soon.'

Over the wire there came the same level, quiet voice. 'She's starting on her run now, making straight for the two lights down on the shore. She's about halfway across the Sound. Now she's lifting – she's in the air now, up over the lights.' There was silence for a moment. 'Stenning! Can you hear what I'm saying? The machine is in the air on the return journey now. You've got that? Good. She went straight up over the lights and then swung round to the right, out to sea. When I saw her last she was heading about due north, and still turning. I can still hear the engine, but it's getting fainter. It's up to you to have a go at her now.'

'Right you are,' I said. 'I'll do my best. But it'll be damn dark when she gets here.'

He spoke again. 'They've still got the landing lights showing.'

'They'll probably leave those out for a bit,' I said. 'A dud engine might bring her back.'

'So much the better, if the launch isn't in a hurry to leave,' he said. 'We don't want the aeroplane to see my rocket or the searchlights if we can help it. I'd like to give her at least ten minutes to get clear.'

'Wait till you see them take in the landing-lights,' I suggested. 'They can't leave those on the beach.'

I held the line and waited. There was absolute silence in the tent; I could feel them looking at me expectantly. Presently I nodded to my mechanic, and looked again at my watch.

'In about twenty minutes' time,' I said quietly. 'Get her going at about four, or a little after.'

He grinned at me and nodded. 'All ready to start up any time,' he said. 'Not half a moon out here. You won't want no lights for taking off.' He expectorated cheerfully. I saw the corporal look at him askance, and resented it. I liked my mechanic. He had been with me on several long trips abroad.

He was a man of my own type. We laughed at the same things, and at the same people.

Then Norman spoke again. 'I'm going to let her go now,' he announced. 'I can't hear the seaplane any longer, and the launch seems to be moving about a bit. I think she must be well clear now. Yes, I've got a rocket here all ready. I'm going to poop it off. Hold the line, and I'll tell you what happens.'

I have always wondered at his nerve. The men in the launch were only three hundred yards away; he knew that they must be armed. He knew that as soon as his rocket went up they would know what had happened, would know that he was there, would know that they were caught. He banked everything on their first impulse being to escape to sea. He bet his life on that. As it turned out, he was right; they only fired one or two shots at the place where the rocket had gone up from, and he had arranged that ten or fifteen yards away to his flank.

I heard the rush of the rocket clearly through the telephone. Then Norman was back again, speaking in his quiet, level tones.

'Stenning there? It's going all right, I think. Did you hear them shooting? Only one or two, and nothing close. The launch is off – left the lights on the shore and making for the open sea all out. Oh, good, sir! Damn good! What? The sloop and the destroyer are out there – I can't see which is which, but they've got their searchlights on a vessel. Yes, she's well inside the three-mile limit. A small tramp, with one funnel in the middle. They're closing on her now. I think they've got her all right.'

'Oh, damn good,' I cried. 'Damn good work!'

He spoke again. 'I think they've got the steamer now,' he said. 'Look here. Do what you can with the aeroplane. The odds are about five to one against you, but do what you can. Don't worry if you lose her – there'll probably be evidence on the steamer that will help us with the English organization. The Navy are coming to fetch me off from here as soon as

204

they've made sure of the steamer. Are you all right? Have you got everything fixed up as you like it?'

'I'm all right,' I said. 'I'll get into the air pretty soon, I think, and get my wireless going.'

'Right you are. I'm packing up now. We've got that ship all right; I can see the destroyer alongside, and the sloop standing off a little way. Cheer-oh, and good luck.'

'I'll need it,' I said, and put down the instrument. I turned to the Sapper officer and told him briefly what had happened, that we had got the vessel that had brought the dope to England.

'That's the stuff,' he said phlegmatically.

I left him and went out to the machine. It was a little before four o'clock; it was time I got under way. I talked for a minute or two to the mechanic; then he left me and went clambering about over the engine. I took my leather coat and helmet from the lower plane and began to dress.

It was getting a little grey towards the east. The moon was still high and there was plenty of light for me to see to get off the ground. The subaltern came out and watched me as I made my final preparations. I talked to him for a little about the wireless and the reports that he was to put through to me. He wished me luck.

'Ready when you are,' said the mechanic.

I clambered up on to the rounded fuselage of the machine and slid heavily down into the cockpit. I busied myself there for a minute or two, head down in the cockpit, settling into my seat and peering at my faintly luminous instruments. Then I sat up.

The mechanic was standing ready by the propeller.

'Switch off?'

'Switch is off.'

He began to turn the propeller slowly, blade by blade. I stared round over the field, looking more spacious than it really was in the dim light, and decided which way I would take off. There was very little wind.

The mechanic stopped turning the propeller, settled one blade into a convenient position, and stood waiting for me, both hands grasping the blade above his head beyond the long tapering nose of the machine.

'Contact.'

I thrust an arm out of the cockpit and fumbled with the switch on the fuselage.

'Contact,' I said. 'Let her rip.'

He flung the propeller round and swung clear; the engine fired with a cough and steadied into a regular, even beat. I left her to warm up for a little; then ran her up to full power and throttled down again.

I waved my hand and the mechanic pulled the chocks from under the wheels. I settled my goggles securely on my helmet, and nodded to the officer. Then I opened the throttle a little and we went rolling over the grass towards the hedge.

Close to the hedge I swung her round and faced up into the wind. Before me the field stretched, wide and dim. I remember that I was glad to be flying again. I was getting back to work that was peculiarly my own. On the ground I was one among many, but in the air it was different. There weren't many people in England that were better in the air than I. That heartened me, but there was another point, I remember, that appealed to me very strongly at the time. It's not often that people like me get a chance of doing something that's worth while in England. We knock about, fly, make money and lose it, get drunk, get sober again, play golf ... and do damn-all good to ourselves or anybody else. But just once and again we get our chance – the chance to do with our cunning hands what the whole world of cunning heads cannot achieve.

I pushed open the throttle, and we went rolling over the grass and up into the air above the shadowy hedge. I let her climb on steadily straight ahead as I always do when flying at night, and looked back to mark the faint glow of the lighted tent. The country was in utter darkness. I saw one light in what I imagined to be Taunton, and then I picked up one or two coloured lights from the railway signals. For the rest, it was as black as the pit below me.

I turned and flew back over the tent at about a thousand feet. Then I set about winding down my aerial and getting into touch with the wireless. I got through to them without difficulty. As soon as I plugged in my telephones and switched on I heard the voice of the corporal monotonously droning from the tent his call signal and my own.

I spoke to the officer, and as I did so I turned again in the dim light and made for the north coast, near Watchet, climbing steadily as I went. A glance at the map will show that the peninsula of Devon and Cornwall narrows considerably in the region of Taunton, forming a sort of neck barely thirty miles from north to south, from Watchet to Lyme Regis. It was for this reason that we had chosen Taunton. Travelling all out I could cover that thirty miles in about a quarter of an hour; in daylight I should have the whole of it in view from the sea on one side to the sea on the other at any height above three thousand feet, given decent visibility. It would be luck if I succeeded in picking up the seaplane, but I had a good sporting chance.

The east began to show very grey. I kept in conversation with the subaltern as I flew on. There was very little cloud about to worry me; I climbed to about seven thousand feet and steadied her at that. It was high for observation in the half light – very high. I had two reasons for it. In the first place, putting myself in the other man's shoes if I had to fly over land unostentatiously I should fly high, and it seemed to me that I ought to be above him at the beginning of the pursuit. The second reason was that if I were well above him I should have an additional advantage of speed over him, in that I could gain an extra ten or twenty miles an hour by putting my nose down and gradually losing height.

When I was nearly up to Watchet the Sapper broke off the desultory conversation that we had been keeping up. In a minute or two he spoke again.

The sound-ranging people had reported an aeroplane near Padstow. They had not sighted it, but reported that it appeared to be travelling northwards along the coast. They identified it with the machine that had gone down before.

The time was then twenty minutes past four. I scaled off the distance on the map, made a guess at the speed of a float seaplane with a Rolls Eagle, and came to the conclusion that she would pass Taunton a little before five. I asked the Sapper to wake up the look-out on Hartland who had missed the machine before, and set to patrolling between Taunton and Watchet.

We had great luck with the weather. The dawn came up in yellow streaks, and practically cloudless. I could see that visibility was going to be good and got the wind up that I should be seen by the seaplane before I could see them, and climbed to about eleven thousand feet. I thought I should be pretty safe up there; I didn't think that the seaplane would be able to get up so high as that without a great effort. I put six or seven thousand as her comfortable height.

We got no report from Hartland. Later we discovered that the seaplane turned inland in the neighbourhood of Boscastle and never went near Hartland at all. We should have done better to have planted more posts inland; as it was, it was the ones along the Exeter–Barnstaple road that really pulled us through. At about a quarter to five one of them rang up from a point a few miles south of Barnstaple.

The seaplane had passed about a mile to the north of him, he said. He had seen it clearly. It was flying high, but when questioned he could not say how high. We pressed him for a rough guess, and extracted from him the opinion that it was about as high as a cloud on a fine day.

I edged down towards Taunton, and began searching the horizon and the ground for any sign of the seaplane creeping slowly over the fields. It was a heart-breaking task. The light was fairly good by this time, but the detail of the ground, the pattern of the fields and woods and hedges confused the eye. I

208

could see nothing of the machine. Time slipped by, and still there was no sign. I was getting thoroughly worried when the subaltern spoke through the telephones into my ear.

'We can hear an aeroplane here,' he said. 'I'm not sure that it isn't you. Where are you now?'

I leaned forward and spoke into the mouthpiece strapped to my chest. 'I'm about three miles south of Watchet,' I said. 'I'll throttle my engine – see if you hear the note change. It'll take a minute or two before you hear it, remember. I pulled the throttle back and put the machine on the glide. 'I've throttled down now. I'm making practically no noise at all.'

'Right you are,' he replied. 'Now wait while we listen.'

I sat up and looked anxiously all round ahead of me. Without my engine I was losing height rapidly, at the rate of about a thousand feet a minute. I kept glancing at the slow movement of the second hand of my wrist-watch. When a minute and a half had gone by I leaned forward and spoke again.

'What's happening now?'

'The noise is still continuous.'

'It's probably the seaplane. I'll give it half a minute more for luck before I switch on my engine. Go on listening.'

We sank lower and lower. At about nine thousand feet I tried again.

'What does it sound like now?'

'The noise is still quite continuous. I think it must be the seaplane – can't be anything else. I've got all the men out looking for it, but we haven't seen it yet. It sounds as if it was to the south of us.'

I opened my throttle, shoved the nose of the machine down, and went full out for Taunton, losing height as I went. I was halfway there and doing a hundred and forty miles an hour at six thousand when the subaltern spoke again.

'Captain Stenning. Can you hear what I am saying?' He spoke very distinctly. 'We've sighted the seaplane. Your man saw her first. She's about three miles due south of us now.'

'Keep her in sight,' I said. 'I'm going to come right over

you. Be ready to give me a compass bearing of her when I'm directly above you. What height is she?'

There was a pause. 'Your man says she's about four thousand feet up.'

I shoved my nose down a bit more and raced full out for Taunton. I had revised my ideas about height. I should be coming up on the seaplane from behind; in that position I should be less conspicuous if I were below her, hidden by her own tail and with a dark background of fields. Moreover, it would be easier for me to pick her up if she were silhouetted against the sky. I kept in touch with the ground, and passed over the tent at about a thousand feet.

As I drew near they gave me a course and a distance – southeast by east about six miles. I swung the machine round on to the course and went full out along that line, heading for Yeovil.

The voice of the subaltern spoke clearly into my ear. 'Turn about ten degrees more to your left,' he said distinctly. 'You are aiming behind her.'

I swung round a little, and then suddenly I saw the seaplane clearly outlined against the sky.

'Right you are,' I said. 'I've got her now.'

She was two or three thousand feet above me and several miles ahead; I was creeping up on her fast. To reduce my speed I climbed a little and finally took up a station a couple of miles behind her and fifteen hundred feet below; I knew that in that position I would be practically invisible from her. While I was getting into position I thanked the Sapper for his help and told him to tell the Bournemouth Broadcasting Station that I was trying to get in touch with them. We had arranged that several stations in the south should be standing by, and we had an inspector at most of them.

The Sapper said that my mechanic wanted to speak to me before they shut down, and in a minute I heard him on the phone.

'Is that Captain Stenning? It's me speaking – Adams, sir.

You come quite close here – we seen you swing round and go after them a fair treat. Don't forget that what I told you, about not running her too slow. It's the perishing oil they give us – all right in the winter. Keep her going and she won't give you no trouble. You give them blighters 'ell, sir. That's right, you give them 'ell.'

With that as a valediction I switched off; soon afterwards I picked up Bournemouth and spoke for a little to the superintendent there. We passed directly over Somerton and began to follow the railway in the direction of Frome. It was pretty obvious by that time that we were making for Salisbury Plain; indeed, I had been privately of that opinion all along. There was really nowhere else that could give the secrecy in landing that they would require. I felt this so strongly that I made the Bournemouth people switch me through to Salisbury by a land line, and spoke a few minutes to the superintendent there. He told me that he had motors and police in readiness at Salisbury and at Devizes, and that the Air Force were standing by with a couple of machines at Upavon.

We passed over Bruton. I was sure from the steady course that the seaplane was keeping that I hadn't been spotted. I had done everything that I could to ensure them a warm reception; my only duty now was to keep Bournemouth informed of the course that we were heading. I had leisure now to study the seaplane more closely; suddenly I realized what she was, and why she had seemed vaguely familiar.

She was the old *Chipmunk*. She was the only one of her sort, built to the order of a wealthy young coal merchant just after the war. I don't know who it was who first called her the *Chipmunk* – her owner repudiated the name vigorously. (He called her *Queen of the Clouds*, and had it painted on the fuselage.) There was something about her tubby lines that suggested a chipmunk, and it was as the *Chipmunk* that she was universally known. She was very slow. For five years she had been entered for every King's Cup race, ambling round the course at a speed that defied the most benevolent efforts of the handicappers. I knew that she had been sold, and I knew to whom she had been sold – a young chap called Bulse who described himself as a stockbroker. He was always about at Croydon. It was the *Chipmunk* all right. She had suffered a sea change; her wheels and undercarriage had been removed and floats substituted, probably with wheels incorporated to make her into an amphibian. But there was no doubt about her.

I passed this information on to the superintendent at Bournemouth, who forwarded it to the Yard. That gave us one good line to put us in touch with the organization in England, at any rate.

We followed the railway as far as Bruton, but here we left it as it trended a little to the north, and took a course that would carry us a little to the south of Warminster. I got pretty busy with the wireless again. Before us I could see the great rolling deserted stretches of the Plain. I knew that the *Chipmunk* might be landing any time now.

We passed a mile or so south of Warminster. Directly we were past the town the *Chipmunk* changed direction and headed a little more to the north. I watched her intently, half afraid that they had spotted me. Then as I watched I saw her tail cock and her nose go down into a glide, and she began to lose height. She was going down to land.

I became furiously busy on the wireless. Everything was ready; I had only to tell them the exact point of landing. I kept my eyes fixed on the *Chipmunk* as she slipped rapidly down on to the Plain, and turned away from her, in order that they should not see my machine till they were actually on the ground. I turned almost at right-angles and watched her as she landed beyond my wing tip, and all the time I was telling Salisbury about it. Then I saw her touch the Plain, run along, and come to rest.

Within half a minute I had given Salisbury the map reference, and the first part of my job was done. I knew now that the police were on the way.

I was then at about a thousand feet and two miles to the east of the *Chipmunk*, now stationary upon the grass. I reeled in my aerial, swung the machine round towards her, and put my nose down to go and have a look-see.

The machine had landed about three miles southwest of the little village of Imber. There was a road that ran from Imber to Warminster across the plain, and there were three touring cars halted together on this road at the point nearest to the machine. The *Chipmunk* was stationary on the grass about two hundred and fifty yards from the road. As I got closer I saw that there was a ditch running across the plain that had evidently prevented the pilot from landing in a more convenient position for the cars, or from taxi-ing towards them.

I don't know when they first realized that I was there. I came on them from the east travelling at a hundred miles an hour or so at a height of about a hundred and fifty feet, and flying erratically as I craned over the side of the cockpit to have a good look. I saw the *Chipmunk* standing on the grass with her engine stopped, and I saw a little crowd of eight or nine men standing beside her, all looking up at me. Then, as I passed over them, my eye travelled on to the three cars on the road, a good two hundred and fifty yards away.

The cars were deserted.

I don't generally pride myself on rapid headwork, but when I saw that, I crashed my hand down upon my thigh and broke into a burst of laughter as I heaved the machine round in an Immelmann turn and dived straight on to the *Chipmunk*. I saw at once what had happened. All the men in the cars had run over to meet the seaplane when she landed, and there they were, with a good two hundred and fifty yards of open grass between them and their cars. To get away in the cars they had to cross the grass.

'By God!' I laughed. '*We'll* show these ruddy Dagoes what's what!'

I dived for the seaplane with my engine full out and pulled up over her at the last minute, missing her top plane by a few feet. I saw the little crowd shrink close into the shelter of the seaplane as I dived on them, and then I was up and away, and turning round in the cockpit to watch their fright. I was really quite close to them for a moment, and as I swept up over them laughing like hell I caught them looking up at me, and I knew that they had seen me laughing. Then I thought of all that I must mean to them – defeat, imprisonment, ruin, perhaps even death itself. And then I thought of how they must have felt when they saw me laughing at them, and I laughed again.

I should like to be able to record that I took what followed in a serious vein. I can't say that. There is an elation in the dangerous game of stunting an aeroplane close to the ground that quickly becomes overpowering. I can only remember two sensations clearly during the next ten minutes. The first was that I was laughing almost continuously, and the other was that when I was not laughing I was singing the unexpurgated version of a popular song.

I zoomed up from the *Chipmunk* to a hundred feet or so and swung round towards the cars again, watching them over my shoulder as a cat watches a mouse that she has let free for a moment. I turned again beyond the cars, and hung about there for a little.

In a minute they did what I had expected. They seemed to hold a little consultation, and then three or four of them left the seaplane and began to run across the grass towards the cars.

Instantly I heaved the machine round, shoved open the throttle, thrust her down, and dived on to them, singing lustily all the time:

> *'Some girls work in factories,*
> *And some girls work in stores —*
> *And my girl works in a milliner's shop*
> *With forty other working ladies.*
> *Oh, it ain't going to rain no mo', no mo',*
> *It ain't going to rain —'*

I was on them then. They were running in a little group. I was barely a foot above the ground when I was fifty yards away, and I flew straight at them like a tornado. I suppose my speed would have been about a hundred and thirty or so. It was tricky work, because I didn't mean to kill them. For a tiny moment they stood their ground, thinking to call my bluff. Then they broke and threw themselves sideways on the ground in all directions, and I shot through among them and rocketed up over the seaplane. I skidded round in the quickest and lowest turn I had ever done in all my life, and dived on them again.

> *'Some girls work in factories,*
> *And some girls work in stores ...'*

They had hardly time to regain their feet before I was on them again, driving straight for the thick of them with my engine roaring and the propeller screaming like a good 'un. One or two of them were still staggering to their feet, very unsteady; I didn't want to have an accident and began to rise before I reached them. Again they had to throw themselves in all directions, but I was higher this time and missed them by a good three feet, I suppose.

Flesh and blood weren't made to stand that sort of thing. They broke up, and when I came round for the third time most of them had regained the shelter of the *Chipmunk*. There were two stragglers still in the field, both running for shelter. I chased one of them as he ran as if to catch him in the back with the tip of my port lower plane; he heard the machine screaming after him and looked over his shoulder as the wing bore down upon him. I hope I may never see such a look on a man's face again. It was only a momentary glimpse; the next instant I had rolled the machine and the wing passed a foot above his head. By the time he had realized he wasn't killed I was fifty feet up in the air again, and laughing at him over my shoulder.

They stayed close under the shelter of the *Chipmunk* then. They knew I couldn't get at them there.

I had won the first round and retired over behind the cars to wait for the next. I watched them carefully as they stood under the shelter of the seaplane; they seemed to be arguing the toss with someone in the middle of the crowd. For a little while they made no move. I looked at my watch, and found that the whole affair had taken rather under three minutes. I realized that I should have to play them for an hour or so, and came to the conclusion that I should have my work cut out. I knew that the trouble would come when they realized that I had no intention of killing them.

For what seemed a long time – perhaps a couple of minutes – they made no move. Then a little squad of them came out from the shelter of the machine and spread into open order, for all the world like infantry attacking a position. There were six of them in the line; they spread themselves out and began to run slowly out into the open. Behind them came a man in a green raincoat, for all the world like an NCO.

I dived towards them. They waited till I was fifty yards away and then deliberately lay down; the last man to go down was the man in the green coat. He seemed to be encouraging them. I was worried about this. I could have killed any one of them just as well when he was lying down as when he was standing up, by lurching the machine down on to the ground as I passed over them. But I didn't want to hurt them, and to frighten them back to the seaplane was by no means so easy when they were regularly manoeuvring in open order.

I swept over them about two feet above the ground. By the time I could look round they were on their feet and running forwards again.

They ran about thirty yards, and then I was coming at them from a flank; they lay down in an uneven line. I didn't try to frighten them this time; I thought it would do them more good if I showed them what I could do to them if I tried. I approached them at a slower speed than before and aimed so that the wheels of my undercarriage would pass a yard or two in front of their faces as they lay on the ground; in that way the wing passed about three feet above their bodies. As I passed down the line I gently 'felt' the wheels down on to the ground, so that I passed over them in a succession of gentle hops very close before their faces, at a speed of about sixty miles an hour. A rabbit in line with my undercarriage could not have escaped, let alone a man.

I think they saw the point. With the exception of the man in the green raincoat they were very slow in getting to their feet, and they turned to argue with him as they rose. By the time they were on their feet I had made my turn and was sweeping down on them again, the propeller screaming like a six-inch shell. There was a bit of the metal tipping with a jagged edge on one of the propeller blades that made a wonderful scream when she was all out.

That dive settled it. They weren't ready for me, engrossed as they were in arguing with the man in green. They flung themselves in all directions as I swept through among them, and when I looked round they were all on their feet again and racing back towards the seaplane. They had farther to go this time, and I got in two dives at them to chase them home. I went too close altogether to one of the men, and for a moment I had a sickening feeling that I must have hit him. I hadn't, but I must have been very close.

On the second of these runs I suddenly became convinced that they had been shooting at me. I had seen nothing hit the machine, but somehow I knew that they had been firing.

I knew that I couldn't keep them there for long. I knew that I had frightened them badly, but with all that they had at stake it could only be a matter of a minute or two before they tried again. It struck me then – I think it probably occurred to them at the same time – that if only one of them could get across to the cars he could drive one of them across the grass to the seaplane; then they could all get away in safety by walking beside the car on its return journey. Obviously I couldn't dive on to a car. I should come off worst if I hit it.

They had been quiet by the seaplane for some minutes now. I flew towards them close to the ground to see what had happened. I was about a hundred yards away from them when they opened fire on me, and opened fire with something uncommonly like a machine-gun, too. I saw the steady flashes from among the crowd, and I heard or felt one or two of the bullets whip past me, and I saw a couple of strips of fabric leap up from one of the planes where the bullets passed through. Then I was up and over them, and circling at a safe distance to see what they would do next.

I saw the gun later. It was one of the Bartlett guns that the Australians tried to sell to the Riffs in their show against Spain. It was more of a pistol than a gun, though it was fired from the shoulder; it loaded with a clip like an automatic pistol and went on firing till its twenty shots were done.

I hadn't long to wait for developments. A man came out alone from the shelter of the seaplane and began to run towards the cars, and I saw at once that it was the man in the green raincoat.

I swung the machine round and dived on him.

> '*And my girl works in a milliner's shop*
> *With forty other —*'

I wasn't ready for what he did then. When I was still some distance from him he dropped on one knee; I saw then that he had the gun. I saw him take aim deliberately, and wrenched the machine from side to side in a zigzag path. In a moment the shots were flying all around me; one went home into the fuselage just behind my seat. He threw himself on the ground as I approached, and I lurched the machine down as close to him as I dared; then I was up and away again. When I looked round the man in the green coat was on his feet and running forward.

I had not been hit, but I had had a great fright. Suddenly I knew as clearly as if I had been told who it was that I was up against. There was nobody else that it could be.

I think it was that that stiffened me. I was miserably afraid of being killed. But as I swung the machine round to dive on the man in the green coat again I thought of Compton, and I remember thinking something about dope, and I know I remembered for a moment the girl that I used to go about with that first wonderful summer after the war, and the fine times we had had together. All that must have passed through my head pretty quickly, because by the time I was straight and diving on Green Coat again I knew that I simply mustn't let him get to the cars. It was up to me.

I made a fool of myself then. I came at him straight from a good two hundred yards away instead of swooping down on to him from above. That gave him a fine target. For five seconds or so I was heading straight for him and unable to dodge to any great extent, and in that five seconds he raked me from end to end. How he missed the engine is a mystery. He was nearly halfway to the cars; I saw him drop down on one knee and then the bullets came crashing home. They all came from the left side. One cracked in my left shoulder and out through the shoulder-blade, and knocked me flying back in my seat; at the same moment another went through my left forearm, breaking one of the bones. A third ripped my breeches on the left side from the knee to the seat and only grazed the skin without drawing blood, and a fourth chipped a bit off the heel of my boot. The instrument-board in front of me stopped several; there were three bullets in the revolution counter when we came to take it down.

I'm really damn proud of what I did then, though I say it myself. I had only one hand to fly with; my throttle hand was hanging loose and dangling till I managed later to put it into the front of my coat. But I was flying straight for Green Coat when I was hit. I know the machine lurched horribly for a

219

moment, but I pulled her straight again and went on. He threw himself flat as I came at him. I pushed the machine down carefully, as carefully as if I had been fit, as if my cheeks had not been quivering, my head swimming, and the blood running down my back. I cleared him by a few inches as he lay on the ground. I could have killed him with the tiniest pressure of my thumb. If I had allowed the tremors that were shaking me to reach my hand he would have been dead, but I steadied the stick against my knee. I only frightened him. I had meant to clear him when I started on the dive, and clear him I did. I shall always be proud of that.

I swung up from that dive, sick and dizzy, and turned slowly when I had reached a sufficient height. Green Coat was on his feet again and running towards the cars. I could only think of one thing – that at all costs I must head him off. It was up to me. I thought that I was going to be killed, but this had become a personal matter now and I could no more let him get away with it than I could have put my left hand to the throttle. I must have another shot at him, and I flung the machine round and dived on him again.

He was very near the cars now. As soon as he saw me coming he dropped on one knee again and took deliberate aim. I was too far gone to do much in the way of dodging and swerving, and bore straight down on him, waiting miserably for the next burst of shots. He opened fire – and then one of those little things happened that really make a man believe that somewhere, somehow, there must be a God. The gun fired two shots, and jammed.

I could see that something had happened. I could see him kneeling up and wrestling with the gun, his head down over it, not looking at me. I knew that he would throw himself flat before I reached him, and I lurched a little lower in a final attempt to frighten him from the cars.

He was still kneeling up when the nose of the machine hid him from my view.

At the very last moment I got the wind up, and heaved

violently on the stick to pull the machine up. I hadn't seen him lie down.

It was that last-minute effort to save his life that probably saved my own. But for that the machine would have crashed down on to the grass and gone flying head over heels. I say now what I have said all along, at the inquest, at the private police inquiry – that I never meant to hit him. I should have said that anyway, I suppose. But as it happens, it's true. I know that Joan believes me, and I think Sir David Carter does.

I had thought that he would lie down, as he had done all along. He didn't.

I had pulled her up and she was rising, when she lurched heavily forward and to starboard. I pulled the stick violently over to the corner of the cockpit and gave her full rudder, but she struck the ground, not very hard, but with a wrenching action that pulled the tyre off one wheel and left it lying on the grass. She bounced up heavily, staggered, side-slipped, scraped the grass again, and rose into the air, under control once more.

It had been a bad moment while it lasted. I couldn't turn in my seat, and I was feeling so sick that it wasn't till I was well over a hundred feet up that I dared to risk turning the machine to look what had happened. And then I saw what I had done. The man in the green raincoat was lying crumpled up over the grass, face downwards. I flew low over him half a dozen times, craning painfully over the side of the cockpit, but I never saw him move.

That was the end.

I flew round and round the seaplane for a quarter of an hour after that, determined not to give in and land till the pain and my growing faintness forced me to do so while I still had my wits about me. But the little group under the shelter of the seaplane never stirred. They had had their lesson; they had seen one man killed and that was enough for them. If I had landed unprotected they would have rushed for the cars, and they might not have been above the odd spot of murder – there were some ugly-looking coves among them. It was certainly up to me to keep in the air for as long as possible.

That wasn't very long. It was about a quarter of an hour afterwards that I looked up and saw aeroplanes overhead, three Siskins manoeuvring down in ever-widening circles. I don't think I wasted much time in landing. I was sitting in a pool of blood by that time, and the shoulder was giving me hell. The arm hurt very little.

I landed about a quarter of a mile behind the seaplane, and so aimed my run that I finished up not very far from the cars, and about a hundred yards from the dead man. I had been afraid that my undercarriage was so damaged that it would collapse as I landed, but nothing happened; I came to rest normally and remained sitting in the machine.

In a few minutes one of the Siskins landed close beside me; the other two kept circling low overhead. I saw the pilot of the machine that had landed looking across to me curiously as we both sat doing nothing. I stopped my engine and waved my sound hand to beckon him near. He taxied his machine close, heaved himself up out of the cockpit and jumped down, and came across to me.

He helped me all he could, but it was a painful business getting out of the cockpit and down on to the ground. He cut my coat free and lashed up my shoulder stiffly for me, and put the arm in splints with a couple of spanners and his scarf. He had just finished doing this when the police arrived in a couple of cars, and went over to the seaplane to take possession of the prisoners.

Two of them helped me to walk to one of the cars. They didn't like letting me walk farther than was necessary, but I insisted on making a detour to where there was a little crowd of men standing in a group about something huddled on the ground.

The little crowd parted as I came near.

It seemed that I had hit him on the shoulder as I rose, that I had as nearly as possible missed him altogether. There was very little to show the violence of his death; the green raincoat was not even torn, but they told me that his back was broken. One of the men was examining the gun.

I stooped painfully over the body. The face was strangely dignified and, in some queer way, attractive. It was the face of a man rather over forty years of age; the hair was already a little grey about the temples. It was a powerful face, clean-shaven, with lines about the mouth that I thought suggested humour. I could see the resemblance to Compton in him, but in the great strength of the jaw he was different. It was the face of a man who could have done anything.

That was the only time I ever saw Mattani – Roddy, they had called him.

They were escorting the prisoners back from the seaplane to the road, each in the charge of a constable. They had to pass close to where we were standing, and suddenly I saw Bulse, the pilot of the seaplane.

I had met him once or twice at Croydon. He nodded to me, and they let him pause a minute.

'Morning, Stenning,' he said. 'So it's you. I knew it must be either you or Padder by the flying. Sorry to see you're hurt.'

I looked down to the grass. 'It's a pity this happened,' I said, and he followed my glance.

'It was a fair show,' he remarked. 'He seems to have shot you up all right. It looked to us as if you didn't mean to do it.'

I shook my head. 'It's probably better this way,' I said slowly. 'It was a hanging matter if we'd got him.'

He started. 'Good Lord – I didn't know that.'

I looked at him closely. I knew that he was speaking the truth. 'I don't suppose you did,' I said at last. 'But one way and another he was a pretty bad lot.'

He may have been, but I was to have a curious proof of the great personality and charm that had endeared him to every-one with whom he came in contact. One of the prisoners heard what I said in passing, and halted in defiance of his escort. I heard later that he kept a small chemist's shop in Blackpool.

'Who are ye calling a bad lot?' he snarled. 'Ye're a liar, and ye know it. Mister Mattani was a champion man.'

He shot a swift glance at me, extraordinarily vindictive.

'Ye bloody murderer!' he said.